The Daring Heart

1

"Look, Geraldine! It's finished at last. Aunt Amelia will scarcely believe me." Lucilla Prior's beautiful violet eyes sparkled with triumph. She gathered up her skirts and ran delightedly across the room to the Honourable Geraldine Childs, proudly holding out the embroidery for her friend to see.

"Tell me the truth. What do you think?"

A puckish smile danced around the corner of Lucilla's pretty mouth as she spoke, for embroidery was not among her talents, and her efforts usually caused more mirth than admiration. Stitching was too slow a pastime for Lucilla's quick nature. She would far rather have been cantering across the countryside on her mare, or, when forced to remain inside, playing whist or quadrille.

Normally, Geraldine would have responded with words of encouragement. But today she hardly seemed to hear what Lucilla was saying. She held in her hand a letter which she had just finished reading. Her deep brown eyes glowed, and a faint tinge of colour spotted each pallid cheek.

Lucilla looked with concern at her friend. Geraldine's expression worried her. She tossed the embroidery upon a dainty satinwood worktable, then ran to Geraldine and placed an arm around her, fearing that the letter contained bad news.

"What is the matter — tell me?"

Geraldine gently freed herself and smoothed out her beautiful satin dress, which Lucilla had slightly crushed.

"Nothing to be alarmed about," she replied with a calm smile as she meticulously traced out the little creases with her index finger. "It is simply that I am so astonished that I can hardly believe my eyes."

Unlike the volatile Lucilla, Geraldine had an even temperament and was not easily ruffled, so her friend knew that the letter must indeed contain remarkable news.

Several possibilities raced through Lucilla's mind before she heard Geraldine say, "My cousin, Rupert Lennox-Childs, is coming to stay to help me sort out father's business affairs. Oh, Lucilla, he is quite the most wonderful and most handsome of men . . . and so busy. To think that he is putting himself out in this way just to help me!"

Lucilla immediately understood why Geraldine was so astounded. Her friend's cousin was a man of great importance and high repute, and, even more intriguing for Lucilla, he was also described as "one of the most eligible bachelors in all England." Upon the recent death of Lord Childs, Geraldine's father, he had inherited the title.

Geraldine had been utterly shattered by her father's sudden death only two months before, as had been the entire county of Surrey, for dear, generous Lord Childs was a much loved and respected figure with countless friends.

Geraldine had witnessed the accident herself — a terrible sight — just as the hunt had rounded a precipitous bend of a steep hill. The horse upon which Lord Childs was riding had suddenly faltered on an uneven surface, and he had been thrown clear over the beast's head into a treacherous ravine below, from which fall he had never regained consciousness. His death had been mourned by friends throughout the length and breadth of the country, and the Prince Regent himself had sent a letter of sympathy.

After the funeral, Geraldine had been very ill, and seemed almost to lack the will to live. She had only started to recover when her dearest friend, Lucilla Prior, had come to stay with her.

Lucilla's high spirits always cheered Geraldine. The two girls were very close, and had known each other since childhood. Perhaps the fact that they were both motherless had created a bond between them; that, and because their fathers had known each other as schoolboys and had remained constant friends ever since.

Because Rupert Lennox-Childs was one of the wealthiest landowners in the country, with three vast estates and a palatial London house, Lord Childs had thought fit to leave his entire fortune to his daughter Geraldine.

However, the complex business matters which Geraldine had so suddenly inherited needed immediate attention, and, fearing that even lawyers were not always entirely to be trusted, she had been at a loss to know to whom she could truly turn.

The new Lord Childs, upon receiving a letter from her in which she told him of her worries, had gallantly come to the rescue by insisting he stay at Langley House, her sumptuous Surrey home, for a few weeks, during which time he would be able to sort out her business affairs, as well as ensure that her vast Surrey estate be placed in reliable hands to maintain it in the future.

"It is so kind of him," said Geraldine softly, "to leave his own interests in order to assist me. After Papa died I was so worried . . ."

"Dear Geraldine, pray do not upset yourself now," whispered Lucilla tenderly, for she could see that tears were already forming in her friend's eyes at the thought of her father, and she could not bear to see her cry.

"Come — cheer up. This news is splendid. Lord Childs might even escort you to London. It is high time you were out and about again."

Her words succeeded in having an effect, for they brought a slight flicker of anticipation into Geraldine's eyes. In her quiet way, there was nothing Geraldine liked better than London society.

Lucilla quickly noticed her reaction and hurried on persuasively. "If you keep on crying, Geraldine, your eyes will become as red and puffy as my Uncle Matt's before he died of drink. You don't want to look like that when you greet Lord Childs."

The remark worked like magic. Gingerly, Geraldine began to dab her eyes with her delicate lace-edged handkerchief, at the same time making a valiant effort to stifle her sobs. She had only met her cousin a few times before, the last being eighteen months previously, but she had been greatly impressed by this debonair man whose integrity was reputed to match his immense charm.

Like Lucilla, who was the daughter of a local parson, she had no brothers and sisters. In fact, she was not really Lord Childs' daughter. Her mother had been Lord Childs' sister and had died when she was born, while her father had quickly followed his wife to the grave after contracting smallpox.

It had seemed the most natural thing in the world for old Lord Childs to adopt Geraldine as his own daughter, since it had been one of the greatest sadnesses of his life that his own deceased wife had never borne him a child. So Geraldine had grown up an only and often lonely child in the vast house, longing for brothers and sisters. Thus she warmed to the idea of having her cousin to stay, since she would dearly have loved to have a brother at this troubled time. Her old nurse, away at the moment tending a sick relative, had reared her since a babe, as, in Lucilla's case, had her Aunt Amelia.

"You are right, Lucilla," Geraldine said sensibly. "Since my cousin is taking the trouble to travel all the way from Northumbria, the least I can do is to receive him looking my best."

"When does he say that he will come?"

"Oh, he does not say for sure. He writes that he will start out as soon as possible and to expect him any time . . ."

"Well, then," said Lucilla jumping up energetically, "whatever are you thinking of, Geraldine, just sitting there? You should be discussing his rooms with the housekeeper. He may have started on his journey even as we sit here gossiping."

Geraldine smiled at her friend's enthusiasm.

"Calm yourself, Lucilla. I have every intention of dealing with the matter. I had already decided, in any case, to give Rupert the best suite of rooms we have — those overlooking the main gardens. They are always kept in good condition and need but a little airing. I shall see to it that fires are lit immediately."

"Ooh! Those beautiful, magnificent rooms! How he will love them," declared Lucilla, her large eyes wide with delight. She lived in a small rectory herself only a few miles away, since her father, the Reverend George Prior, although well connected, possessed but a modest income.

"I hope so," replied Geraldine, a little uncertain. "Remember he is used only to the very best, and his own home in Northumbria is almost a mansion, or so I gather."

As she spoke, she picked up the piece of discarded embroidery which Lucilla had thrown down on the table.

"Well?" asked Lucilla, watching her questioningly.

Geraldine's head was bent over the work so Lucilla could not see by the expression on her face what she was thinking.

"Mmm — it's an improvement," said Geraldine discreetly. "Some of the stitches are, well, quite neat. And the colours are definitely very fine and harmonious."

"You need say no more," said Lucilla, taking the embroidery from her. "I can tell by the tone of your voice that you think little of it."

"I said nothing of the sort."

"No — but you thought it. Come, tell me the truth."

"It is an improvement. Truthfully."

"Geraldine, your act is positively touching," said Lucilla with a ripple of laughter. "You know quite well that is a perfectly hideous piece of work. Why, the roses look more like a bunch of radishes!"

Geraldine burst into laughter as well, a thing she rarely did these days.

When they had both stopped laughing, Lucilla held the embroidery out at arms length and gazed at it. "Still, I shall keep it," she declared firmly. "I shall keep it for posterity. Who can tell that some future generation might not find it charming? After all, hung on a wall and looked at from a distance, it would appear quite attractive — nobody would see the stitches!"

When Amelia Prior, who had accompanied her niece to stay at Langley House, entered the room a few moments after the two girls had left it, she did not share either Geraldine's or her niece's opinion of the hastily stitched piece of embroidery.

She placed her spectacles carefully upon her nose and peered at it critically, before shaking her head resignedly and returning it with a sigh to Lucilla's workbox. She had quite given up trying to get her niece to take more trouble with her stitches, for the more she tried the worse they seemed to get.

Amelia Prior, nonetheless, was extremely fond of Lucilla. Her brother, the Reverend George Prior, had sent for her when Lucilla's mother had died, and, being a spinster with neither money nor looks to her credit, she had somehow, to her brother's relief, remained at the rectory ever since.

She had not found it very easy to rear the spirited Lucilla, a wilful girl whose adventurous nature had led her into many a scrape. Yet, the girl had such a loving, affectionate side to her that she could wind most people around her little finger without even knowing it, including her aunt.

Aunt Amelia had watched her niece grow from a lovely child into an even more beautiful young woman, slender and exquisitely proportioned, with quick, lissome movements. Her face, dominated by enormous violet eyes, was delicately heart-shaped with a tip-tilted nose and full, pretty mouth. Lucilla's hair, both her crowning glory and a cause of chagrin, since it would never stay in place, was the colour of ripe corn, tumbling to her shoulders in curls and waves. She was just nineteen years old.

Lucilla had many admirers, but as yet had shown none of them any particular interest. This secretly pleased Aunt Amelia, for she was sure that Lucilla would do very well for herself and make a superb match, if only she could mix in the right circles before falling in love with some nonentity.

It was partly because of such ambitions that Aunt Amelia was pleased that Lucilla had remained friends with the Honourable Geraldine Childs through the years, although she was also very fond of Geraldine, who was nearly two years older than Lucilla. Often, in fact, she found Geraldine easier company and far less trying than her own niece.

Aunt Amelia approved of Geraldine's gentle temperament. This quiet girl, beautifully brought up and with exquisite manners, could be guaranteed to behave with the utmost grace at any social function and on any occasion.

Geraldine's strongly defined sense of etiquette could always be relied upon, whereas Lucilla, with her quick, spontaneous nature and sense of fun, could be shatteringly unpredictable. Nonetheless, Aunt Amelia had thankfully observed that Lucilla had improved considerably of late, since coming to stay at Langley House. The two girls certainly made an attractive pair, one so fair and delicate and the other dark-haired and olive-skinned. Geraldine was several inches taller than Lucilla, well rounded, with beautiful shoulders. Her larger build accentuated Lucilla's slender frame when they were standing side by side.

Plump Aunt Amelia settled herself comfortably by the roaring fire with a look of utter contentment upon her round face. She was thoroughly enjoying her stay at Langley House, and hoped for several more weeks of such comfort before returning to the more austere conditions of the rectory. She popped a sugared almond into her mouth and started her sewing.

Lucilla had decided to accompany Geraldine on her inspection of the suite of rooms which was to be prepared for Lord Childs. The rooms had not been open since the death of Geraldine's father, and she did not want their forlorn emptiness to upset her friend.

They were certainly the finest rooms in this grand house, beautifully proportioned with intricate, gilt cornices and matching architraves. The finest of French wallpaper had been used throughout, and the curtains of heavy silk were headed by elaborate festoons and flounces in a complementing shade. The furniture varied from fashionably elegant and ornate pieces to those more substantial items which had been handed down through the generations. Everything was of superlative quality.

"It seems damp," declared Lucilla. "What a horrid, frousty smell." She turned up her pretty nose, sniffing disapprovingly. "This won't please Lord Childs."

Geraldine looked worried.

"It's worse than I thought," she admitted. "But perhaps if the windows are opened wide and the doors thrown apart, the fresh air will blow away the smell."

"We could put bowls of lavender and potpourri around afterwards," declared Lucilla cheerfully. "Then with the warmth from the fires, and the smell of the burning logs, the place would quickly seem normal again."

Geraldine nodded and proceeded to instruct the housekeeper who had accompanied them. The good woman had already decided to do so anyway, and was only waiting for the word from her young mistress before setting to work at once with as many underservants as she could muster to clean the rooms from top to bottom.

Lucilla ran to one of the large sash windows which over-looked miles of soft, wooded countryside. It was a bright, still day, and here and there she could see straight wisps of smoke from the chimneys of the isolated cottages dotted around the estate. She longed to be out on her mare, but realized that Geraldine was far too preoccupied with her news to consider accompanying her. Sadly she dismissed the idea of a ride, for she would not leave Geraldine alone.

"Tell me more about Rupert Lennox-Childs," she urged her friend as they linked arms and sauntered through the rooms.

"There is little to say, for I hardly know him myself. Yet, when I last saw him . . ." Geraldine paused as if searching for words, and Lucilla gave her a mischievous little smile. "I was so struck by his fine qualities that I urged dear Papa to invite him to Langley House one day. If Papa had only lived — "

"But his fine qualities were not all, were they?" Lucilla interrupted with a twinkle. "I have heard you mention often his handsome looks and fine demeanor."

Geraldine coloured up very slightly.

"Nobody could help but notice such things," she said quickly. "They would strike anybody, they are so exceptional. But pray remember, Lucilla," she added in the elder-sister tone which she sometimes adopted when she was on her dignity, "that Rupert is my cousin. I have no romantic notions concerning him."

Geraldine was well known for being choosy with the opposite sex, and might have married any one of several well-connected young men already. But there was always something which did not quite please her. It had become quite a joke with Lucilla and her Aunt Amelia.

"Lord Childs is turned twenty-seven, is he not?" asked Lucilla.

Geraldine nodded.

"Well, it cannot be much longer before he chooses a bride. I wonder who it will be, and when."

"Really, Lucilla, I am surprised that you should sink to idle speculation," snapped Geraldine crossly.

Lucilla shrugged her shoulders.

"I only said it because it seems to me that his attraction will lessen considerably once he has taken a wife," she retorted, "as I think you will discover for yourself in the fullness of time, Geraldine."

An impish smile lit Lucilla's face. She had just come from Geraldine's bedroom and had been astonished to find her friend prostrate upon her bed with two thin slices of cucumber beneath each closed eye.

Lucilla had entered the room silently, having first been bidden come in by Geraldine, who had thought her to be the chambermaid.

"What do you want?" Geraldine had demanded in the tone she used to address servants when she was annoyed at being disturbed, her eyes still closed.

"To ask if you wished to play backgammon, as it is such a dreary afternoon," Lucilla had replied, trying hard not to laugh.

"Oh! It is you, Lucilla — I thought it was Violet."

Geraldine opened her eyes, removed the dank cucumbers and sat up.

"Having a little rest?" enquired Lucilla tactfully.

Geraldine ignored the question and replied coolly, "You saw perfectly well what I was doing. Since it was you who mentioned in the first place that my eyes might grow puffy after so much weeping, I decided to try this old remedy which is supposed to remove such signs."

"I see . . . and does it work?"

Geraldine cast her a meaningful glance. "You need to keep the cucumber there for several minutes — had you not disturbed me — "

"Pray do not let me do so further," interrupted Lucilla, still managing to keep a straight face. "I'll wait for you in the drawing room and set up the backgammon table."

She had sped from the room before she laughed, but once outside she had given way to her mirth. A smile still lingered on her face as she moved the little games table closer to the fire.

Two weeks had passed since Geraldine had received the letter from Rupert Lennox-Childs, and they expected him any day. Geraldine had become increasingly fussy about all sorts of things. The flowers in the house had to be just so; the silver must be cleaned and polished until it glistened and gleamed; the grand hall must be immaculate; and now her latest whim was with her own appearance.

The mourning she still wore made her look pale and tired, she said, so she decided to rest every afternoon. Now Lucilla knew the reason why. Never would Geraldine have admitted to anything so vain; she was no doubt furious at being discovered, neither would she deign to reveal how excited she was about her cousin's imminent arrival. To show outward signs of such emotions was to reveal a distinct flaw in the strict code of good breeding. Geraldine had been taught that a lady always remained calm and never showed her feelings, and with very few exceptions she adhered to this.

Lucilla paid small attentions to such niceties. She openly admitted that she could not wait to set eyes on Lord Childs. She had seen a miniature of him upon Geraldine's dressing table, but only after the arrival of the letter had she paused to give it a closer look.

As with Geraldine, she could not help but be impressed by what she saw. He really was exceedingly handsome — that is, if the miniaturist had not been indulging his imagination as he painted. Lord Childs' looks were of the aristocratic type, with an aquiline nose, fine bone structure, and firm mouth. It was difficult to tell what his eyes were like in such a tiny portrait, but they looked as though they might have an interesting expression in them, and certainly the painter had captured something of the man's engaging smile.

Lucilla had not thought it fitting to ask too many questions of Geraldine about her cousin, since he was a bachelor and she, herself, was unwed. Her curiosity was satisfied, however, because Geraldine often spoke about him, and seemed very happy to do so, and already Lucilla's romantic nature warmed to him. Influenced by Geraldine, she, too, was beginning to think of him as the most gallant and wonderful of beings.

Not that Lucilla nurtured any false notions about the gentleman's susceptibility to the opposite sex, as Geraldine did. Aunt Amelia had discreetly confided in her niece that she had heard stories concerning Lord Childs, but she would say no more, and merely accompanied her vague words with a knowing nod of the head and a pursing of the lips.

Geraldine looked upon her cousin as a veritable knight in shining armour, come to rescue her from the ordeals of dealing with solicitors, bailiffs, and stewards. A man who could do no wrong, and whose every deed was one of chivalry and gallantry.

Lucilla set up the games table and sat waiting impatiently for Geraldine to join her. Outside, the rain pelted down, and, shivering slightly, she moved closer to the fire. She was glad when the maid brought in the gleaming silver tea tray, laden with hot scones and caraway seed cake.

Geraldine made a languid appearance shortly after, and Aunt Amelia began to pour tea. Lucilla was ravenous and ate heartily, but Geraldine seemed to have little interest in the food. From time to time she wandered to the window and peered out into the gloom of the dying afternoon. It was not late, but the low clouds and torrential rain had hastened on dusk.

Lucilla watched her uneasily. It was not like Geraldine to be so restless. Aunt Amelia also glanced at her. She worried that Geraldine might be sickening for something, or was it the thought of Lord Rupert's arrival that had made her agitated?

Geraldine must have read her thoughts. She turned away from the window with a sigh and murmured, "I do hope Rupert comes soon. If we have more of this torrential rain, the rivers will flood the roads, and they will become impassible. It will delay his arrival even longer."

"Since he did not deign to say when he would start out, he may still be in Northumbria for all we know," declared Lucilla as she munched her way through her third scone. "There is no way of telling."

"I am sure he would have worded his letter differently if

that were the case," said Geraldine. "No, I feel that he started out soon after he wrote to me. I am sure he will come soon." She returned to the window as she spoke and looked into the deepening gloom.

"Have some fresh tea, Geraldine," said Aunt Amelia, eyeing with disapproval Geraldine's half-consumed cup. "Lord Childs will not come any faster if you stand all evening by the window, and I am sure he would not want you to go off your food."

"I am not off my food," declared Geraldine with dignity, annoyed that Amelia Prior spoke to her as though she were an excited child.

To prove that she was nothing of the sort, she returned to the fireside and helped herself to the last scone, consuming it down to the last crumb even though it tasted like cotton. Neither did she decline the piece of seed cake proffered firmly by Aunt Amelia, although, happily, the events of the next few minutes prevented her from eating it.

Lucilla had just wiped the last crumbs from her mouth and sipped the remainder of her tea, when a sudden noise outside cut through the stillness of the room. Horse's hoofs could be heard approaching along the drive. They came so quickly that, for a moment, all three women were startled.

Lucilla was the first to recover. She ran nimbly across to the window and uttered an excited cry of delight. Geraldine joined her in moments. Aunt Amelia placed her teacup upon the tray with a hasty rattle and hurried to another window.

There on the forecourt stood a large carriage. They could just make out the shape in the gloom of the lights from the house. Already, servants were appearing with flickering lanterns, for the driver had lost no time in jumping down and thumping on the door. Geraldine had warned the household that Lord Childs might arrive at any time. They had stood at the ready for days.

Within only a short while the carriage was surrounded by a throng of menials lifting out travelling chests and bags. It was only then that Lord Childs appeared. The bright light thrown from the open doors of the hall, together with that from the numerous lanterns, enabled the three women to see him quite clearly.

Rupert Lennox-Childs alighted from the carriage with an easy grace. He was very tall; far taller and broader shouldered than Lucilla had imagined. Unhurriedly, he turned to the servants to instruct them about important pieces of his baggage before glancing critically at the house.

He did not seem to be in undue haste to enter and looked around him for several moments. Neither did he seem to be fatigued by the journey, which, in fact, he was not, having slept most of the afternoon and only awakening when aroused by the noise of the servants outside the carriage. Nonchalantly, he sauntered towards the large doors of the house, both of which were thrown open to receive him.

Then he disappeared inside.

Lucilla turned excitedly to Geraldine.

"Come — let us go and welcome him!" Her eyes sparkled and she caught hold of Geraldine's arm, urging her towards the door. She could not understand why Geraldine had not run to greet him as soon as they had seen the carriage.

Aunt Amelia understood. Geraldine, always calm, preferred to exercise more decorum in such an important matter. She had instructed the servants days ago that they were to announce Lord Childs in a manner which befitted his title and rank, as soon as he arrived, no matter at what time of day.

"Restrain yourself, Lucilla," Geraldine replied serenely. "The servants will announce him soon enough . . . and please do something about your hair. It is so untidy!"

Lucilla glanced quickly at her immaculate friend and put her hand to her head. Several tresses of the fine golden hair had evaded the hairpins she thought she had fixed firmly.

She flew to the ornately framed pier mirror which hung between the two windows and began to unpin and rewind the curls. Within moments the recalcitrant strands were tucked securely where they belonged. She had just finished when the double doors were thrown open and Lord Childs was announced.

There was no doubt that he was devastatingly good-looking, and even more handsome than the miniature which stood upon Geraldine's dressing table.

His hair was raven black, immaculately brushed back from the high, intelligent forehead. His eyes were of a most incredible shade of blue, far deeper than the usual tone, with a penetrating look which could quickly change to one of amusement. His nose was straight and his nostrils finely chiselled. The cheekbones and general bone structure were superbly aristocratic, and the firm mouth was well shaped yet sensual.

To Lucilla, his looks were everything she desired most in a man, although she would never have admitted it. For already bitter disappointment had quelled her enthusiasm. Within seconds, his arrogance had infuriated her enough to make her dislike him immediately.

The cursory glance which he bestowed upon her, sweeping her from head to toe and taking in her shape, cut of her dress, and quality of the fabric incensed her. The next moment, he had dismissed her from his mind and had stepped forward to greet Geraldine.

He clasped her in a brotherly embrace, kissing her punctiliously.

"Dear cousin," breathed Geraldine with just a slight loss of her usual composure. "Welcome to Langley House — I hope your journey here has been a pleasant one."

"The journey went swiftly for the most part, but I'm glad to be here at last, my dear Geraldine," he said, standing back from her. "How good it is to see you again — yet, you are pale, my dear. Now that I am here to watch over you, I hope that the colour will soon return to those cheeks." He had an impeccable speaking voice, with perfect pitch.

"I feel better already, Rupert," replied Geraldine as she gazed up at him with obvious admiration, "and I am sure that if anybody can restore my spirits, you can. Although I have not been alone during my period of mourning, my good friend Miss Lucilla Prior has been staying with me together with her aunt, Miss Amelia Prior."

He bowed pleasantly to Aunt Amelia and asked her a few questions about her brother's parish in a perfunctory manner, then he turned to Lucilla.

"It is a pleasure to meet such a good friend of my cousin's, Miss Prior," he said graciously, "and I hope that you will remain here as long as you are able. Do not let my coming disturb your stay in any way."

Lucilla thanked him and gave him a beguiling smile, suspecting that he would later question Geraldine about her means and position in the town, not realizing that he knew already. Geraldine had mentioned in her letter to him that Lucilla's delightful nature amply made up for her modest social position.

He could see by Lucilla's simple dress that she was far from wealthy. But he had not been prepared for her exquisite beauty. The delicate complexion and violet eyes, such bright, sparkling eyes, and the corn-coloured hair were all quite breathtaking. He found it hard to take his eyes off her.

"I long for a bath," he said, turning to Geraldine, "but I shall look forward to joining you all at dinner."

"Everything is prepared for your comfort, Rupert," replied Geraldine, ringing for the servant as she spoke.

When the door closed behind him, she turned to Lucilla and declared with an elated sigh, "Did I not say what a fine figure of a man he was? How good it will be to have him here. I can take all my problems to him."

Lucilla smiled at her. It delighted her to see how uplifted Geraldine's spirits were, and she could see that Lord Childs would never be able to do any wrong in his cousin's eyes. She glanced warily at her aunt to see if she could discern what that good lady thought of Lord Childs. By the look of agreement with Geraldine's remark on her aunt's face, it seemed that she shared Geraldine's impression.

Lucilla vowed that she would keep to herself how she really felt about Rupert Lennox-Childs. His haughty demeanor and appraising glances seemed only to have been perceived by herself.

"You are lucky, indeed, Geraldine," said Aunt Amelia approvingly, "to have somebody of Lord Childs' calibre to whom you may turn."

Lucilla knew instinctively that Geraldine was waiting for her to pay a similar compliment. She faced her friend with a smile and said truthfully, "I have never met anybody quite like your cousin before, Geraldine. It is not difficult to see why you are so fond of him. He is so perfect a gentleman, and so considerate towards you, that you must consider yourself most fortunate to have him here.''

"Ah! I knew that you would like him the moment that you saw him," declared Geraldine happily, well satisfied with her friend's remark, and quite missing the fact that Lucilla had said nothing of the kind.

2

Lord Childs had been at Langley House for several days already, and Lucilla had to admit that he was every bit as charming as Geraldine had said. He could also be witty and amusing, although Aunt Amelia did not always see the joke, and Geraldine, too, sometimes appeared puzzled. At other times he was cold and restrained, particularly towards Lucilla.

He had entirely captivated Aunt Amelia, who thought him one of the most amenable and mannerly of men, even though he did not go out of his way to charm her, while Geraldine absolutely adored him and was never happier than when singing his praises.

Yet, Lucilla's first impression remained. She could not bring herself to like him fully. Moreover, she had noticed a curious change come over him since his arrival. It was hard to define, and certainly she would not have dreamed of saying anything to Geraldine or her aunt for fear of upsetting them. But it was as though he had some hidden worry. A brooding expression would cloud his face from time to time, and often she felt he was paying only scant attention to the conversation.

She had noticed it first after he had been with them for a day or so. More than once she had seen him staring forlornly into space as he took a pinch of snuff from his sumptuous gold snuff box, or while playing backgammon. Lucilla suspected that something had happened to upset him deeply and this constantly rankled him. She alone seemed to notice it.

But a more entertaining incident had occurred to overshadow her preoccupation with Lord Childs. Lucilla had overheard Violet, the chambermaid, chatting with another servant about a band of gypsies who had arrived in the area.

Violet had prattled on with giggles about a certain fortune-teller who travelled with them. She had seen the old woman at Dorking Fair when the gypsies were last in town, and was determined to pluck up the courage to have her own fortune read this time.

Lucilla pricked up her ears when she overheard the young girls talking. Fortunetelling appealed to her own sense of fun, for she was not much older than the two maids herself. At home such an opportunity would never present itself, for her father would have frowned on such a venture. Since she was now at Langley House, there was nobody to stop her.

She decided to suggest a visit to the fair to Geraldine, although she suspected that her friend might be a little shocked at the idea.

She chose her time with care, during a happy morning when they were both out riding. The two girls cut a fine picture in their fashionable high-waisted jackets, full skirts and wide, wavy-brimmed hats.

"Now that Lord Childs is here, Geraldine, will you not relax a little and come with me to Dorking Fair next week?" Lucilla asked eagerly.

Geraldine did not answer at once. She seemed to be turning the question over in her mind.

"There will be all sorts of things to see," Lucilla continued with enthusiasm. "I might even have my fortune told — "

"How can you, Lucilla?" Geraldine interrupted her in horror. "As likely as not, you would catch something horrid from the wretched gypsy. Anyway, I do not feel like the bustle of a fair at the moment."

"Come Geraldine, where is your sense of fun?" Lucilla laughingly persisted. "Behaving like a dowager duchess before you are even betrothed? No harm will come to us if we take care — and it will be so exciting . . . there is a travelling pedlar with fine ribbons and nicknacks, which they say he brings from France," she added temptingly.

A flicker of interest showed on Geraldine's face.

"I will see," she said guardedly. "Perhaps I might take the carriage into town that day to buy some silk for a new dress."

Lucilla smiled to herself and let the matter drop, knowing full well that Geraldine would be unable to resist the temptation of sorting over the pedlar's ribbons.

She was right. That evening as they sat by the fire, Geraldine raised the matter herself.

"I have decided to go to Dorking," she said suddenly.

Lucilla looked up in surprise. She was replacing the beautiful little mother-of-pearl counters in their box. They had just used them for a game.

"Oh, I am so glad — I am sure you will enjoy yourself. There will be so much to see . . ."

"But do not think that you will get me to visit that vile

gypsy," Geraldine added quickly. "Nothing would induce me to go near the creature."

"That's a pity," said Lucilla, showing her disappointment. "Still, perhaps, I will go by myself."

"As you wish," shrugged Geraldine. "I cannot stop you, but I think you would be ill-advised to do so." She let the matter drop, but the annoyance in her voice revealed only too plainly how she felt.

The day for the visit to Dorking dawned bright and clear, and, although it was cold, the two girls were snug in their fur-lined cloaks with fur-edged hoods. Each carried one of the large muffs so fashionable at the time, and Lucilla was especially proud of hers since it had been an unexpected Christmas present from Geraldine.

"Is this not fun?" Lucilla laughed, her eyes sparkling as the carriage swept out of the drive. Her face was alive with excitement for she meant to enjoy herself, although she wished that Geraldine would be less sullen.

"I shall try to find some blue and pink ribbons on the pedlar's tray which will match my two nightgowns" Lucilla said brightly. "Old Mrs. Lacey can stitch them on. She works neatly and needs the extra money."

She chatted on lightheartedly, although it was not easy, for her mind was really on the gypsy fortuneteller. As soon as she had escorted Geraldine to the shoemaker, she intended to hurry off to find the gypsy tent. There was no point in her staying with Geraldine, for she had already spent the small allowance which her father allowed her for clothes.

Geraldine's quiet mood persisted. There was something on her mind.

"Do you not think, Lucilla, that it is time I came out of this dark mourning and gradually returned to lighter colours?" she suddenly asked.

Lucilla looked at her, first in amazement, then in delight. As for herself, she was heartily sick of the black satin and brocade dresses which the local seamstresses had run up for her and longed to return to normal clothes.

"Rupert mentioned that it would be proper and timely only yesterday," continued Geraldine, "and, well, black does not become me very well."

A slight flush had spread over Geraldine's face when she mentioned her cousin, which puzzled Lucilla. She could not know that Lord Childs had said that he would take Geraldine to a wonderful ball in London the following month, but that, surprisingly, he had not included Lucilla in the invitation. Geraldine knew how disappointed Lucilla would be and it was this which had been preoccupying her. She felt almost guilty because of it.

"How lovely it will be to wear ordinary clothes again," said Lucilla happily, "although I think you look beautiful in that pretty black velvet turban with the three feathers."

"Well, then, it is settled," declared Geraldine, her face breaking into a smile at last. "I shall start replenishing my wardrobe this very day."

Lucilla had begun to swivel her head around to catch a closer sight of the fair, for they were already approaching the town of Dorking, and the market sprawled along stubbly fields on the outskirts. She was hoping to discover the location of the gypsy tent so that she could make straight for it without wasting time, since she did not wish to leave Geraldine for too long.

"What a bustle it all is," said Geraldine, following her

gaze and eyeing the market folk with distaste. "They all look so dirty, particularly those disgusting gypsies over there."

She had spotted them straight away and Lucilla rejoiced inwardly to see the fortuneteller sitting outside a shabby tent.

"Dirty, yes, but so alive," retorted Lucilla. "Just listen to their funny calls and watch the strange way they twist their mouths as they shout out their wares." She stopped and did a perfect imitation of one of the vendors, much to Geraldine's amusement.

Glancing at Geraldine's pale complexion, Lucilla suddenly wondered whether her friend would be up to the pushing and shoving of the crowded fair. Her illness had left her very delicate.

"If you like, I'll bring the ribbons from the pedlar's tray," she offered kindly. "Why not go and take tea with the seamstresses? It will be more restful and you can have a look at the latest French fashion dolls."

Geraldine gave her a thankful look, for she had been dreading the crowds. However, she was anxious about Lucilla.

"You won't do anything reckless, Lucilla, will you?" The question sounded silly but she knew her friend only too well. Lucilla's exploits had got them both into trouble in the past. Her sense of adventure often got the better of her judgment, and Geraldine did not want her to do anything which would upset Lord Childs. She suspected that he was not altogether sure about Lucilla, and she also wanted to persuade him to take her friend to the ball.

"Reckless?" Lucilla burst into a ripple of laughter. "What do you mean? What sort of reckless thing would I do, pray?"

"You know very well what I mean," retorted Geraldine, unamused. "Really Lucilla, surely I don't need to warn you. Remember we have my cousin with whom to contend now, and not dear, easygoing Papa. Rupert will not understand one little bit if you do something silly." A querulous tone had crept into her voice, so Lucilla thought it best to drop the subject.

The carriage shortly drew up before the premises of the town's shoemaker and the two girls alighted.

"Will you come inside with me?" asked Geraldine as the carriage moved off. "It would be helpful to have your advice, since I need several pairs of slippers and shoes." Lucilla had excellent taste, and Geraldine liked to discuss colours with her.

"Not if you wish me to buy ribbons from the pedlar."

"I do. Yes, indeed. I would much rather you went to that horrid fair without me, but I'd love these colours." Geraldine, always well organized, handed Lucilla part of her shopping list.

"Mmm — you certainly want a lot," murmured Lucilla as she glanced at it.

Geraldine thrust a sovereign into her friend's hand. She knew that Lucilla would not be able to afford everything that she wanted as well as buy ribbons for herself and Aunt Amelia. Lucilla took it gratefully and placed it carefully in her reticule.

"You are quite sure you don't wish to come?" she asked. She knew that Geraldine loved to buy ribbons and lace from the travelling pedlars.

Her friend shook her head emphatically, so Lucilla bade her good-bye and hurried back along the narrow high street towards the noisy fair where villagers from miles around thronged to buy and sell their produce. Already she could hear their loud, vying calls, offering everything from goose eggs to indispensables.

She pushed her way through the crowds, taking care to watch out for pickpockets, since she had no intention of losing Geraldine's sovereign and her own meagre amount of money. Then, at last, she heard the call which brought a tingle of excitement rushing through her body.

It was the high, lilting tones of the gypsy fortuneteller, loud and clear it rang out above the others: "Fortunes for a farthing! Know your fortunes, pretty ladies! Let old Meg turn your luck! Step up! Step up!" The singsong voice droned on hypnotically, guiding Lucilla through the crowds to the gypsy tent.

But progress was slow. It was a big fair and a popular one. It stretched out over the less fertile fields in a higgledy-piggledy fashion, a sea of booths and stalls accommodating traders of all kinds up from the coastal ports and down from London.

Everybody had come to enjoy the fun of the fair, and the noise was shattering. Many were drunk already, and the jostling and pushing was almost impossible to fight. Violence was never far from the scene, and angry scuffles broke out all along the way between both men and women at the slightest provocation.

At last, Lucilla broke free of the mass of people, emerging at a bedraggled clearing on the edge of the fair. There stood the gypsy tent she had seen from the road with Geraldine. Her heart gave a strange jump as she saw before her a gnarled old woman hunched over the outstretched palm of a rosy-cheeked girl. A few feet away stood a younger gypsy, probably the old woman's daughter, singing out the fortuneteller's mystic powers in the persuasive voice which had lured Lucilla to the spot.

The woman glanced across to the fringe of the crowd at that moment and spotted Lucilla. At once she noted her as a lady of quality, perhaps good for as much as a sixpence. She stopped her trilling and stealthily made her way towards Lucilla.

"Does this lovely lady want her fortune told?" she asked softly as she edged towards her, for she knew how reticent gentlefolk could be, and she did not want to frighten this one away.

Lucilla hesitated. Suddenly she felt both frightened and silly. For a brief moment, she remembered Geraldine's disapproval. Perhaps her friend was right. She drew back. But it was already too late. The woman had drawn closer.

"Don't be shy, young lady," she wheedled. "You can go inside, yonder, if it pleases you better." She jerked her head in the direction of the tent.

"I'm not sure," stammered Lucilla. "I was only passing by . . ."

Her words sounded feeble and unconvincing. The woman gave her a toothy grin, the disbelief showing only too clearly in her eyes.

"Don't you want to know who your husband will be, you, such a pretty one?" A coaxing tone had crept into her voice. "Old Meg'll be able to tell you. No need to stay longer than a few minutes."

As soon as the woman mentioned time, Lucilla remembered that the minutes were all-important. She had but a short while at her disposal before she must return to Geraldine. She drew her breath in sharply and turned to the woman.

"Very well. Take me inside the tent. But I have only a moment to spare." She glanced uneasily around as she spoke, fearing the somebody she knew might see her.

It was then that she saw the man standing a little distance away from the crowd, engaged in conversation with a bad-tempered looking gypsy. Why, he appeared to be none other than Lord Childs! She could not be absolutely sure, since she could not quite see his face.

The gypsy woman had seen her startled expression and had followed her gaze. Quickly, she realized that the fine-looking gentleman was known to the young woman and that if she did not act quickly she might lose her prey. Before Lucilla could stop her, the gypsy had grasped her arm and drawn her inside the gloomy tent.

Old Meg had watched from hooded eyes. As soon as she saw that Lucilla was netted, she brought the fortune she was casting to a speedy conclusion, grabbed her money from the bewildered farmer's wife who was sitting with her, and hobbled inside to Lucilla.

" 'Tis a lucky face you have, as well as a lovely one," she cackled, holding Lucilla's small white hand tightly in her sinewy grasp. "Aye — the palm is just as lucky, too."

Lucilla peered at her hand and wondered how the old gypsy could see anything in the gloom of the filthy tent.

The gypsy was shrewd enough to see that Lucilla would need more convincing than most people.

" 'Tis all here," she cackled. "You'll wed within the year, my pretty one, and he'll be handsome. He'll be as fine a man as any in the land."

She sat rocking herself from side to side as if in some sort of coma. It was an act which never failed to impress.

"I see riches . . . riches galore. Fine jewels and gems. A

ball and you dancing with splendid gentlemen. Aah —
what's this? One is finer than the others. He is different . . .
he wears a crown — "

"A crown?" interrupted Lucilla impatiently, for, up until
then, she had been believing the old woman. "You mean I
am to attend a ball at which the King will be present? Well,
he is nearly past dancing, so I think you should look again."

A strange expression swept the gypsy's face.

"Mock me not, lady, I say only what I see. And I tell you
that there will be a grand ball where all eyes will be turned
on you and your partner."

"Perhaps," retorted Lucilla. "I go often to balls, and there
are many gentlemen who ask to dance with me."

"This one will be different — you'll see. Old Meg knows.
She's never wrong when she feels it as strongly as this.
Anyway," she added ominously, "you may lose your fine
love — the line is broken, see!" She thrust Lucilla's palm
under her eyes, pointing to something which Lucilla could
not find.

"How? Since you know so much — tell me how?"

"You're stubborn and headstrong — that's why. You'll
very likely not be guided by your heart when the time
comes. Watch out for a letter, for it will tell you all . . ."

But Lucilla had had enough of the old woman's meander-
ings.

"Well, if I'm to lose such a fine man, there is no point in
my being told about him. And you can keep your character
reading for somebody else!"

Without waiting for the old woman to reply, Lucilla
sprang up, groped inside her indispensable reticule for a
coin, thrust it at the gypsy, and ran swiftly into the fresh air.

She had spent too long away from Geraldine already, and

she still needed to find the pedlar for the ribbons.

The crowd was becoming even more dense, and was almost impossible to push through in a hurry. The place reeked of the smell of people and the stench of greasy food and beer. Lucilla felt sick. She held her cambric handkerchief to her nose, thankful that Geraldine had not accompanied her. She had quite lost her sense of direction. The crowd seemed to be sweeping her along. She began to wonder how she was ever going to find her way back.

In desperation, she looked around for somebody who seemed reliable enough to ask. A leering drunk watched her from a nearby booth and gave her an insolent smile as he lurched towards her. She fled into a clearing by the side of the stalls in fear, and threaded her way back through another avenue of booths. Then she saw the muffin man. Almost sobbing with relief, she jostled towards him. She tossed him a small coin and asked if he had seen the pedlar. He gave her a cheeky grin and jerked his finger over his shoulder.

There stood the pedlar, surrounded by a throng of eager buyers, his tray covered with gleaming ribbons, novelty hair-pins, cheap jewelled combs for the hair, feathers, and nick-nacks of all kinds. Lucilla wished that she had brought more money with her.

She pushed her way to the front of the crowd and stood gazing at the sea of colours. It took time to sort out the ribbons that Geraldine wanted, then there were those she needed to buy as a surprise for her aunt, to say nothing of her own small requirements. At last she had finished. She half ran back through the town, arriving at the seamstress's house which had been Geraldine's last call, just as her friend was taking her leave.

"You look very flushed," declared Geraldine in alarm,

upon seeing Lucilla. "Oh, dear, I do hope you have not picked up some malady from the crowds. I asked you not to go."

"Fiddlesticks!" retorted Lucilla. "The fresh air has brought the colour to my cheeks, that is all."

Geraldine pursed her lips, but let the matter rest, for she was in a good mood. Her morning had been very successful. At the shoemaker she had ordered some charming sandal shoes, cut low over the foot and tied on by delicate criss-cross ribbons over the instep and round the ankle. She had also bought two pairs of slippers, one in palest blue and the other in lemon, both daintily trimmed with roses and ribbon ruching. Apart from these, she had been delighted by some of the new fashions she had seen.

"The dressmaker had some enchanting moppet fashion dolls," she declared enthusiastically, when they had settled in the carriage and were on their way home. "It was a good idea of yours, Lucilla, to suggest that I visit her. I saw one ballgown in particular which I should love to have copied."

"Had you any particular ball in mind?" asked Lucilla curiously.

"No . . . well, not yet, that I know of for absolute sure, that is," said Geraldine, looking confused, and rather wishing that she had not mentioned the gown to Lucilla before she had tried to persuade Rupert to invite her friend as well.

Lucilla sensed that something was afoot but dismissed it. Her thoughts were still back with the fortuneteller, and she could not resist a quick smile when she recalled the old woman's predictions.

"Did you go to the peddler for the ribbons?" Geraldine asked eagerly as the carriage moved swiftly along the deep, tree-lined lanes away from Dorking.

"Oh, yes! He had such wonderful colours, and so many. It was quite a tease to choose. Look — are they not fine?" Lucilla took them out and held out the colourful array of gleaming ribbons for Geraldine to see. They were indeed beautful. Like an exotic waterfall, they suddenly unwound from their neat circles and cascaded to the ground.

"They'll get spoiled," cried Geraldine in alarm, and leaned to rescue them from the floor of the carriage.

Hardly had she done so, when it jerked suddenly to a halt. Men's voices were heard outside, and Lucilla recognized one of them as that of Lord Childs. Soon, the door was flung open and he peered inside.

"May I join you, Cousin? My horse has gone lame and I have left him with my groom." Although he smiled with his customary charm, Lucilla sensed that he was in one of his brooding moods.

Before Geraldine had time to reply, he had jumped inside and seated himself opposite Lucilla.

"We were returning from Dorking," he explained, "when it happened — the poor beast seemed in great pain. We had gone to inspect some hunters. You need new blood in your stables," he said, turning to Geraldine.

He had been looking at the ribbons which Geraldine still clasped.

"I see by your shopping that you have had a good morning," he added, with just a touch of male condescension.

Geraldine did not notice it.

"You are right, Rupert," she replied happily. "I have seen such lovely gowns on the fashion dolls that I long to have them all."

"Where was this, pray?"

"At the seamstress in Dorking. She has only recently

received them from Paris," explained Geraldine eagerly, "and so they really are the very latest Paris fashions."

"The local seamstress, eh? And is this where you usually have your clothes made, Cousin?" he enquired loftily.

"Not always, Rupert," replied Geraldine, looking slightly abashed. "When I go to London, I seek out a dressmaker I know. But the seamstress in Dorking is very good for all that."

Lucilla had listened to the conversation in amusement. She had often wondered, herself, why Geraldine, with so much money to spend on clothes, should choose to patronize the local seamstress. Had she been in Geraldine's place, she would have delighted in travelling to London specially for her gowns.

She was not surprised, therefore, when Lord Childs continued, "In future, Geraldine, I think it would be advisable if you employed the Dorking person for only minor garments. When I escort you around London, you will meet ladies of the highest fashion who spend lavishly on their outfits. The homespun efforts of your Dorking woman would look ridiculous in such company. You must order an entirely new set of gowns as soon as we arrive in London. I shall treat you to them myself."

Geraldine's crestfallen expression was transformed to one of rapture. She spent several moments more than necessary thanking him profusely for his generosity. He seemed to grow bored with the subject and waved her thanks aside with a dismissive gesture.

He turned to Lucilla almost as if with relief. "And you, Miss Prior, what have you been up to this morning? Have you also been viewing moppet dolls with such pleasure?"

Lucilla met his steady gaze unblinkingly. She smiled at

him disarmingly, a beautiful smile which seemed to light the entire carriage. For a brief moment, he seemed to be captivated by its purity. Then his usual set expression returned. It hardened as she answered his question.

"No, Lord Childs, I did not accompany Geraldine. I could not resist the fun of the fair."

He gave her a withering glance.

"Then you are extremely foolish, Miss Prior. Such places teem with vagabonds and robbers. You were lucky not to have your money stolen and your jewellery filched."

Lucilla threw back her head and laughed — a sweet, girlish laugh which bubbled up with all the exuberance of youth.

"My money or my jewellery stolen, indeed," she replied with mirth. "Why, Lord Childs, I have little jewellery to speak of, so I treasure what I have and left it safely under lock and key in my casket. As for money — I am hardly over-endowed with that commodity, so I took only a little with me. It would be a sad day for the thief who picked my pockets, I assure you, for his family would starve."

Lord Childs' lips twitched and he turned away quickly, but not fast enough for Lucilla's quick eyes, and she caught the amused look.

The next moment, however, she felt sure she must have been mistaken, for when he turned back to her, his deep blue eyes showed no trace of humour, and there was scorn in his voice as he replied with indifference, "It is up to you how you conduct yourself, of course, Miss Prior, but I cannot help thinking your father would disapprove if he knew that you were in the habit of wandering around rough fairs by yourself. Few gentlefolk — be they ladies or gentlemen — would be so foolish as to move among gypsies alone."

His tone confounded her, but his words brought a sudden vivid picture into her mind. She glanced at the clothes which he wore and remembered the man she had seen talking to the gypsy close by the fortuneteller's tent. She had thought it was Lord Childs then, and now she could see by the clothes that it was.

Lucilla was tempted to say something immediately, but a surreptitious poke in the ribs from Geraldine's elbow warned her to say no more on the subject.

Lord Childs noticed nothing, and Geraldine, eager to change the subject, prompted him to tell them about his Northumbrian estate, which he did with great feeling, for he obviously loved the place, and even Lucilla was captivated by his fine descriptions of the vast house built during Queen Anne's reign for his illustrious ancestors. Geraldine's delight showed clearly in her eyes.

Noticing this, Lord Childs declared expansively, "You shall journey north with me, Cousin, at some appropriate time in the future, and see for yourself."

Lucilla observed, without surprise, that he did not include her in the invitation.

Although she realized that Geraldine had been annoyed with her in the coach, for the nudge in the ribs was clearly indicative of this, Lucilla was not prepared for her friend's temper when they were alone. Geraldine turned on her, in one of her rare furies, accusing Lucilla of provoking her cousin's ill will.

"I don't understand — " Lucilla replied in astonishment.

"Then you are stupid, as well as being insensitive to the type of man my cousin is," snapped Geraldine.

"What do you mean?"

"How could you flaunt your reckless actions before him? Surely you could have guessed that he would disapprove of your visit to the fair?"

"I did not think he would react quite so strongly — and I needed to tell him."

"And why, pray?"

"Because it is possible that he saw me there!"

"What nonsense is this? How on earth could he have seen you?" demanded Geraldine.

"I am sure that I saw Lord Childs talking to a gypsy near the fortuneteller's tent . . . such a bad-tempered looking vagabond, too, he was . . ." Lucilla's voice trailed off as she beheld the fierce look of disbelief in Geraldine's eyes.

"Lucilla, if I did not know you to be such an honest person, I should have said that you made that up," declared Geraldine furiously, as she fanned herself irritably with quick, nervous movements, her black fan resembling the movements of a quarrelsome jackdaw.

"Is it likely," she persisted, "that Lord Childs would be doing any such thing? Why, the idea that my cousin would demean himself like that is ridiculous."

"I know. And please believe me, I was truly astonished myself."

Lucilla could see how upset her friend was, so she added as an afterthought, "I must admit that I did not see his face, for it was turned away from me."

"Well then! You silly goose, you were obviously wrong."

Geraldine snapped her fan together with a quick, decisive movement of the wrist as if to denote an end to the subject, crossed the room and kissed Lucilla on the cheek. She loathed any sort of discordance and wanted to let Lucilla see that she bore her no ill will.

"Let us forget the matter," she said, as she seated herself at her dressing table and tidied her hair. "Only, you see, I do not want you to upset my cousin in any way at the moment."

Lucilla raised her prettily shaped eyebrows in surprise.

"He has been annoyed enough already — and I wish to ask him for a favour on your behalf."

"A favour? I don't understand."

"Let me explain. I am to accompany Rupert to a wonderful ball at the London house of the Duke of Sedgeley. Oh, Lucilla, I do so want you to come as well, and I know that Rupert received a third invitation — one for his sister, but she has broken her leg."

"But why did he not ask me when he mentioned it to you?"

Geraldine shrugged her shoulders.

A cloud had crossed Lucilla's face.

"Thank you, Geraldine," she said quietly, "but if Lord Childs did not think fit to ask me in the first place, he must have had his reasons. I don't want you to plead for such favours on my behalf. The matter is best left as it is. Perhaps my background is too modest to please your cousin."

"You are wrong! How could you even think such a thing. It is probably that it slipped his memory."

"Lord Childs is not the sort of person who allows things to slip his memory," asserted Lucilla with a proud gleam in her eyes. "Believe me, I do not wish you to mention the matter to him."

Geraldine could see that Lucilla felt strongly, and decided to let the matter drop for the time being.

"You went to the fortuneteller — what did she say?" she asked, changing the subject.

Lucilla's face broke into a smile.

"Ah, now, that is something worth talking about, for I am to be married within the year!"

Geraldine's eyes opened wide.

"Within the year! La! You had best make haste, then, Lucilla, if you are to get one of your admirers to propose in time."

Both the girls began to giggle at the thought.

"Moreover, he will be rich and handsome," added Lucilla, "although he may slip through the net if I don't watch out."

"How disappointing for you," said Geraldine with mock concern, "but forewarned is forearmed, so, no doubt, you will be able to prevent it."

Lucilla nodded and was about to tell Geraldine of the rest of the gypsy's prediction, including the prophesy of a royal ball, but she managed to stop herself in time. Coming so soon after their discord over the ball at the Duke of Sedgeley's house, it hardly seemed a tactful thing to say. And, anyway, it was all rather silly, she decided, since there could not be the remotest possibility of such a prediction materializing, no matter how vividly the gypsy had seen it in the future.

3

Aunt Amelia swept forward in a cloud of black taffeta. She was annoyed, and it showed on her plump face. She had remained at home by herself at Langley House the entire day, and was impatiently awaiting to hear Lucilla's news and to see what shopping her niece had done in Dorking. But Lucilla was nowhere to be found. Yet she knew that the two girls had returned, for she had seen them alight from the carriage.

To add to her chagrin, she had met Lord Childs on the stairs and he had passed her without a word, inclining his head in only the merest of nods. It was so unlike him, for his manners were impeccable, that she had wondered just what had happened in the carriage on the way home, for she had seen him, too, alight with the girls.

Since it was one of the few places she had not looked on the ground floor, she decided to see if the girls were in the library. With a sigh, she retraced her footsteps through the main hall. It was then that she heard their laughter and chattering. The voices came from upstairs, which puzzled Aunt Amelia, for she could not understand why the girls should be there. It was usual for them to take tea in the drawing room before they changed.

Geraldine had guessed that Aunt Amelia would be waiting in a predatory fashion for Lucilla and had whisked her friend away to her boudoir for the chat she wished to have with her, which was just as well, since it would have been unpleasant if Aunt Amelia had witnessed their small disagreements concerning the fair and the ball. Now the two girls came laughing and talking downstairs as though nothing had happened, and Lucilla ran to her aunt and kissed her upon the cheek.

In an instant, Aunt Amelia's black mood was dispelled and her kindly face lit up with a smile.

"Do you not fancy any tea, then?" she asked. "I could not find you anywhere — where did you disappear to, pray?"

"We are longing for our tea, Miss Prior," said Geraldine sweetly, "and we have only been chatting in my boudoir. Look, we have sorted out the ribbons that Lucilla bought and these are for you."

"I thought they would cheer up one or two of your mobcaps," added Lucilla to Aunt Amelia's delight, for she was among the older women who still preferred to wear a cap when at home. She did not feel comfortable or dressed without one, she said, although Lucilla and Geraldine both knew that the real reason was her thinning hair.

"Aah!" Aunt Amelia gazed at the exquisite shades with delight, palest pink down to deepest red, and three tones of blue. "I will put them away until we are come out of mourning," she said, as she thanked her niece.

"There will be no need to wait, Miss Prior," said Geraldine, "for my cousin thinks it quite timely to end the mourning period already."

The relief showed on Aunt Amelia's face. The few black dresses in her meagre wardrobe had been well worn before she came to Langley House, and, of late, they had grown positively shabby. To replace them would stretch her slender means unbearably.

"I think Lord Childs is right," asserted Aunt Amelia, as she carefully replaced the ribbons in their wrapper, "and, since spring is not far away, you will be able to buy the new colours which are in fashion."

She had been so engrossed with her present that she had nearly forgotten to tell Geraldine that her old nurse had returned while she had been in Dorking. The old woman had been looking after the sick niece of whom she was so fond. Geraldine loved her old nurse who had been her sole companion for so many years, and, as soon as she had finished her tea, went at once to see her, since the old lady was tired after her long journey.

Lucilla chatted on to her aunt about her morning in Dorking, but, at the back of the mind, she was still thinking about the ball to which Lucilla would be going with Lord Childs. She told herself it did not matter that he had not asked her, and that it was silly to expect an invitation to such a grand event. After all, she could not hope to accompany Geraldine everywhere, least of all to events for which Lord Childs was responsible.

Aunt Amelia saw that there was something troubling her niece.

"So you really enjoyed yourself, today, my dear?" she asked, as she rang for the maid to remove the tea tray.

"Indeed I did, Aunt," replied Lucilla, "and should like to go again . . . I was so pleased when Geraldine told me in the carriage that she is coming out of mourning. I loathe these dresses. Oh! How I wish I could order a whole new wardrobe, as Geraldine probably will when she goes to London . . ."

Aunt Amelia glanced quickly at her niece and wondered if this could be the reason for Lucilla's strange mood.

"And you envy Geraldine her fine outfits, no doubt," she said, not without a certain amount of understanding.

"Oh, no! Certainly not, Aunt. How could I envy Geraldine anything? She is such a good, kind friend."

"But there is something, is there not?"

"Well — it is not that." Lucilla's face clouded. "But I admit that I am a little upset . . . I cannot understand it, Aunt, yet I am sure that Lord Childs dislikes me."

"I am sure that he does no such thing," declared Aunt Amelia, momentarily astonished.

"Well, his manner is always so severe with me. He is so unbending, and — "

"Yes?"

"He is to take Geraldine to a magnificent ball in London. Oh, Aunt, even though he had three tickets, he did not think to ask me to go."

Having said what was on her mind, Lucilla felt a little better.

"My dear, you should not let such a small thing upset you," replied her aunt soothingly. "I am quite sure it is not because he dislikes you. He probably has other reasons of his own." Although she would never have said so, Aunt Amelia had formed the impression that Lord Childs quite admired her niece. She had often caught a quick look of pleasure pass over his face when Lucilla had entered the room.

"Perhaps," said Lucilla flatly, "but I do not think so. Geraldine had made up her mind to ask him to take me also, but I could not bear her to ask such a favour on my behalf."

"No — I am quite sure you could not," replied her aunt, who knew enough of her niece's proud nature to understand.

Lucilla gazed out of the window dismally. Living so splendidly with Geraldine in the grandeur of Langley House often caused her to forget how modest her own means were by comparison. Geraldine could expect a glittering future, but there was no such outlook for herself.

As soon as Geraldine left Langley House for London with her cousin to enjoy the splendours of London society, she would return with her aunt to the solitude and quiet social life of the rectory, and, although she loved her father dearly, his retiring habits and simple pleasures were not enough for a young woman of Lucilla's spirited nature.

Aunt Amelia guessed what was going on in Lucilla's mind. Carefully, she selected a lemon thread from her work basket to embroider a bunch of primroses, before she asked: "Does Geraldine say why she thinks her cousin did not ask you to attend the ball?"

"Oh, she feels that he has simply overlooked the matter, but I do not," asserted Lucilla with feeling. "I know him to be so haughty that he would not wish somebody from a modest background such as mine to even be seen in his company."

"Bosh!" Aunt Amelia said the word so violently that she pricked herself, which was almost unheard of for her.

"What utter nonsense you talk, niece. I am ashamed of you. And, of course, you are completely wrong."

"I do not think so," said Lucilla petulantly, wandering listlessly back from the window and watching her aunt as she deftly applied her needle.

"You have too much imagination," snapped Aunt Amelia. "Why Lord Childs knows perfectly well that your family connections can bear more than a close scrutiny, even if your father's means are but modest. Just think how respected your uncle is. Remember that Sir Ralph Stavely has long been among the most respected ministers in the land." And this was true, for Sir Ralph, who was the brother of Lucilla's mother, had been, at one time, Privy Counsellor and First Commissioner of the Treasury.

"Well, then, there is some other reason why he does not like me," shrugged Lucilla.

"Come — be honest — is not the real reason for your despondency simply because you will be losing Geraldine's company when she goes to London? The ball surely is of secondary importance," declared her aunt sensibly.

Lucilla puckered up her little nose like a small child, but said nothing. She could not understand, herself, why she was in such a mood.

"Ah! I thought so," said her aunt, assuming that Lucilla's silence meant agreement. "Tell me, my dear, where is this important ball to be held? Who is giving it, pray?"

"The Duke of Sedgeley — "

"Gracious heavens! Why did you not say so in the beginning?" Aunt Amelia was so surprised that she dropped the needle she had been endeavouring to thread. "The Duke of Sedgeley — well, if it is he, you may be able to attend your fine ball, after all."

"But how, Aunt? What do you mean?"

"Simply that Sir Ralph Stavely has been a close friend of the Duke's for many years. I can assure you, Lucilla, that if the Duke is giving an important ball like this one, your own uncle will be high on the list of those invited, and if he is invited so will his wife be — "

"But my aunt is bedridden and stays always in the country," interrupted Lucilla.

"Precisely."

"Aunt, oh! You are not thinking of writing to Uncle Ralph to ask if he will take me instead?" breathed Lucilla, guessing her aunt's reasoning and unable to believe her good fortune.

"Naturally. Since it means so much to you. Moreover, I shall go to my room and put pen to paper this moment." She was already rising from her seat as she spoke.

"Find that needle I have just dropped," she commanded, "and put my embroidery away in my work basket."

"Of course, Aunt . . ."

"The sooner I send the letter, the better. We do not want him to refuse the invitation before he receives my letter."

Aunt Amelia sped from the room as fast as her large frame would permit. Lucilla let out a whoop of delight and skipped around the room like a school girl.

She did not notice Lord Childs appear in the doorway, nor did she see him enter. She had danced to the other end of the room in her ecstasy, and it was only when she turned to come back that she saw him.

In between the elegant chaise longue, designed especially by Mr. Thomas Sheraton, and the delicate writing table which stood to the side of it, Lucilla skipped to a halt. She threw back her head to toss the golden hair from her eyes and brushed it smooth with her hand, and turned round.

The look of elation was transfixed on her face when she beheld Lord Childs.

He had already changed the clothes which he had worn into Dorking and stood elegantly clad in fashionable tight-fighting breeches of deep blue velvet, matching double-breasted waistcoat, and a stylish white silk cravat tied in a floppy bow. He gazed at her coolly.

Lucilla felt flushed and untidy, and very stupid. She had on the unbecoming black dress which she had worn to the fair, having had no chance to change into anything else. The dress was crushed and creased, and the dainty shoes she wore still bore ample signs of the trek she had made through the muddy fields at the fair. She braced herself and sailed towards him.

"Pray, do not let me interrupt you, Miss Prior," he said disarmingly, taking out his snuff box, opening it and then snapping it closed again, as if changing his mind.

"You did not do that, Lord Childs," she replied quietly, "I was just about to take my leave."

"Ah! After the . . ." he waved his hand as if trying to pluck a suitable word from the air, "solo dance perform-ance, I presume." He gave her a quizzical look.

Lucilla realized how ridiculous she must have looked as he walked into the room, but was determined to regain her dignity.

An impish sparkle came into her eyes as she replied calmly, "Dancing echoes the way one feels, Lord Childs. One does not need to be at a ball to feel like dancing. If there is nobody with whom to dance — then why not dance by oneself?"

"And you felt like dancing at that moment — I see. I can only assume that some good news or other led you to feel so elated at that moment, then."

"Perhaps," she replied with a touch of mystery, at the

same time giving him such a beautiful smile that it would instantly have thawed the hearts of most men.

Whatever he may have felt as he gazed at the exquisite little heart-shaped face smiling up at him, Lord Childs showed no outer sign. He merely cleared his throat, as if trying to give himself a few moments grace before speaking, and then said, "Well, happily, your high spirits are infectious, Miss Prior, for already my cousin seems cheerful and sanguine again. I am indebted to you for your help."

"Thank you, My Lord. Geraldine is my dearest friend. I can assure you that it brings me great pleasure to see her more like her normal self again."

"Where is my cousin?" he asked suddenly, as if to bring an end to the conversation.

"She will be down shortly, Lord Childs. Her old nurse returned while we were in Dorking, and Geraldine went to see if she was comfortable after her long journey. Shall I tell her that you are here?"

He shook his head. He seemed to be preoccupied, and, for a brief moment, she wondered if he was going to raise the matter of the fair.

"No. Do not disturb her now. It is of no great importance," he said shortly.

"Then I shall take my leave of you, My Lord, for there are several letters to which I must attend."

With relief, Lucilla gathered up her aunt's embroidery, picked up the needle which she had spotted on the floor near the chair and replaced them in her aunt's workbox, then she walked gracefully from the room.

Her pace changed as soon as she had closed the door behind her, however, and, holding up her skirts, she ran lightly along the corridor to the grand staircase. She was impatient to see how far her aunt had progressed with the letter to Sir Ralph.

Long experience had taught Lucilla not to run up the stairs at Langley House. It was a beautiful, elegant staircase, much admired by all who came to the house, but she had discovered that it was the easiest thing in the world to trip on the stairs, since they seemed deeper than they actually were. Once she had done precisely that, and the pain of her sprained ankle which resulted from the tumble lived long in her memory.

She ascended the stairs, therefore, rather more graciously than had been her speedy journey along the corridor. Nobody would have guessed, had they watched her, with what impatience she made her ascent.

Aunt Amelia's room was at the back of the house, a small but pleasant room with red flock paper upon the walls, and a large painting, showing the exterior of Langley House, hanging above the marble fireplace. Aunt Amelia sat at a small writing table with her spectacles upon the end of her nose, assiduously penning her letter.

Lucilla had knocked quietly. At first, her aunt had not heard her, so Lucilla had half opened the door, peered round, then knocked again. Her aunt guessed at once who it was. She knew how impatiently Lucilla would be waiting for her to dispatch the letter.

Without looking up, she said mildly, "Come in, Lucilla, and close the door — there's a draught."

Swiftly Lucilla did as she was bid.

"If I am disturbing you, I'll go away," she said peeping over her aunt's shoulder.

"No, my dear, sit down by the fire. I've nearly finished.

There is no need to write a long letter since I let Ralph have all the news quite recently."

Lucilla sat for a while gazing into the dancing flames.

"There, it's finished!" Aunt Amelia removed her spectacles, sealed the envelope, and handed the letter to her niece.

"Take it downstairs and place it with the others," she said as she handed it to Lucilla. "And let us hope that it brings you luck."

"Oh, Aunt! Thank you so much. If only Uncle Ralph will take me. I have never had such an opportunity before. It is something of which I have always dreamed." Lucilla clasped the letter to her bosom, her eyes shining, as she spoke.

"Well, don't get too excited, just in case he has decided to take somebody else. Try to forget it for now. You don't want to be too disappointed."

Lucilla nodded.

"And I had better not mention it to Geraldine until I am sure, either."

"Indeed not." Aunt Amelia looked alarmed. She did not want her niece to look foolish if Sir Ralph Stavely should decline to take her. "The least said about that subject to Geraldine the better. You have said quite enough already, Miss."

The letter had been placed on the silver salver with the other correspondence, to be attended to by the servants, and Lucilla was retracing her footsteps upstairs. Now, at last, she could change for dinner. She knocked at Geraldine's door as she passed it, to see if her friend was dressed yet and to discover what Geraldine was wearing. Lucilla did not wish to look too inferior in front of Lord Childs if Geraldine made an appearance in one of her more beautiful gowns. She had a feeling that her friend would discard her mourning clothes immediately.

Geraldine bade her enter. The moment she saw her, Lucilla was thankful that she had come. For Geraldine, resplendent in a most delightful silk dress of palest apple green, with a cascade of small satin bows down the front and around the sleeves, sat at her dressing table having her hair twirled into small ringlets by old Nurse Hargreaves.

"Look! Do you not think this dress is perfect to wear, now that I am finished with mourning — not too bright, but a pretty colour?" Geraldine addressed the question to Lucilla's reflection in the mirror.

"Oh, yes. It is so delicate," replied Lucilla, examining the dress. "I have not seen it before."

Geraldine sat very still. She did not want in any way to spoil the effect which her nurse was creating so adeptly. The old woman had dressed her young mistress's hair with great expertise for years and knew just how to get the best from it.

"La! The dress is quite old," she retorted carelessly. "I have had it at least a year. But there has been little opportunity for me to wear it."

Lucilla turned to Nurse Hargreaves and kissed her on the cheek. "Welcome home — Geraldine has been quite lost without you, Nurse. I hope your niece is fully recovered."

"Thank you, Miss Lucilla. My niece, thank the good Lord, is well on the road to good health again — although it was touch and go, I can tell you . . ."

"Heavens above, Lucilla!" interrupted Geraldine, turning round for the first time and looking at her friend fully. "What on earth have you been doing? You look frightful.

Your face is shiny and smudged, and your hair, well, words escape me. You look as though you've been dragged through a bush backwards."

"I know," replied Lucilla, as she peered at herself in Geraldine's mirror, "but I assure you it will not be for long. I am going straight away to have a bath and change into another dress." She eyed Geraldine's gown as she spoke, for she knew that there was nothing in her own wardrobe to match its beauty.

Nurse Hargreaves saw the wistful expression. She was fond of Lucilla and knew her well. "Since Miss Geraldine is come out of mourning, why do you not do the same, Miss Lucilla?" she asked kindly. "Have you a dress aired?"

"Mmm — I think so, but I haven't really looked yet."

"What a pity we are such different sizes," said Geraldine, "or you could borrow something of mine. But please feel free, Lucilla, to go to my cupboard and select anything which you may fancy — a pretty jacket or a sash, perhaps."

Nurse Hargreaves looked pleased. She had always tried to bring up Geraldine in an unspoiled manner and liked her young mistress to be generous.

"Oh, Geraldine, you are so kind. It would be a great help. Some of my dresses are a bit, well, uninteresting. Papa says I may have some more in the spring — but it seems a long way off."

Lucilla threw open the doors of Geraldine's large cupboard and gazed with admiration at the rows of exquisite gowns. There were so many delightful accessories from which to choose that she did not know where to begin.

Geraldine's old nurse came up beside her, having finished Geraldine's hair and left her young mistress admiring herself critically in the mirror.

"Try that blue dress there, Miss Lucilla," she said, pointing to a pale blue silk gown at the far end of the row. "The colour would look lovely on you — most becoming."

"No, it would not fit me. Geraldine's dresses never do. I'll look for a pretty sash."

"Ah! You are wrong. This one will — try it and see. Here, let me get it out for you." And she pulled it out before Lucilla could stop her.

It really was a lovely dress, with a low, scalloped neckline and a wonderfully full skirt, tied at the waist with a wide sash.

"See — it was made for Miss Geraldine two or three years ago, when she was far slimmer and not nearly so tall as she is now. You can pull the sash in to fit any waist, even your tiny one, Miss Lucilla."

Lucilla took her dress off in a flash and slid the luxurious gown over her head. Nurse arranged the sash and tied it for her. The dress fitted perfectly and looked lovely.

"There! What did I say," declared the old woman triumphantly. "Off you go now and take your bath. Why, Lord Childs won't recognize you when he sees you at dinner."

What Lord Childs thought when he beheld Lucilla was never recorded for posterity, but Aunt Amelia, who happened to be descending the stairs to dinner at the same time as her niece, had plenty to say. Her amazed expression was quite comical, and Lucilla could not help laughing.

"Really, Aunt dear, don't look so surprised. You look as though you are seeing things that aren't real. Do you not like what you see?"

"Tush! Of course I like it. I just wonder whether it is

really my niece inside it. Well . . . now that I look longer, I realize that it is *my* niece wearing one of her friend's dresses. I wonder whether she is also wearing her friend's beautiful manners!"

Having reached the bottom of the staircase, Aunt Amelia turned to her niece and bade her swivel round so that she could see the dress from all angles.

Lucilla did so with a smile on her face.

"Hmm, very nice indeed. You always looked good in blue. But don't let it go to your head, for you know what your dear Papa preaches about vanity," Aunt Amelia sniffed, as if to acquiesce. Secretly she was enraptured with what she saw, and thought that the fullness of the dress, caught at the waist with the sash, accentuated marvellously her niece's tiny waist. The girl looked perfectly beautiful in the delicate shade of blue, more beautiful than her aunt had ever seen her appear before.

As she did not want to give Lucilla inflated ideas of herself, she merely nodded approvingly and added, "Aye, you'll do, niece. Just try to make sure that your quick tongue lives up to the dress, that's all. There's no good in looking like that if you immediately say something to upset Lord Childs." And on this warning note she swept forward into the dining room.

Geraldine and Lord Childs were already seated at the long table. Geraldine eyed her friend with surprised approval. Even she had not suspected that Lucilla would look so exquisite in a dress which she had long discarded because it was unfashionable.

Lord Childs rose from his seat as the two ladies entered the room. He had quickly concealed his first amazement on seeing Lucilla. Her beauty astonished him. He had not seen her in a colour before, and the fragile shade of the blue dress showed to perfection her delicate rosebud complexion and golden hair. Her large, wide-set eyes seemed bluer than ever. They looked at him now with a questioning, slightly mocking expression, and he realized that he had been staring at her.

"Now that the two girls have come out of mourning, Lord Childs, I confess I feel positively dowdy," declared Aunt Amelia, who had not thought it necessary to change the dress she had planned in the morning to wear for dinner.

For once, he was thankful for the older woman's chatter. It helped to divert the attention from Lucilla and the fact that he felt she knew she had made an impact upon him.

"You look charming as always, Miss Prior," he said graciously to Aunt Amelia.

"Why, Aunt, that dress always becomes you," said Lucilla sweetly. "You need not feel that the lack of colour lessens its attraction one little bit."

Lucilla turned away from Aunt Amelia to reach for the salt, and as she did so her eyes met those of Lord Childs. He was staring at her in such a strange way that she wondered if there was something wrong with her appearance. She had taken special pains to make sure that her unruly hair would stay in place, and had chosen the simple necklace which encircled her white throat with infinite care. Surely, she thought, seeing what she interpreted as a critical expression, he has not found something to dislike already.

She could not know that he was wondering where, only recently, he had seen a young woman of whom she reminded him. Where was it? His brow furrowed. He could not quite recall. Then, suddenly, his mind cleared. It had been near the gypsy tent. He was sure he had seen Lucilla there. But had she seen him?

"You both appear to be in excessively good humour this evening," he remarked as the girls laughed and chatted among themselves. "May I know the reason for such levity?"

Geraldine shot Lucilla a guarded look which Lucilla either did not see or chose to ignore.

"Lucilla amused me earlier with one thing and another," Geraldine answered vaguely, before her friend could reply. She helped herself to the rich game soup from the silver tureen, thankful that Lucilla had not spoken. But her thanks were short-lived as she heard Childs speak again.

"Indeed, Miss Prior, no doubt you amused Geraldine by recounting your exploits at the fair."

Lucilla took her time in replying, then she answered in a cool, clear voice, "How perceptive of you, Lord Childs, for I was doing precisely that. Geraldine found several things hard to believe, though."

"Really! Then your adventures must have been truly exceptional." His face was impassive, but there was a sarcastic edge to his voice.

"Perhaps, sir, perhaps . . ." And she would be drawn no more.

Geraldine sighed with relief and gave her friend an approving glance. For a brief moment she had thought that Lucilla would burst out with her fortunetelling incident, or, even worse still, say that she had actually seen Lord Childs at the fair. Lucilla's measured approach came as a pleasant surprise. Perhaps, at last, thought Geraldine, she is learning discretion.

They ate mostly in silence for a while, and Lucilla could

not but help notice that a brooding expression had clouded the face of Lord Childs.

"Have you news of the lame horse, Lord Childs?" she inquired as the servants removed the remnants of the succulent roast goose and apple chutney. "I hope that the poor beast is not badly hurt."

"Ah! He is one of the very best horses in the stables, Miss Prior, and it would deplete the stock sadly if we had to have him shot. At the moment it looks as though we may escape this, for the groom feels it is only a temporary lesion."

"What good fortune it was that our carriage passed by just at that moment to give you a lift home," observed Geraldine. "We might easily have missed you, Rupert. In fact, you must have left the fair at about the same time as Lucilla."

"Fair!" he ejaculated angrily. "I did not go to the fair. I have already told you that I went only to the horse breeder on the other side of the town."

"Of course — I meant to say Dorking," said Geraldine in slight confusion. "I cannot think why I uttered the word fair. How silly of me — what on earth could I have been thinking about?"

He did not deign to reply, but sullenly helped himself to an ale fritter without a word.

Lucilla's large eyes narrowed.

"La! Mistakes like that are easy enough to make, Gerald-ine," she said consolingly, taking a few sugared cherries and a comfit. "Why, I made a similar one myself only today . . . I thought I actually *saw* Lord Childs at the fair."

Geraldine dropped her spoon with a clatter. Aunt Amelia's eyebrows shot up, and Lord Childs looked thunderstruck.

"Yes — I had it in mind to visit the fortuneteller, Aunt," continued Lucilla calmly, ignoring their expressions. "Such things she told me, too. Anyway, I could have sworn that Lord Childs was standing nearby talking to an unpleasant-looking gypsy."

"You went alone to a gypsy fortuneteller — fie on you! You stupid girl!" Aunt Amelia was so beside herself that she was almost speechless. "What would your dear father say if he knew?"

"Bosh! I was perfectly safe," retorted Lucilla with spirit. "And I'm glad I went. For now I know that I am to be married within the year to a gentleman of vast fortune." She could not resist a ripple of laughter.

"Then I hope that he will be able to control you, Miss," declared her aunt hotly. "Why, you might have been robbed or half murdered."

All the time, Lucilla had been keeping a wary eye on Lord Childs, who, after the first dark look at her words, had quickly regained his usual composure.

"And is that all the gypsy predicted?" he now asked, having finished his food. "Hah! She does very well for a sixpence a time then, telling the same story to each gullible young woman silly enough to visit her."

"No, it was not *quite* all," retorted Lucilla, "but, since nobody here seems to believe in fortunetelling, I see no point in revealing all my secrets. Still you will have to eat your words when you receive the wedding invitation!" She returned to her cherry, which she munched with relish, a mischievous expression on her elfin features.

"Let us hope that the bridegroom will have more substance than the phantom person you mistook for myself at the fair, Miss Prior," said Lord Childs with a cold smile.

Geraldine giggled.

Lucilla lowered long lashes over her beautiful eyes. She did not reply immediately. She calmly wiped her mouth with the delicately embroidered table napkin, looked Lord Childs straight in the eyes as she glanced upwards, and said: "Oh! I hope so, Lord Childs, especially when he stands at the altar. It would be so irksome to marry a man who *imagined* himself to be somewhere else."

"I did not imagine I was somewhere else, Miss Prior," said Lord Childs, rising to the bait. "I was never at the fair . . . unlike you, I do not thirst after cheap adventure."

For a brief moment their eyes met — hers with a candid, steady gaze, and his as hard as granite.

"For all that — the man I saw was so like you that he even had the same taste in clothes. In fact, they appeared identical to the ones in which you returned from Dorking," said Lucilla with an innocent air. "Still, it is not likely that I shall see him again, for I have a feeling he will keep well out of my way another time."

Then, with a demure smile, she promptly excused herself from the table before Lord Childs had time to reply, and swiftly left the room.

4

Lord Childs strode into the room with a thunderous face. Geraldine had never seen her cousin like this before, and it alarmed her. She suspected already that she knew why he had asked her to wait upon him punctually at eleven of the hour that morning, stressing she was to come alone. She was sure that he intended to discuss Lucilla's behaviour of the previous night, and in her heart of hearts she could not blame him, for she, too, had been infuriated.

In fact, Geraldine had scarcely slept a wink that night. She had been beside herself with disappointment at Lucilla's total disregard to her feelings, for she had made it perfectly clear to her friend, during their disagreement, that she did not want her cousin provoked.

She could not understand why Lucilla had persisted so at the dinner table with the ridiculous story that she had seen Lord Childs near the gypsy tent. Geraldine had tossed and turned all night in her luxurious bed with its domed canopy of embroidered silk and flounced lace trimmings.

The more Geraldine thought about it, the more perplexed she had become. Yet, because she had so recently had a confrontation with Lucilla, she refused to have another scene, since she abhorred them so, and had eventually decided, therefore, to say no more for the time being.

In the morning, however, Lord Childs' manservant had delivered a note to her boudoir requesting this meeting in the library. She had hurried there anxiously, making sure to be well in time, for she knew that her cousin was not the sort of man who took kindly to being kept waiting. She had hardly seated herself when he had strode into the room.

Having bidden her a brisk good morning, he got to the point without any preliminaries.

"You have known Miss Prior for many years, I believe," he said, "and your dear father was fond of her also."

Geraldine nodded emphatically.

"Indeed he was, Rupert. Why, dear Papa thought the world of Lucilla, and was never happier than when she came to stay here with me."

"Have you no other friends with whom you are close — surely there are others in the locality more of your social standing."

"Why, yes. There are several families highly thought of in the town . . . but still . . . there is nobody quite like Lucilla . . ."

"Hmph!"

He stood with his back to the elegant Adam fireplace and avoided her eyes. He knew that what he was about to say was bound to upset her, which was why he hesitated.

Geraldine toyed nervously with the frilled cuff of her gown and studied it apprehensively, waiting for her cousin to speak.

"I will put it to you honestly, Geraldine," he said at last. "I do not care much for Miss Lucilla Prior's attitude, and I marvel that your late father thought any good of her at all.

She is not without charm, I admit, but this is overshadowed entirely by the way in which she delights in crossing one. She is too bold by far, and it is a quality which one does not like to see in a lady."

Geraldine was stunned. She stopped fidgeting with her cuff and stared at him in astonishment. She was not sure how to combat his words. To openly disagree with her cousin would only lead to an unseemly exchange of words. She loathed the idea. Yet, on the other hand, she could not allow her friend to be spoken of so without defending her, even at the risk of crossing him.

"Lucilla is high spirited, I agree," she said at last, choosing her words slowly, "and, indeed, it was this very quality which dear Papa most admired. Lucilla used to amuse him no end with her pranks, and even the scrapes she got us both into seldom made him cross for very long . . ."

Lord Childs gazed hard at her. He said nothing.

"She has been such a dear friend to me over the years, Rupert, that I appeal to you to try and forgive her. It is not easy, I know, for she can be most unpredictable, and, of course, her behaviour at table last night was unforgivable. Still, for my sake, Cousin, if you would but try . . ."

Geraldine looked up at him appealingly.

Lord Childs cleared his throat as if to say something, then changed his mind. He did not want his cousin to think of him as a hard man, and, indeed, he had no desire to be one. He certainly did not wish to deprive Geraldine of her friend, yet he felt the girl might be a bad influence on her. He would not admit to the fact that he found Lucilla's irresistible beauty very distracting, or that her impetuous nature had a strange fascination for him, for he was genuinely worried that her spirited nature might in some way adversely influence Geraldine. He sought only to protect his cousin.

"Perhaps if you had a quiet word with Lucilla, Geraldine," he said at last. "If you tried to guide her a little in the way things are handled in a more mannerly fashion, she might listen to you. Truly, she needs to be spoken to. High spirits may be admirable in a child, but not in a young lady of Miss Prior's age," he added, thinking to himself, nor in one of such remarkable beauty.

"I will certainly see what I can do, Rupert," replied Geraldine, looking worried. She could hardly tell him that she had already tried but without success.

He noticed the slight pucker which had appeared between her eyes and could see that something troubled her. He half guessed that Geraldine doubted her ability to influence Lucilla.

"Perhaps it might be an even better idea to speak tactfully to her aunt," he suggested wisely. "Miss Amelia Prior is a sensible person and will quickly see the value of such advice. If she cannot guide her niece, then who can?"

Geraldine's face brightened. She would much prefer to raise the matter with Miss Prior, for the lady was always most amenable.

"I shall do so at once, Rupert," she exclaimed, showing her relief. "I am sure it is quite the best way of doing it. And then Miss Prior can speak to Lucilla. Oh, yes, I am sure it is the only way."

Lord Childs was appeased. He left the room looking almost benign. As for Geraldine, she was delighted that the matter had been so easily resolved. But even so, Lucilla's conduct still rankled her, and she kept well out of Lucilla's way for the time being, which was not difficult, since Lucilla

had left the house earlier for a gallop across the country on
her mare.

The two girls did not see each other for any length of time
until the evening meal, and still Geraldine was restrained.
Lucilla half guessed the reason, and shrugged it off, telling
herself that her friend's glum moods always took time to
dispel, and that, no doubt, Geraldine would be quite normal
again the following day.

However, for once, Lucilla was wrong. Geraldine's mood
persisted, and Lucilla finally realized that this time she had
upset her friend rather deeply. She sought out her aunt and
told her.

Aunt Amelia's plump face had a hard look about it as she
listened.

"There is nothing, absolutely nothing, I can do to cheer
up Geraldine," declared Lucilla as the two sat alone in the
drawing room sorting out silk thread for her aunt's embroidery. "She has become so morose and scarcely says a
word. In fact, she almost seems to go out of her way to
avoid me. What can have upset her so?"

"La! If you do not know, Miss, then your head is empty
beneath those curls, and I do not really think that it is,"
declared her aunt tartly.

"Whatever do you mean?"

"Your trouble, Lucilla, I am afraid, is that you refuse to
learn. Do you think that your dear, gentle friend enjoyed
that ungracious scene in the dining room? Could you not
see how she writhed, and how angry you made Lord
Childs?"

"Nonsense! It was all a joke. It was only a little tease. No,
Aunt, you must be mistaken. There must be something
else."

"Shame on you — how can you be so insensitive, Lucilla? Lord Childs spoke himself to Geraldine about the matter, and she came pleading with me to talk to you about it, otherwise she feels that Lord Childs may request that you leave this house!"

Lucilla jumped up horrified.

"But why did she not say something?"

"She says that she has already tried," replied her aunt with tight lips, "all to no avail."

Lucilla turned a forlorn face to her aunt.

"It is true — we had words on the day we went to the fair, but I did not take them too seriously."

Aunt Amelia patted the back of her mobcap and poked a few stray wisps of graying hair beneath the floppy rim before saying anything.

"I fear your friendship with the sweet girl may be drawing to an end," she said at last, "unless you change your ways smartly."

"Oh, Aunt, such an idea is unthinkable. I shall go to her at once and apologize with all my heart. Moreover," added Lucilla with resolve, "I shall go to Lord Childs, and apologize to him, too."

"And in future," declared her aunt, "try a little more sweetness and a little less of your audacity, my girl."

Lucilla crossed the room and kissed her aunt.

"I am sorry," she said contritely, "for causing so much worry, Aunt dear. It was thoughtless and silly of me. I see that now. And I shall try my hardest to please Lord Childs in future. I shall do it for Geraldine's sake. It is the least I can do after her many kindnesses to me in the past."

Lucilla kept to her word, and, as soon as she had left her

aunt, went in search of her friend. Geraldine had been torn and unhappy during the past few days. It had pained her no end to feel estranged from Lucilla, yet she could not help but see the sense in her cousin's words. Lucilla's high spirits were an embarrassment, and could become more so in society. She must learn to curb them now. For all that, Geraldine loved her friend, and life without her would seem extremely dull.

Geraldine was sitting in the library with a small volume of poetry in her hands. The verse had been written by her own dear father, and, of late, she had taken to reading it in solitude there. Lucilla seldom read, and, since Geraldine had wished to keep out of her friend's way for a while, the library had offered her both seclusion and a certain amount of safety from a confrontation with Lucilla.

Geraldine looked up as the door suddenly creaked on its hinges. Only yesterday she had told the housekeeper to get it oiled, for it had grown progressively worse during the recent damp weather. The library was in the older part of the house which constantly needed attention.

She was surprised to see Lucilla peeping cautiously around the door.

"Ah, there you are, I have searched everywhere for you, Geraldine," said Lucilla softly, entering the room. Somehow or other, the library always made her speak in a hushed tone. It was so peaceful there, more like a church than a room in a house, that it seemed the right thing to do.

Geraldine gave her a faint smile and laid the book on her lap. Something in Lucilla's manner told her that Aunt Amelia had already spoken to Lucilla. At least, she hoped this was the case.

"I have been sitting here for some time," said Geraldine

sweetly. "It is so peaceful, hardly a sound to be heard. I have been reading dear Papa's book of verse . . ."

Lucilla nodded, observing her friend's pale face, and thinking, as she did so, that it would have been better by far for Geraldine to have been out in the fresh air. She wandered over to one of the shelves and took a book.

"See, Geraldine, it is the one which Aunt Amelia used to read to us when we were children. The one with poems and riddles," remarked Lucilla as she crossed the room and handed the book to Geraldine.

Geraldine's face broke into a smile.

"Why, I have not looked at it for years, Lucilla. What made you go straight to it, I wonder. I had quite forgotten that it was kept on that shelf."

"Oh, I remembered because it was one of the few books that I ever really enjoyed," laughed Lucilla. "Its place in the library was firmly fixed in my memory."

"What fun we had in those days," declared Geraldine with a faraway look in her eyes.

"Oh, we did. We did, indeed," retorted Lucilla with enthusiasm. "And we shall have even more fun in the future — just wait and see."

She ran across the room to her friend.

"Geraldine, dear Geraldine," she cried, unable to contain her feelings a moment longer, "please forgive me. I am truly sorry if I have made you unhappy these last few days. Aunt Amelia has been talking to me — I see now how selfish and thoughtless I have been."

Her rush of words was so unexpected that Geraldine was quite overcome. For a moment she did not quite know what to say.

"Forgive? Indeed I will, with all my heart," she declared,

catching hold of her friend's hand. "Only promise me, Lucilla, not to provoke dear Rupert again. He was furious with you — I did not know how to defend you."

"I do promise, Geraldine. I swear it. You will be quite surprised at the change in me — wait and see!"

"Then pray replace these two books on their shelves, and let us take a stroll in the garden," exclaimed Geraldine, her eyes shining. "I think that I have seen enough of the library for the time being."

"Oh, I am so happy — it was horrid to feel that I had made you so miserable," said Lucilla with relief. "Why, such a thing has never happened to us before."

She took the books from Geraldine and half skipped across to the shelves where they were kept.

Geraldine could not resist smiling at her jocular movements. Then the two girls linked arms and sauntered happily from the room.

"There is something else," said Lucilla, as they strolled through the gardens.

"Oh?"

"Yes, to show you that I am truly sorry, I intend to go to Lord Childs and apologize."

"Lucilla! Will you really? Oh, I am sure it would make such a difference if you did — it would show him that you care."

"Precisely! In fact, I cannot think why I am dallying here with you, Geraldine, when I could be with him now. I shall go at once and search him out," declared Lucilla with a resolute tilt of her head. "There is absolutely no point in delaying the matter. Have you any idea where your cousin is likely to be at the moment?"

"Mmm — I believe he is in the stables," replied Geraldine

uncertainly. "He said something about going to look at the lame horse — he is quite worried about it, for it is one of our best beasts."

Without waiting to hear more, Lucilla untwined her arm from that of her friend, and set off immediately in the direction of the stable block, the cupola of which could just be seen through the trees.

"Wish me luck," she called over her shoulder to Geraldine. "I hope that Lord Childs is in a forgiving mood . . ."

Geraldine did not catch the rest of her sentence, for Lucilla was already out of earshot, which, perhaps, was just as well, for Lucilla had added, "Heaven help me, if he is not!"

The stable hands had been busy in the stable block that morning. The entire yard and most of the stables had been sluiced down by an army of menials who were bearing the brunt of the head groom's fiery temper. This, in its turn, had been ignited by scathing criticism on the deplorable state of the stables by Lord Childs himself. It was utterly disgusting, he had fumed, a positive disgrace, and if things were not put right by the end of the morning he would dismiss the whole lot of them.

The head groom, a lazy and surly man, had glowered, but had held his peace until Lord Childs had departed. Then he had let fly at the under-groom, who had promptly sworn at the stable lads and set them to work with buckets of water and large brooms, sluicing down the stable yard and stables for all they were worth. Bales of fresh straw and hay had been fetched to replace the old, which was being carted away to a massive bonfire.

When Lucilla arrived on the scene, the job had just been completed. She paused in momentary amazement, for she had never seen the place looking so pristine. Then she cautiously proceeded on tiptoe over the slippery cobbles. She needed to watch her step, for murky rivulets were still trickling over the uneven surface, and one wrong move would have brought the water squelching into her dainty shoes.

Because her head was bent, she did not see the tall figure of Lord Childs swing out of the tack room, at which door she had just arrived. A collision was unavoidable, and she would have been sent tumbling to the ground had he not caught hold of her at that moment.

She hardly realized what was happening. All she knew was that two arms enveloped her just as she was about to sway and topple over, and, although she staggered a little as she felt a sharp pain shoot through her ankle, his support prevented her from crashing to the ground.

Lucilla was vaguely aware of a fine woollen material brushing against her face and the firmness of two strong arms which encircled her. A little cry of pain escaped her as her ankle gave beneath her, then she heard a man's voice and looked up into the eyes of Lord Childs.

"I have you — you cannot fall. Lean on me," he said reassuringly. "These dratted cobbles need to be relaid, every one of them. The place is in a deplorable condition — everything is worn. Small wonder that people trip and hurt themselves."

She nodded, but could not speak, for the pain was quite severe, and she was fighting hard not to cry.

"Are you all right?" he enquired anxiously.

"Yes . . . but I am not sure that I can walk yet. It is my ankle."

He glanced impatiently around for help, but nobody was to hand at that precise moment, then, to her surprise, he lifted her gently into his arms and carried her into the tack room.

He placed her carefully on a bench and bade her not move until she was really ready.

Lucilla sank back thankfully.

"You are not dressed for riding — what were you doing here?" asked Lord Childs curiously, and without his customary aloofness.

Lucilla had momentarily forgotten the reason until then; the pain in her ankle had sent it from her mind. This, and the way in which Lord Childs had carried her into the tack room, had left her in quite a flutter. She recalled the soft touch of the woollen stuff of his waistcoat, and glanced at it now, the deep shade of blue which he often wore. She remembered the warmth from his body and coloured up as she answered, "I had come here to find you, Lord Childs."

"Me? And how did you know that I would be here, pray?"

"I asked Geraldine — she thought it likely."

"Ah! The matter was of some urgency, then."

"It was something which I wanted to say as soon as possible, yes."

He looked down at the heart-shaped face with its large, serious eyes gazing up at him so intently, and was struck again by her incredible beauty. Usually the face was alight with laughter, and the eyes had such a glow as to set any man's thoughts turning to romance, but today they were troubled, and Lord Childs was strangely touched by their expression.

"I have come to apologize, Lord Childs," continued Lucilla, looking him full in the eyes, "for my unpardonable behaviour at dinner recently. I was thoughtless, and it was silly of me, for I not only upset you, but also caused Geraldine and my dear aunt to be unhappy."

"Is that all!" The relief sounded clearly in Lord Childs' voice. "My dear Miss Prior, I thought by the grave look on your face that something tragic had happened."

His eyes began to twinkle, and Lucilla thought again how devastatingly handsome he was.

"You are forgiven — if that will make you happy, for I cannot bear to see you so serious. But there really was very little to forgive. I quite enjoyed our . . . er . . . amusing banter. Although, I admit, I did mention the matter to Geraldine. You really went too far, Miss Prior, and in most circles such conversation would be far from tasteful. Such lack of tact can be infuriating."

Geraldine would have been astonished to hear him so benign. She could not have been blamed for not recognizing the reason for his change of heart, for even Lord Childs, himself, did not know it. Truth to tell, he had, quite unwittingly, succumbed temporarily to Lucilla's innocent charm, and had Lucilla but known it, she could have asked anything of him at that moment. He had never smiled at Lucilla quite like this before. His arrogance had completely disappeared, and, for the first time, Lucilla felt at ease with him.

"You have made me very happy, Lord Childs. Indeed, I am quite overcome," she exclaimed with sudden warmth. And the thought passed through her mind that it was quite worth slipping on the cobbles to see him in such a pleasant humour.

"How is your ankle?" he asked, bending over her with concern. "You must not walk at all if there is the slightest pain."

"The pain is nearly all gone, I do assure you, sir," she said, gingerly testing it.

"Here, take my arm," he commanded. "Lean on me for support."

She did as she was bidden and began to limp slowly towards the door.

"Oh, I am sure that I can manage," she said after a few paces.

But Lord Childs was not convinced.

"Perhaps — nevertheless, I shall accompany you back to the house to make sure. We shall walk very slowly, and you must promise me that the moment you feel any real pain you will stop."

She took his proffered arm, and they began to walk slowly across the cobbled yards towards the lawns that led to the gardens surrounding the house. There was no doubt about it, the ankle did hurt, and quite considerably. But Lucilla only laughed and joked the more, for she was determined not to give in to the pain.

Thus it was that Geraldine and Aunt Amelia, on looking out of the drawing room window a little while later, were amazed to see the unlikely sight of Lucilla and Lord Childs walking happily towards the house. He had his arm around her (for he was still carefully supporting her), and they were engaged in what appeared to be an amusing conversation, for their faces were wreathed in smiles.

It was then that Aunt Amelia had a sudden premonition. It flashed into her mind as she saw the couple so contentedly together, that they would make a remarkably handsome and well-suited pair. But she immediately swept the thought aside as being ridiculous, for it seemed almost presumptuous even to link Lucilla's modest name with that of the wealthy Lord Childs. She felt guilty for even thinking such a thing.

"Well, Lucilla has certainly made a fine job of a mere apology," she heard Geraldine remark dryly.

"What was that, my dear? I don't quite understand."

"La! She was so contrite and upset when I last saw her that I felt truly sorry for her. Now look — she seems to have not a care in the world . . . and why . . . has my cousin placed his arm around her?"

"Well, it is obvious that he has forgiven her," admitted Aunt Amelia unnecessarily, for she did not quite know what to say since she was as surprised as Geraldine at the sight. She peered out of the window, narrowing her eyes in an effort to catch a closer glimpse of the expressions on their faces as they drew nearer. She was very shortsighted, and had left her spectacles in her bedroom.

"More than that — it looks as though they have never had a disagreement in their lives," declared Geraldine incredulously. "Just see how they laugh together, 'tis amazing. Oh, look! Whatever has got into my cousin?" she cried. "He is lifting her up . . . he is carrying her into the house!"

Geraldine turned quite pale and clutched Aunt Amelia's arm, she was so shocked at her cousin's surprising and unseemly behaviour.

Miss Prior suddenly came into her own. For once her mind moved quickly.

"My niece must be unwell," she declared firmly, her good common sense prevailing. "Come, we must go at once and see if she needs assistance."

Without waiting for Geraldine to reply, she hurried from the room anxiously, wondering what her niece had been up to this time.

"Fiddlesticks!" Lucilla's young voice rang out clearly. "I tell you, Aunt, that my ankle is perfectly recovered now. There is no trace of pain whatsoever — I am sure that Lord Childs saved the ankle just in time by carrying me to my room."

"That he did," agreed her aunt. "But you should still rest it for a few days more. If you are too active upon it," she persisted, "the swelling will more than likely return. I have seen it happen before."

"Nonsense! See, I can dance and jump on it if I wish which proves that it is normal again — there is not the smallest twinge." To demonstrate the point, Lucilla sprang up and pirouetted across the room.

For several days she had rested the ankle, and had permitted her aunt to fuss over her as much as she pleased. Now her patience was at an end. She was determined to be treated as an invalid no longer, even though it had been almost pleasant being the centre of attraction with regular visits even from Lord Childs, who seemed quite changed towards her these days.

On awaking that morning, she had run to the window, flung it open, and longed to be out in the bright sunshine. She simply could not bear to be shut up in the house for one moment longer. She had decided there and then, even before seeing her aunt or taking breakfast, that she would take her mare and ride across to the forest at the edge of the lake, one of her very favourite haunts. She did not care how much her aunt objected, she had vowed that she must somehow persuade the dear soul. Geraldine, Lucilla knew, had a sore throat, because she had said so the day before, so that she would not be able to accompany her. She would, therefore, have to ride alone, which did not worry her one bit, since she almost preferred it.

"Do not worry, Aunt dear," Lucilla continued. "I would not dream of riding if I felt the ankle could not stand the strain. Believe me, I do not enjoy it when my foot and lower leg look like a bloated melon!"

Aunt Amelia seemed only a little convinced, but she could tell by the headstrong mood in which she had found Lucilla that morning, that she stood little chance of stopping her.

"Oh, very well, then," she replied a trifle impatiently. "Since nothing I can say will make you see sense, you had better go for a ride . . . but only a very gentle one, mark you."

Lucilla was across the room in a trice.

"I promise you I will not stay out very long at all," she called over her shoulder. "Just a little fresh air and I'll come straight back."

It did not take Lucilla more than a few minutes to change into her riding habit and tie a steinkirk loosely at her neck. She cut quite a dashing figure in her sky-blue habit, scarlet sash, and green hat. Then, glancing across at the bright sun streaming in through the window, she promptly removed the hat and flung it on the bed, letting her long golden hair fall loosely around her shoulders.

Lucilla was down the stairs and across to the stable block in no time, and anybody seeing her speed along would never have suspected that she had only recently hurt her ankle.

The groom was in another of his black moods. He had not expected Miss Prior to appear and demand that her horse should be saddled that morning. He had understood that she was indisposed. He had only just attended to Lord Childs, who was in a temper, and had been promising himself a bit of a break. There was a comely new wench recently arrived to work at the dairy, and he had thought of sauntering over there to try his luck.

He obeyed Lucilla's request with ill grace. But, since he wanted to be about his own affairs as quickly as possible, he worked speedily, and Lucilla was able to jog out of the stables, quite unknowingly, only a short while after Lord Childs had left.

It was a perfect morning for a ride, warm enough to be hatless, as Lucilla had suspected, with a slight breeze which blew her thick hair behind her, tingling her cheeks, and bringing back their colour. Her eyes sparkled as she rode, and she felt at perfect peace with the world, so much so that she sang catches of her favourite ballads from time to time.

The small wood for which she made was on the perimeter of the estate, but on the side which was nearest to the house, so that it was almost with regret that she saw it coming within sight as she rode to the top of a hill. She had enjoyed the ride so much that she would love to have gone further afield, but, since she had promised her aunt not to stay out for long, she reined in her horse and reluctantly slowed down as she approached the thicket which surrounded the wood, intending to rest for a while before returning to the house.

She spotted a suitable place where she could dismount, and was just about to do so when the stillness was suddenly broken by men's voices. They were raised in anger, and Lucilla was thankful to be hidden by the trees. She glanced nervously around but could see nobody. She could not catch what they were saying, but momentarily, as the wind wafted the voices in her direction, she realized with amazement that one of them was Lord Childs'.

She sat transfixed upon her mare, not knowing what to do. Gradually, it became clear that there were only two men — their raised voices had made it seem like more. Then followed a sternly delivered monologue by Lord Childs, carried out in such a low voice that she could not catch a single word. After this, the men continued to talk in normal tones.

At first, when Lucilla had heard the voices she had feared for her safety, suspecting them to be vagabonds or even rough poachers. Then, when she had discovered that one of the men was none other than Lord Childs, fears of a different nature entered her mind. To move into sight would possibly cause him acute embarrassment, for there was something definitely clandestine about the two men meeting alone in the wood. Also, if he saw her, the present good relationship which she had with him might well be jeopardized. Yet, she hardly fancied staying concealed where she was like some common eavesdropper.

Lucilla therefore determined to move off without more ado, and, as soon as the men seemed really engrossed in what they were saying, she began to ease more gently along the more grassy paths of the thicket, doing so as silently as she could. Each time that the beast trod on a twig and it snapped, her heart stood still, in case she had been heard. But the noise did not appear to carry, and gradually she cleared the thicket, and, at last, emerged on the edge of the meadow which ran along the side of it.

Pausing to glance only hastily over her shoulder to make sure that she had not been observed, she was about to gallop back to the house when, to her horror, the man to whom Lord Childs had been talking suddenly appeared.

He did not see her, for his head was lowered and he was making off in the direction of the village. Lucilla, however, could see him very clearly, and what she saw made her gasp, for the man was none other than the mysterious gypsy to whom she had seen Lord Childs talking on the day of the Dorking Fair. Now she knew that she had been right, but it was imperative that Lord Childs did not realize this, since he had denied it so adamantly, for there must be some very good reason for such strange reaction. Lucilla did not stop to see more. Her one thought was to put as much distance as possible between herself and Lord Childs. She turned the mare in the direction of the house and made off at a gallop, praying that Lord Childs was not following.

5

Lucilla all but threw the reins of her horse at the stable lad when she arrived back at the stables. The thought of coming face to face with Lord Childs horrified her. She had consoled herself as she rode by thinking that, perhaps, he might not return immediately to the house. All the same, she was determined to take no chances, for she could not bear to think what he might say if he realized that she knew of his latest encounter with the gypsy.

She made sure to enter the house by a small side door. She did not want her aunt or Geraldine, if she was about, to see her flushed and so out of breath, for they would immediately start asking questions, and, although she would not lie to them, she had vowed to herself that never again would she mention the gypsy in connection with Lord Childs. Too much trouble had already been caused by her rash words on the subject.

She sped upstairs as fast as her legs would carry her, and stood for a few moments out of breath with her back to the door of her room, as soon as she had closed it safely behind her. It took a little time to regain her composure, then, quickly and nimbly, she removed her riding habit, splashed ice cold water over her face to reduce its heightened colour, and patted her skin dry with a soft towel. She reached for a brush, and dealt with the heavy mane of golden hair which had become tangled in the wind as she rode, sprinkled jasmine water over her neck and wrists, and changed into a demure cotton dress which she sometimes wore in the mornings. She emerged from her bedroom within half an hour or so, looking as though she had been at home the entire morning, and proceeded to make her way downstairs to find her aunt.

She had just arrived at the foot of the impressive staircase in the hall when the main double doors leading to the exterior portico were flung open, and Lord Childs stood framed between them. Lucilla grabbed the banister, more for moral support than anything else, and prayed that he would not guess what she was thinking by the look in her eyes. She was never good at hiding her feelings.

But she need not have worried. He hardly seemed to notice her at all. He gazed ahead as though seeing nothing, and there was such a look of foreboding on his face that a chill struck at Lucilla's heart. She did not know whether to speak to him or slip quietly past.

"Good afternoon, Lord Childs," she said, at last, in a meek voice.

He glanced at her as though he had only just noticed her.

"Miss Prior . . ." he said bowing stiffly. "Good afternoon. Forgive me, I did not see you. My mind was on another matter."

Before she had time to reply, he had strode past without giving her a second thought.

Lucilla continued on her way, perplexed and worried. Whatever it was that he had discussed with the gypsy must, indeed, be serious, if it could so deeply disturb a man of Lord Childs' nature. She wished with all her heart that she had somebody with whom to share her secret, but that was impossible, for neither her aunt nor Geraldine would believe her.

Geraldine had no such worries on her mind. Her excitement, albeit well concealed beneath her calm exterior, was growing daily. The marvellous ball, which she was to attend with her cousin, was now but a few weeks away, and she was to leave Langley House at the end of the week for London with Lord Childs. She was totally occupied with her wardrobe and the sort of gown which she would choose for the grand occasion, and had few thoughts for anything else.

Lucilla shared her excitement, for she still waited impatiently for a letter from her uncle to see if she, too, would be attending the ball. But she had done as her aunt had bid and not mentioned the possibility to Geraldine, although she hoped fervently that she would have his answer before her friend left for London so that she would be able to tell her.

"I have almost definitely decided on apricot silk for my ball gown," declared Geraldine as the girls sat discussing the event that afternoon, Geraldine's sore throat having disappeared. "Do you fancy the shade on me, Lucilla?"

"Mmm — either apricot or pale green," Lucilla replied thoughtfully. "But will the dressmaker be able to make it in time — there is so much work in the pattern you have chosen."

"Oh yes. There's no need to worry about that. I have already written to the best dressmaker in London, and, although I have never been to her before, she cannot refuse to help me, since Rupert's sister is one of her best clients. The woman will be glad to take me on, as, indeed, she should be," she added with an autocratic toss of her head, "for I shall be spending a small fortune with her during the next few weeks."

Lucilla did not answer. She was wondering how she would be able to raise even a small amount of money for a suitable gown, should her Uncle Ralph decide to take her.

"You are very quiet," remarked Geraldine. She was sitting at a small table upon which were scattered samples of all sorts of silks and materials which she had received that morning, and which had had such a magic effect on her sore throat. Her elegantly coiffured head was bent intently over the stuffs as she painstakingly searched for a suitable colour close to the shade of apricot which she so fancied. "Is something worrying you, Lucilla?"

"Certainly not," laughed Lucilla, pulling herself together. "Why on earth should there be? I was just thinking of your gown, and what a wonderful ball it is sure to be . . ."

It was on the tip of Geraldine's tongue to retort that it was Lucilla's own silly pride which had prevented her from going to the ball herself, but she bit back the words just in time, and answered instead, "I expect there will be plenty of similar occasions in the future. Then, when I am introduced into London society by Rupert, I shall make sure that you are invited."

"I shall look forward to such times," said Lucilla gaily, "for I do not intend to spend the rest of my years living quietly and inconsequentially with Aunt Amelia and dear Papa — as much as I love them."

Geraldine grunted a reply, for she had not really been listening, but, a moment later, she called out with delight in her voice, "Oh! Look at this — it is the very shade," and she held up a small piece of exquisite apricot silk.

"It is precisely what I want," she declared triumphantly, handing it to Lucilla. "What do you think — will it not look superb?"

Lucilla smiled her approval as she took it, for it really was a most delightful colour. She held it up close to Geraldine's cheek, and it enhanced to perfection her friend's fine olive-coloured skin and deep brown eyes.

"I cannot think of anything better," she murmured admiringly. "Oh, Geraldine you are lucky . . ."

Geraldine looked at Lucilla sharply. She caught the wistful note in her friend's voice, and saw the look in her eyes.

"Well, I think it is a shame you are not coming," she said loyally. "But, since there is nothing I can do about that now, I can at least try to cheer you up. Admit it, you are low, are you not?"

She paused, eyeing the stuffs on the table. "I shall be most upset if you will not accept a small present from me, Lucilla. Choose anything you like from these samples and you shall have sufficient material for a dress."

"Gracious — what would my aunt say? I could not dream of accepting such a generous gift," declared Lucilla, overcome by such an offer. Nevertheless, her colour rose quite noticeably, and her eyes brightened at the suggestion. She could see at a quick glance that there were many shades on the table which would suit her admirably.

"La! Do not worry yourself about Miss Prior. You may leave her safely to me," replied Geraldine lightly. "I shall tell your aunt that you seemed depressed, and I gave you the stuff to cheer you up. She will quite understand.''

"Well . . ."

"Come over here and take my place," urged Geraldine. "Sit down and choose something quickly before I change my mind." She rose graciously from her pretty little chair with the shield-shaped back, and stood behind for Lucilla to take it.

Hesitantly, Lucilla did as she was bid. She felt deceitful at not being able to mention to Geraldine the possibility of attending the ball, particularly as this very material might be used for her dress.

"Who knows — perhaps a miracle may happen, and I shall be able to come to the ball after all," she said at last, as she sorted through the samples.

Geraldine really felt quite sorry for her. Such a likelihood was so remote as to be ridiculous. Still, she did not wish to hurt her friend's feelings, so she merely nodded indulgently as she replied, "Who can tell? And should such a thing come to pass, you can use my gift for your gown."

Geraldine stood by the side of Lucilla watching her friend sort through the samples.

"This would look perfection on you!" said Geraldine, holding up a small swatch of silk which Lucilla had not seen. It was the most delicate shade of turquoise possible, and perfect, indeed, for Lucilla's fine colouring.

"I remember you once had a party dress in a similar tone when you were about ten years old," said Geraldine. "I thought of it the moment I saw the colour — you looked so pretty when you wore that dress."

"Oh, it would look wonderful on most people," retorted Lucilla, taking it from her, "but it looks as though it's particularly expensive to me . . . I really could not accept it." She began to stroke the fine silk with the tips of her fingers. "Feel how soft it is," she said. "Why, it would be like wearing swan's down."

"I shall send off for the stuff this very day at the same time as I order my own," declared Geraldine with finality. "I shall ask for yours to be sent straight to your own house, since we shall both be leaving here shortly."

"Oh, Geraldine, I don't know how to thank you," cried Lucilla, running to the window with the silk to see the shade in natural light. "And you know — there is just a faint possibility that I may still be able to attend the ball," she added, a little guiltily, "but the chance is so remote I do not really wish to talk of it."

Geraldine was busy replacing the samples in a large canvas bag. She looked up absently at Lucilla's words.

"How very mysterious," she murmured with a soft laugh as she placed the apricot silk next to the turquoise sample which she had taken back from Lucilla. "I hope for your sake, then, that this . . . er . . . faint possibility materializes — and, if it does, you will most certainly need this stuff, so I had best order it at once."

By the end of the week, when Geraldine departed for London with Lord Childs, Aunt Amelia had still not heard from Sir Ralph Stavely.

Lucilla stood sadly on the steps of Langley House, waving farewell to her friend as the carriage clattered off down the long, winding drive. It was a dreary, rainy day, and her mood matched the weather. Yet, although she was miserable to see her friend depart, Lucilla was quite relieved to be seeing the last of Lord Childs for the time being. His good humour with her had proved, after all, to be only temporary, and, of late, he had become unbearably sardonic and aloof again. It was as much as she could do to keep up the sort of behaviour which she had promised both her aunt and Geraldine, for she longed, more than once, to be her usual forthright self during the conversation.

She had hoped and prayed that a letter would arrive from her uncle before Geraldine left, but now she wondered whether she had not been unduly optimistic, for surely he would have replied promptly if he had been able to take her.

Lucilla returned disconsolately to her room to complete her packing. The following day, they were to leave Langley House themselves. Aunt Amelia had already finished her packing, and was at that moment in the large kitchen with the housekeeper, sorting out dried herbs which Geraldine had insisted she take home. For the little herb garden at the rectory, over which Aunt Amelia presided, had fallen prey to insects the previous season.

Lucilla had nearly finished her packing at last. She stood in the middle of the room with a bundle of silk stockings and garters, wondering which valise to bundle them into, for all were crammed to overflowing, when Aunt Amelia appeared.

Her aunt surveyed the scene in horror.

"Heavens, Lucilla, what a dreadful mess! If you would only fold your garments carefully, you would find that everything would fit in quite nicely," she scolded, as she proceeded to remove some of the hastily crumpled dresses from a valise and refold them.

"What does it matter — they will have to be pressed in any case when we arrive home," replied Lucilla crossly. She loathed it when her aunt fussed over such trivial things.

"Nonsense! If you fold them carefully, the creases will fall out when you unpack, and it will be less work for the kitchen maid — you know very well that we only have the one girl for this sort of job," her aunt retorted sharply. "Your dear father cannot afford the army of servants you have become used to at Langley House to cater for your every need."

Lucilla did not reply. She was not really listening, but was wandering aimlessly around the room thrusting small oddments into the valises where she thought there might still be any room, thinking, as she did so, of Lord Childs and what a strange, moody man he was. She picked up the small sample of silk which Geraldine had cut off the piece she had sent back when ordering the material, and sighed to herself.

"Scatter this lavender between the clothes," ordered Aunt Amelia, handing her a small bowl which she had brought up from the kitchen. Then she glanced up and saw the piece of silk in Lucilla's hand.

"Oh, so that's it, miss. I wondered why you were mooning around in this dilatory fashion. You're upset because we have not heard from your uncle — you were hoping to have that silk made into a gown for the ball, I know."

"I was hoping to do so, yes," replied Lucilla ruefully, "but I don't see much likelihood of it now. Oh, Aunt, it would have been ideal . . ."

"Well, no news is good news," retorted her aunt briskly. "I am quite sure that we shall hear any day now." She enjoyed packing and was happy to be going home. She was also not the slightest bit worried that Sir Ralph Stavely had, as yet, not replied. "Perhaps your uncle has been away," she added as an afterthought.

But Lucilla's despondency continued, and even the

thought of seeing her father again did not raise her spirits.

"Perhaps it is just as well," she remarked, as she sat with her aunt the following day in the carriage which Geraldine had insisted they use to convey them home.

"What, dear? What is just as well?" her aunt asked. She had been staring out of the window wondering in what state she would find the rectory, for, without her supervision, many of the chores which she considered essential were sometimes neglected by the servants.

". . . that my uncle cannot take me to the ball, of course," retorted Lucilla irritably.

"Any why is that, pray?"

"Well, I am not really used to such grand company — it would be humiliating to be ignored because Lord Childs did not consider me important enough, or too insignificant, to introduce to his famous friends."

"Ho! As if you could be insignificant *anywhere*, Niece," exclaimed Aunt Amelia with a chuckle, peering from the window as she spoke, for the carriage had just turned into the narrow lane which approached the rectory. "You usually have your fair share of attention, my dear, no matter who else is present."

Lucilla did not reply, for she doubted that this would be the case in the sophisticated circles in which Lord Childs mixed. She, too, was gazing from the window to see if her father might have walked along the lane to look out for their carriage.

The Reverend George Prior was an absent-minded man, given to moments of incredible vagueness. But he adored his daughter, and had marked today's date with a heavy cross in his diary so that he would, on no account, forget to be at home when she arrived.

All that morning, he had been hovering in the house awaiting her, and, as soon as he heard the carriage enter the gates at the end of the short drive which led up to the rectory, he was at the front door in moments, his face beaming.

Lucilla ran to him with arms outstretched. Despite the fact that she had hated leaving Geraldine and Langley House, she was now truly happy to be home with her father, whom she adored.

"Dearest Papa, how good it is to see you," she cried as she hugged him.

"Ah, I thought that you had deserted me for good this time," declared her father, as he added teasingly, "a little bird told me of all sorts of fine plans you have for the future — why, I'm quite surprised to see you here at all."

"What's this?" asked Aunt Amelia, giving her brother a perfunctory peck on the cheek as she joined them. "Fine plans, eh? I should like to know who has been filling your head, George, with such a notion."

"A very good authority, indeed, Sister," he replied with a twinkle. "But come, enough of this, you need some refreshment after your journey. The cordial is awaiting — unless you would prefer some hot chocolate, and there are cakes and sandwiches."

"Papa," laughed Lucilla, "we have only come ten miles or so, and it was hardly an arduous journey."

"Nevertheless, you must take some form of nourishment. And then, perhaps, a little rest before we exchange all our news."

"Quite right, Brother," assented Aunt Amelia, who was always ready to eat. "I feel quite peckish. Is there any of Cook's meat paste in the sandwiches, I wonder?"

They strolled happily into the small drawing room and Lucilla glanced with pleasure at the old familiar objects, thinking how good it was to be home. Upon a rosewood side table were sandwiches, almond cake, and tiny cherry jam tartlets, the latter having been made especially by Cook, since she knew Lucilla loved them.

Aunt Amelia took one of the cream-coloured earthenware plates from the pile by the side of the food and began to help herself lavishly.

"Ah, freshly baked bread," she murmured with approval, "and those little cherry tarts look as though they've only just come from the oven as well."

Lucilla, as her father had suspected, could not resist a tart, even though she was not the slightest bit hungry.

Her father handed them each a glass of cordial.

"Thought you said you weren't hungry," he chuckled as Lucilla munched contentedly.

"Oh, Papa, this is one thing that they cannot make so well as Cook at Langley House," she retorted with a grin. "Although the most luxurious dishes are prepared in that massive kitchen, the pastry is never as good as Cook's."

"Worth coming home, then, after all, was it not?" laughed her father, taking a tart himself. He then proceeded to tell them all sorts of snippets of local news.

Lucilla was happy to listen, for her father had a knack of turning the most trivial anecdote into something amusing or interesting. As she watched his kind, plump face (for the Reverend George Prior loved his food as much as his sister did) with its sparkling blue eyes and jovial expression, she thought how much she loved him, and how lucky she was to have such a father. Then it was that she remembered the half jest, half tease of the remark he had made when he had greeted them.

"Papa," she said curiously, as soon as he had paused for a while, "what did you mean when we first saw you — about the fine plans you had heard of which we had made . . ."

"Aha, I meant precisely what I said," he replied mysteriously, pouring them more cordial. "This may be only a quiet country rectory, my dear, but I do have important visitors occasionally, you know."

Aunt Amelia had been cutting a slice of cake. She stopped and looked at him with a sudden knowing expression.

Lucilla watched her. She saw the two of them exchange glances, and suddenly she realized what had happened.

She let out a squeak of delight and ran to her father, catching him by the arm.

"Papa, oh, Papa — he has been here has he not, my Uncle Ralph Stavely? Answer me, do. He visited you for some reason, and he has told you about the ball!"

Her father freed himself with a laugh and kissed her affectionately on the cheek.

"Quite so — he was passing through Guildford, and, since you, Sister," he said, turning to Aunt Amelia, "had written that you would be leaving Langley House shortly, he came in and left this for you. But, naturally, Ralph told me of its contents." So saying, he crossed to his bureau and took out a letter which he handed to Aunt Amelia.

"But what did my Uncle Ralph say — do tell, Papa," pleaded Lucilla excitedly, with a touch of impatience, for she could not bear to wait until her aunt had found her spectacles to read the letter.

"Tut! Is it so important to you, my dear?" he asked, peering at her flushed, anxious face. "Do these superficial things mean so much to you?"

"Yes, I'm afraid so, Papa. I am not ashamed to admit it, either. I should love to go to this ball. Oh, it would be one of the most exciting things that could happen to me — I have been wishing every day for it."

"Then your wish has been granted," he chuckled understandingly, "for your Uncle Ralph is going to the ball and says he will be delighted to take you. It is believed that the Prince Regent will be attending, too."

"Oh! I cannot believe it. It's a dream come true," exclaimed Lucilla, giving him a hug then dancing around the room with exuberance.

Her aunt had been reading the letter.

"There is more," she interrupted unexpectedly. "Your uncle has invited us to stay at his London house for a few days before the ball, if we so wish. And I must say," she added, "that it would be a great blessing to be able to do so, since the house, being in Soho Square, is very central."

"There! I am to lose you again and you have only just this minute returned to me," declared Lucilla's father mournfully, but Lucilla could tell by the look in his eye that he did not really mean what he said. She ran to him with a consoling kiss.

"We shall not be gone long this time, dear Papa," she said tenderly. "Only for a few days — then we shall be back again."

"Lucilla must be given her chance in society, Brother," Aunt Amelia declared firmly. "She will scarcely find a husband while she is living quietly with you here in the country — and she is not getting any younger."

Lucilla and her father exchanged meaningful glances and burst into laughter.

"Come, Aunt, I am hardly that decrepit yet," giggled Lucilla.

"And she has plenty of admirers locally," added her father for good measure.

Aunt Amelia sniffed, but she thought it wise not to pursue the subject further lest she upset her brother, for she knew that he did not like the thought of Lucilla's being launched into society just to catch a husband.

"I suppose this grand event will mean an expensive new gown," he said resignedly.

"No, Papa. I already have some fine silk on order, and I shall only need new shoes and a few accessories."

"No need to fuss about that, Brother," added Aunt Amelia. "I have a little money to spare at the moment, and I shall be happy to subsidize things — "

"Oh, Aunt, I could not hear of it," exclaimed Lucilla, greatly touched by her aunt's generosity.

"And neither could I," said her father sternly. "There will be no need for such an exigency, I do assure you, Amelia. Although you mean well, I know."

"Very well, just as you say," Aunt Amelia assented with just a trace of huffiness. "But the child must look her very best, and I have every intention of seeing that she does."

The silk had arrived a few days later, and already it was with the local dressmaker, well on its way to becoming a truly delightful gown. Aunt Amelia had insisted on something simple, for ostentation, she said, would not become Lucilla's delicate beauty. Lucilla had been inclined to agree, but for different reasons. She had remembered a charming style worn by one of the moppet dolls which Geraldine had described to her after their eventful day in Dorking.

Lucilla had a good memory and had managed to sketch this dress down to the last detail. It was supposed to be embroidered on the bodice with small pearls, but, since Lucilla could not afford such a luxury, she had substituted ordinary embroidery and had added a scalloped-shaped neckline. Then she had redesigned the skirt with a scalloped hem, and the whole effect, even Amelia had admitted, was perfect.

They had accepted Sir Ralph Stavely's invitation to stay in his Soho Square house and would be leaving for London within the fortnight. Lucilla was so excited that she could hardly while away the time fast enough. Each day seemed to stretch endlessly before her, and she could not settle down to anything. Her one real pleasure was to ride her mare, and this she did often.

Gossips in the village disapproved of this, considering it most unladylike that the daughter of a parson should spend her time galloping across the country. But Lucilla ignored them, until the matter was brought home to her more forcefully when she overheard a conversation between two tattletale village women as she stood, unnoticed by them, in the haberdashery.

Because of such wagging tongues, she decided to stay away from the environs of the village when she rode in the future, and, one day, chose a particularly remote route in the opposite direction from her customary ride. There were no cottages, and the area was practically deserted except for the very occasional farm wagon.

Lucilla was surprised, therefore, as she rode, to hear the sound of voices, and children laughing and talking. She could not understand what they were saying, for they seemed to be speaking in a foreign language. It occurred to her, as she saw the wisps of smoke rising from behind the hedge, that she had come upon a gypsy encampment.

At the very thought most people would have turned tail immediately, for terrible stories surrounded the gypsies. They had been known to attack innocent travellers in the most barbaric ways, perhaps even murder them for quite trivial amounts. And they were seldom caught for their crime. Lucilla, however, was not the slightest bit alarmed. The strange Romany which they spoke, as well as their nomadic existence, had always fascinated her. She even thought them slightly romantic. She drew up close to the hedge and peered through where the leaves were thinnest, marvelling at the picturesque wooden caravans, and longing to explore their secrets.

Then it was that she saw a lean gypsy emerge from one of them. She drew back at once, for she had recognized him. She was sure that he was the man to whom she had seen Lord Childs speak. She watched him pass by unconcerned on the other side of the hedge, only a few feet from her. He made his way across the field to a stream on the very far side, where other members of the tribe were gathering.

One by one, the gypsies drifted to this spot, leaving the encampment deserted except for a few small children. They seemed to be holding some sort of a meeting. Lucilla's eyes glittered at the wonderful opportunity to take a peek inside a caravan. She longed to see how these strange, independent people lived.

In a moment, her mind was made up. She quickly led her mare around the edge of the field, taking good care to remain out of sight, tethered the beast to the gate post, then ran silently through the farm gate and made for the nearest caravan.

There were two close together, but, since she did not want several ragged children who were playing close by to see her, she made for the nearer one, which happened to be the caravan from which the gypsy had emerged. She was through the doorway in a flash, and stood breathlessly triumphant observing the interior.

But her triumph was short-lived. She realized almost at once that the risk had hardly been worth taking. At first glance, there was little of any interest, just a truckle bed along one side, and a rickety chair with one or two stools beside an old table. On the table were empty trencher bowls from which had recently been eaten greasy broth or stew. The stench of it had pervaded the place and hung every-where.

Lucilla wrinkled up her nose in disgust and began to wander around examining things. She was just about to leave when she noticed a small casket of documents on a shelf. It seemed an unlikely object to be in the possession of an uneducated gypsy who could probably not even read a word. On the floor nearby was a small pile of ashes. It seemed that the gypsy was in the process of destroying them. In all probability, he had stolen the casket along with more valuable items. But if that were the case, Lucilla wondered, why was he doing this so furtively in the privacy of the caravan, and not outside at one of the big campfires?

She gazed at it curiously as she passed by, and, because her mind was still on it, she did not pay enough attention to easing herself between the shelf and the table. She mis-judged the space, and in doing so brushed against one of the documents which was protruding from the casket, sending the entire contents overflowing on to the floor. Horrified, she knelt hurriedly to retrieve them. The floor was filthy, and the documents retained the dust and crumbs. She tried to blow these away, and, as she did so, she noticed the name on one of the sealed items. She almost dropped the entire lot again when she read this.

"It can't be," she whispered to herself in amazement, "I must be mistaken."

With a trembling hand, she replaced the remainder of the documents and then took the named one to the door. Now she could see quite clearly that she had not been mistaken, for it was addressed to none other than Lord Childs.

At the same time, she heard voices drawing near and realized that the gypsies were returning. Without even bothering to close the casket, she let herself out stealthily and ran as fast as she could to her mare.

Her heart was pounding so loudly that she thought it would jump through her ribs. She seemed to be all fingers and thumbs as she tried to untether the beast, and then it was that she realized she still held the document addressed to Lord Childs. She felt like some common thief. Yet, since there was no way in which she could return it without being discovered, she tucked it quickly into the long pocket of her riding habit, mounted her mare, and made off at a gallop across the lonely countryside.

All the time, as she rode, urging her mare on faster, she thought that she heard the sound of horses pursuing her. She was so terrified that she dare not even glance behind. She nearly cried with relief when the rectory at last came in sight, and she was finally within the safety of its precincts.

Having dealt with her horse, she slipped thankfully into the house. All was quiet. Only the sound of the long case clock, ticking placidly from its corner in the hall, could be heard as she closed the door with a soft click. Both her father and aunt were out visiting the sick, but she knew that they would be home shortly.

She had hardly removed her riding habit when she heard voices from outside and saw Aunt Amelia alighting from the carriage. She stepped briskly away from the window, seized the document and thrust it deep into a drawer, patted her hair into order, and hurried from the room. She was just in time. Already, Aunt Amelia was calling her for tea. It was the first thing that her aunt turned her attention to when she returned from her visits.

"Coming, Aunt," Lucilla cried, as soon as she heard her, for her aunt hated the tea ritual to be kept waiting. Then, she ran lightly across the hall to the window and looked out long and hard to make sure that there was no sign of lurking gypsies. She still could not believe that they had not followed her, for she was sure that she had been seen. Having fully convinced herself that there was nobody loitering, she composed herself and prepared to face her aunt.

"Ah, there you are, dear," declared Aunt Amelia, without looking up, as she poured the tea. "I passed the dressmaker on my way home, and thought to call and see if your gown was finished."

"Aunt — tell me — I cannot wait to hear. What does it look like?" demanded Lucilla excitedly, forgetting all about her adventure and the letter addressed to Lord Childs in her eagerness to hear about the dress.

"La! It is quite the most beautiful gown I think that I have ever seen," replied her aunt, with delight on her face.

"Oh, are you sure, Aunt? It does not look homespun or . . . well, provincial, does it? I shall not look like a country bumpkin, all silk and no style, shall I?" quizzed Lucilla anxiously.

"The dress is enchanting," beamed her aunt, "and the

seamstress has made it perfectly. Why, you will look good enough to dance with the Regent himself!"

"Oh, Aunt," Lucilla began to laugh, "it must indeed be exquisite."

6

A log falling in the fireplace awoke Lucilla. She blinked her eyes for a moment, then sprang up and ran quickly to the window.

They had been in London for an entire day already. Lucilla had fallen off into a deep sleep through sheer mental exhaustion, for her excitement had been almost unbearable during the last few days, particularly when they had finally arrived in London and the carriage had made its way across the town to Soho Square where Sir Ralph Stavely's house was situated on the north side. It was one of the smaller houses in the Square, with neat, well-proportioned rooms, and comfortable, rather than elegant, furniture. Its spick-and-span state thoroughly pleased Aunt Amelia, who had inspected everything on arrival with an increasing glow of satisfaction upon her face.

Lucilla had been entranced with everything she had seen along the route, from the fine buildings and lavish outfits of the sophisticated occupants whom she had glimpsed emerging from their grand houses, to the bustling crowds along lesser streets, and the strange cockney calls of the urchins. She had so longed to see inside the shops, which seemed to her young eyes to be positively bursting with tempting folderols, that her aunt had promised to accompany her on a shopping expedition the following morning.

Sir Ralph Stavely had arrived from the country a day ahead of Lucilla and her aunt. He had stood at the door to greet them, a jovial, rounded man, whose twinkling blue eyes and merry smile belied the shrewd political mind which had taken him to the summit of his profession.

Lucilla hardly slept at all on her first night in London, and was up bright and early, dressed, and ready for the outing before Aunt Amelia had even finished her breakfast of toast, spread thickly with a quodeny of plums, which she consumed with several cups of delicious, creamy chocolate.

At last, they had set out for the more fashionable shopping spots, since Aunt Amelia had a fear of dubious side streets, and had no intention of allowing Lucilla to explore such potentially dangerous places. London, to Aunt Amelia, was a town where she suspected treachery and vice lurked around every corner, and, when there, she proceeded with distinct caution.

Lucilla, however, felt no such apprehension. Her eyes sparkled and her cheeks were flushed with expectation as she insisted on peering into every shop window that took her fancy, sometimes zigzagging dangerously across the road between carriages, horses, and carts the moment her eye caught something of interest in a shop window on the other side.

Her aunt had soon become quite weary and had found it difficult to keep up with her. Lucilla, on seeing her lag behind, had escorted her gently through the crowds which thronged the sidewalks. Finally, at an enchanting little frock shop, Aunt Amelia could stand the pace no longer. She had sunk gratefully down on the hard chair provided for tired or elderly customers and let Lucilla peruse the goods by herself.

Aunt Amelia had put a gloved hand to her mouth, and, forgetting that she was a lady for a moment, emitted a long yawn. Then she had noticed the pile of tradesmen's cards on the counter, and had picked one up, adjusting her spectacles to read: *"Mary and Ann Hogarth sell at this address ye best and most fashionable ready made frocks, suits of fustian ticken or Holland stripp'd dimity and flannel."*

The simple words immediately dispelled Aunt Amelia's fatigue, for she had quite forgotten that she had promised herself a simple frock for mornings in the garden at the rectory, and her instinct told her that she would more than likely find the very thing here.

She had been right, and had discovered a sensible blue check dress which was ideal for the purpose and which she bought at once. So her spirits were as high as those of her niece when they had eventually returned home, entering the house just as the clock had struck one of the hour in the dining room.

Although they did not generally eat a big meal at this time of day, they were so famished that they had sat down to hot chestnut soup, followed by baked fish, and, afterwards a good, sustaining milk pudding which had been well spiced with cinnamon and nutmeg.

Then they had withdrawn to the small salon for Lucilla would not hear of taking an afternoon's nap in her room as her aunt had suggested. However, within only a few minutes, Lucilla had dropped off to sleep on the big, comfortable sofa, and Aunt Amelia had tiptoed from the room, having first drawn the curtains together.

Lucilla was annoyed with herself for sleeping. She could not bear the thought that she had wasted precious time which might have been used for far more interesting purposes. Besides, she had promised herself a visit to Geraldine that afternoon. Now, as she pulled the curtains apart, she saw, to her dismay, that the afternoon was already drawing in, and there was no possibility of such a thing.

Why had Aunt Amelia let her sleep for so long? she thought crossly. She could hardly call on Geraldine in the evening. She ran at once to her aunt's room and knocked loudly on the door. There was no reply, only the sound of light, even snores could be heard. She stopped knocking at once, and realized, for the first time, that her poor aunt must have been exhausted after their outing.

Lucilla tiptoed quietly away. She made straight for a small room which adjoined the large salon, for she had looked in there the previous day when they had arrived, and had discovered it to contain a writing bureau. Books lined the walls, and she guessed that her Uncle Ralph used it to withdraw to peace when he wished to deal with correspondence or indulge in a quiet smoke.

Since she could not visit Geraldine, she decided to write her a short note and send a servant with it for, although the two had written to each other, Lucilla had kept secret her good news concerning the ball. She wanted to surprise her friend, and had planned to visit her as soon as she arrived in London to tell the news herself.

Lucilla sat down at the bureau and helped herself to her uncle's plain writing paper, then seized a quill from the silver inkstand, and, with a smile playing around her pretty mouth, speedily penned the following mysterious lines: *"A good friend desires to call upon the Honourable Geraldine Childs concerning a matter of utmost mutual interest. The matter is important and cannot wait. Thus the writer would deem it a great kindness to be able to wait upon her between 11 of the hour and midday tomorrow. Kindly indicate by return messenger your wishes in this respect. Signed . . . a true friend."*

Lucilla cast her eye quickly over the disguised writing and chuckled as she folded the letter and sealed it. Then she rang the dainty handbell which was kept on the inkstand, and sat back with a smile still upon her face, awaiting the servant.

"Make sure that this is delivered at once," she instructed, as soon as he arrived. "You are to wait for a reply, but on no account to reveal who sent you!"

The man looked at her curiously. Sir Ralph never sent him on such strange errands, yet here was this chit of a girl who had only just arrived, giving him orders as though she owned the place.

"It is not usual, Mistress . . ." he began, with disapproval on his face and in his voice.

"Yes, yes, I know," retorted Lucilla, with a mischievous little smile, "but this is a joke. I assure you that Sir Ralph Stavely would see no harm in it if he were here." She smiled at him so beguilingly, and there was such a delightful twinkle in her beautiful eyes that the aloof servant thawed immediately.

"Very well, Mistress," he said with dignity. "I will do as you instruct, and send a boy with it at once."

Lucilla nodded with satisfaction. She returned to the bureau and sat down again. This time, her letter took far longer. It was to her father, and contained every incident and scrap of information that had occurred since she had kissed him goodbye. She was still writing it when Aunt Amelia awoke.

Her aunt was mystified when she did not find Lucilla where she had left her. Then she saw a dim light from beneath the door of the small adjoining room, and guessed at once what her niece was about.

"Why did you not rest, child?" she demanded, a little querulously. "You will be quite wan and pale at this rate, in no time at all. Do you not wish to look your best for the ball?"

"Oh, Aunt, of course I do," retorted Lucilla with a smile, as she signed her letter. "I slept for so long, in fact, that it was too late for me to go and see Geraldine . . ."

"Visit Geraldine!" interrupted her aunt incredulously. "Where are your manners, pray? You are in London now. You cannot just appear without so much as a warning, especially as she does not even suspect that you are here. Why, she may be entertaining or occupied in some other way. Geraldine may be your closest friend, but at least have the courtesy to send a note first."

"Yes," said Lucilla, dimpling, "I do understand, Aunt, and such a . . . er . . . *dreadful* breach of etiquette was thankfully avoided by my snooze, so I have written to her and sent it by messenger. I have said that I will come in the morning if she is free . . . do you feel happier now?"

Aunt Amelia snorted at Lucilla's tone and mumbled something in response. However, Lucilla did not catch what her aunt said, for she was not really listening. Her mind was elsewhere. She was musing over Geraldine's reaction when she received the mysterious note, and was wondering how long it would take her friend to fathom the disguised writing.

Geraldine sat alone in the sumptuous salon of the vast

town house which Lord Childs had inherited only recently from an uncle on his late mother's side of the family. On arrival, she had been dumbfounded by the incredible richness of the decoration and furnishings, and could not see how even the Prince Regent's houses could be finer.

The massive place occupied practically all one side of one of the most fashionable squares. Its vastness had quite taken her breath away, and the size and number of rooms, opening one from the other, had seemed like a continuous gilded maze when she had first arrived.

There was an oriental room which was clothed in a pagoda and dragon wallpaper, where japanned and lavishly gilded furniture of eastern splendour quite took the breath away. Several tables had supports of bronze Chinamen, and fierce, fiery dragons. Geraldine had never encountered such exotic fantasy before.

Another was devoted to an Egyptian style, with an abundance of sphynx heads in the designs of the chairs, tables, and cupboards; a third retained the popular Adam decoration, so much in vogue some years before (and retained because it was a favourite of Lord Childs' aunt, who loved the blue jasper plaques); while a fourth was painted in simulated marble from ceiling to floor, and was simply referred to as "the painted room."

Geraldine had been astonished at such dedication to the whims of fashion. At Langley House, considered by locals to be most splendid, such a thing would have been thought utterly wasteful. New curtains and drapes were not considered essential until the present ones showed distinct signs of wear. She realized, now, that the fashionable wealthy who followed slavishly the exotic tastes of the Prince Regent would happily spend vast fortunes on such refinements.

Even her bedroom had been refurbished in a sumptuous manner, and was dominated by a spectacular bed surmounted by a high dome of cherry taffeta edged with gold braid and tassels. The valance, curtains, and chairs were all of the same colour as was the costly flocked wallpaper.

Geraldine had been whisked into a demanding social life as soon as she had arrived in London. A new side of her cousin's character had become apparent as he had taken her from one fine party to another, thoroughly enjoying himself among some of the noblest families in the land. He seemed to revel in such an environment, and she began to realize how very dull he must have found Langley House.

The social whirl was not entirely continuous, however, for, on certain days, she was left to while away the time entirely by herself. Lord Childs had a habit of disappearing for hours, sometimes entire days, without saying where he was going. Invariably, when he returned he would be in a black mood and would scarcely speak. He seemed like another man.

Such an occasion had just occurred. He had been gone all the previous day, and she had wandered forlornly from room to room, gazing at the incredible furniture. She had looked forward to his company for today's outing, but he had excused himself, saying he was tired.

Geraldine had returned disconsolately to Nurse Hargreaves, who had come with her to London, and the two had taken a solitary walk. Afterwards, the day had dragged on, and Geraldine had tried to read but could not concentrate; then she had picked up her embroidery for a while, but only sat pricking at the material with an empty needle. Her thoughts alternated between the sullen mood of her cousin and Sir David Clifton, the rich and very handsome young man who always seemed to appear at her side at parties. She thought him extremely attractive, and quite the nicest man she had met in London.

Then, quite suddenly, a strange thing happened. A messenger boy had arrived in a livery which she did not recognize and delivered a peculiar message. The writer wished to visit her the following morning, but did not give a name, signing the letter "a friend."

It was strictly against Geraldine's true nature to become involved in anything of an uncertain quality. But today she felt lonely and particularly neglected by her cousin, and, moreover, she was very bored. Since she had just been thinking of Sir David Clifton, it occurred to her that he might be the writer. Sir David had a great sense of fun, she had noticed this from the start, and, while he would not in any way compromise a lady or breach etiquette, he might guess that she would be at home to her friends in the morning, with ample people around to act as chaperones. In any event, she only had to say no to his request if this were not the case. She would dearly love to see him, and surely, if she made sure that her old nurse was in attendance, there could be no harm.

Geraldine swept to her elegant writing table, seated herself with dignity, and wrote calmly but firmly: *"The Honourable Geraldine Childs will be at home to all callers on the morning you mention in your note."* This was not quite true, but she did not want Sir David to think that she was staying in specially to receive him alone.

Nurse Hargreaves was mystified by Geraldine's request that she should sit with her in the magnificent turquoise and gold saloon the following morning. It was most unusual. She dreaded to think what Lord Childs would say if he found her there with her young mistress. She did not relish being scolded by him. Still, she did as she was bid and settled down with her stitching as soon as the clock struck eleven of the hour.

"What you want me for, I don't know," she grumbled. "Why can't you receive your visitors by yourself — it will look very odd having me here . . ."

"Hush, Nurse," said Geraldine. "All is well. I know what I am doing, and I don't ask for favours very often now, do I?"

"Nay," agreed the old woman, "that's true enough. But 'tis the thought of arousing Lord Childs' temper that worries me. If he found me sitting in this splendid place, a mere servant, well, I don't know what he'd say."

"Bosh! He should not leave me alone so much," replied Geraldine petulantly, "and anyway he will not find you here, for he said not to expect him until dinner time."

She had hardly finished speaking when there was a knock at the door. It was a quick flutter of a knock, followed by a cheeky rhythmic rat-a-tat-tat, which no servant would dare to deliver, nor most guests. Certainly it would be totally out of character for Sir David Clifton to announce himself in such a way.

Fear gripped Geraldine's heart, and the colour rushed to her cheeks. She realized that she had made a ridiculous mistake in expecting Sir David. She saw now that the mysterious writer could be practically anybody. Even, perhaps, some common fellow, and she had fallen right into his trap. He might murder the pair of them.

Nurse Hargreaves saw the flustered look of alarm on her young mistress's face, and realized that there was more than she had bargained for behind Geraldine's innocent request to have her there. Her old eyes glanced swiftly in the direction of the heavy fire irons, and especially at the big poker.

Before she had time to think of anything else, the door was opened inch by inch, very slowly at first, until it was flung open with a flourish, followed by a girl's ripple of laughter, and Lucilla stood before them, her face wreathed in delight at their astounded expressions.

"Behold — the mysterious stranger!" she declared with glee, running to Geraldine and kissing her friend soundly on her cheek.

"Come — admit it — you did not guess it would be me, did you? I can see it by your faces."

Geraldine was utterly dumbfounded to see Lucilla. Her first reaction had been one of disappointment that it was not Sir David. Then relief had quickly followed, for it could have been some person of ill intent. Finally, delight had flooded her heart at seeing her dear friend so unexpectedly.

"Lucilla — I am lost for words," she exclaimed. "I cannot believe my eyes. Is it really you?"

"Ho! I thought I would surprise you, and I did," laughed Lucilla, "although I thought that you would soon fathom my disguised writing."

"But how are you here? And why did you not write and tell me in one of your letters?" said Geraldine, ringing for the servant to take Lucilla's pelisse.

The servant was hovering just outside the door. He was worried that his mistress would scold him for permitting Lucilla to announce herself in such a fashion. But Lucilla had asked him so prettily, insisting that she was a very old friend of Lord Childs' cousin, that he could not resist her. He moved uneasily forward to take the pelisse, avoiding Geraldine's eyes. But he need not have worried. Geraldine hardly noticed him. She was so engrossed in conversation with her visitor.

". . . How long have you been in London and where are you staying?" she asked, the incredulous expression still on her face.

"With my uncle — Sir Ralph Stavely — and, oh, Geraldine, I am to go to the ball. My Uncle Ralph is taking me!"

"But Lucilla, this is marvellous news. I cannot believe it."

"Well, it is true. Moreover, dear Geraldine, you may rest assured that your beautiful silk has been made up into the most delightful ballgown," declared Lucilla, with shining eyes.

Nurse Hargreaves had been listening to their conversation with an understanding smile. She had been as amazed as her mistress to see young Miss Prior enter the room, but had been delighted when Lucilla had kissed her and given her a little present of chocolates, which she had bought the previous day when out with her aunt.

The old woman rose unsteadily to her feet, her arthritic knee preventing any sudden movement, and walked slowly towards the door, clutching her stitching and chocolates.

"I shall leave you both to talk," she said, adding with a meaningful look at Geraldine, "now that my part in the proceedings is played."

Geraldine ignored the remark and answered coolly, "Send up some refreshment, please, Nurse dear. I am sure that Lucilla could do with some hot chocolate and buttered Sally Lunns while we chat."

"Aye — I'll see to it," assented the old nurse, thinking to herself as she closed the door, Now you can tell Miss Lucilla who it was you were really expecting.

"If you guessed that the note was from me," said Lucilla

as soon as the door was shut, "why did you look so surprised?"

"Well — to be perfectly truthful, Lucilla, I thought that it had been written by somebody else . . ."

"Geraldine, gracious me! What changes London society has wrought in you, to be sure. You mean that you actually answered my note, not knowing for sure from whom it came? Why, you would never have dreamed of doing such a thing at one time."

Geraldine's usual composure looked in slight disarray.

"Not exactly — I was almost sure . . ."

"Oh? And who else would play such a trick, pray?"

"Lucilla, do not think badly of me, but I . . . er . . . thought it was from a certain gentleman — "

"Aha!"

"Yes. You see, I have met the most charming person by the name of Sir David Clifton, whom I know to have a most wry sense of humour. I thought the note might be from him. That is why I asked Nurse to stay and do her stitching."

"A fitting chaperone," laughed Lucilla. "Oh my, and I thought how touching it was that you had asked Nurse in to welcome me with you." Lucilla's laughter seemed to amaze Geraldine.

"You think it is funny?" she demanded, surprised. "You do not think it was an unseemly thing for me to do! — to await this gentleman in such an unorthodox way?"

"But of course not. I should have done the same thing myself," cried Lucilla, "although probably without Nurse hovering in the background!"

"Oh, Lucilla!" said Geraldine, shocked.

"Mmm — he must have a great deal to commend him, your Sir David Clifton," added Lucilla thoughtfully, "for he has obviously made a strong impression on you, Geraldine."

"Yes, he has very many good qualities which I have observed already," admitted Geraldine, turning a little pink.

"Tell me more about your invitation to the ball," she asked, changing the subject, "for I am still a little puzzled."

Lucilla proceeded to tell her how Aunt Amelia had written to her uncle; how he had taken so long to reply that she could not let Geraldine know when they were at Langley House together; and how her uncle had said that they might use his town house in Soho Square.

"Is your gown ready?" demanded Geraldine practically, for she knew that Lucilla had the habit of leaving everything until the very last moment.

"Quite, down to the last detail," replied Lucilla with a chuckle, "and it is made from your beautiful silk, Geraldine dear."

"Ah, I am so happy for you, Lucilla. We shall be able to meet at the ball, probably after supper, and I can introduce you to Sir David Clifton."

"I shall look forward to meeting this gentleman," said Lucilla warmly, and then she added, as if it were an afterthought, "And your cousin, will you kindly send him my kindest regards, Geraldine? Perhaps I shall see him at the same time . . ."

"Rupert? Oh, of course," declared Geraldine at once, but even as she spoke, Lucilla noticed the look of uncertainty which seemed to cross her face at his name.

"Lord Childs is quite well, I hope," Lucilla said sharply.

"Oh, yes, perfectly," replied Geraldine flatly, "and he has been wonderful to me — taking me out in London society so much that I have scarce had a day's leisure."

"Then why did you look so worried when I mentioned his name?" demanded Lucilla, bluntly.

Geraldine hesitated before replying. But suddenly she thought how good it would be to be able to confide in her friend, so she told Lucilla of Lord Childs' unpredictable, dark moods, and the habit he had of going off on his own.

Lucilla listened. She did not wish to add to Geraldine's worry, so she decided not to tell her that she had noticed the same symptoms when they were at Langley House. Nor did she tell of the strange meetings with the gypsy. She glanced at her friend uneasily, for she was now more sure than ever that some mystery surrounded Lord Childs which accounted for these moods. As she looked at Geraldine's anxious face, she suddenly remembered the letter which she had inadvertently taken from the gypsy's caravan, and which she had meant to bring with her to give to Lord Childs. Until this moment, it had completely gone from her mind. She frowned to herself, at a loss to understand how she could have been so remiss.

Lucilla thought she would try to console Geraldine. "I am sure that you are worrying unnecessarily," she said eventually, when Geraldine had finished talking. "Perhaps he attends to boring business matters and does not wish to trouble you with their intricacies."

"I had thought of that," admitted Geraldine, brightening up a little.

"Well then, I am sure that we are both right. Put it out of your mind and tell me about the parties to which Lord Childs has taken you — they sound wonderful!" Despite her lighthearted tone, conjured up to console her friend, Lucilla felt far from cheerful, for the worry of the letter was nagging at her peace of mind.

7

"By God — you've grown into a beauty, niece. I wish your father were here to see you at this moment, m'dear."

Portly Sir Ralph Stavely stood back, beaming at Lucilla. He had been awaiting her patiently in the hall, and had glanced up as he heard the swish of her skirts upon the stairs, but he had not been prepared for the picture which Lucilla made as she descended.

The finery had transformed her from a most beautiful young woman to a young lady of quite exceptional delicacy and charm. Anticipation of the night's grand ball had made her positively radiant.

Aunt Amelia followed proudly behind her. She, too, was staggered at Lucilla's beauty.

Lucilla's golden hair had been washed and rinsed until it squeaked as the sponge was run through it. Then it had been set into the latest style of ringlets, some piled on her head and others left to frame her face, and now the light caught up the true depth of the burnished tresses.

The exquisite little heart-shaped face, with its tinged rosebud complexion and deep violet eyes, was shown off to perfection by the dressing of the ringlets.

But the *piéce de resistance* was the gown which had been made with such love and attention by the local seamstress. Geraldine had chosen well when she had selected the pale turquoise shade for Lucilla. It could not have been bettered, except that it tended, if anything, to give her an almost ethereal quality which was not quite the real Lucilla.

The bodice was daintily embroidered with tiny flowers, as was the scalloped skirt in layered tiers, which matched the neckline of the same shape. Around Lucilla's slender white throat hung a most beautiful aquamarine and diamond necklace, a loan from Sir Ralph Stavely for the night, since his wife had sent him with no less than four necklaces from which Lucilla might choose. A kindly person, she had realized that her poor niece would hardly be likely to possess any suitable jewellery herself for an important ocassion.

Lucilla's white silk stockings were topped at the knees with garters made from leftover material from the gown, and covered with tiny rosebuds. Her dancing pumps were of a near shade of turquoise, for she had not been able to afford to have these made specially, so the seamstress had stitched a row of ruching and rosebuds around them, and these, too, looked delightful.

"You'll take good care of her, Ralph," said Aunt Amelia, with concern. "Watch her every minute, I beseech you," she added in a whisper, "she is so young and innocent."

"Have no fear, Amelia, I shall let no harm come to her," laughed Sir Ralph, watching Lucilla twirl around gaily before him. "She will love every minute of the evening, and likely remember it for the rest of her life!"

The Duke of Sedgeley was among the top six wealthiest men in England. His estates were vast, and he owned enormous sugar plantations in the West Indies. His huge London mansion matched Carlton House in its luxury and splendour, and his entertaining was equally as lavish. He was a close friend of the Prince Regent, and was often to be seen in his company.

Tonight's ball was exceptional, even for him. It was being given in honour of his daughter's betrothal, and a fortune had been spent on it. More than a thousand guests had been invited, and, as they descended from their carriages and conversed in the main hall, they presented a unique picture, dressed as they were in the finest apparel that money could buy. The men wore court dress (for the Prince Regent was to be present) or uniforms, while the ladies boasted the latest fashions from Paris with all attendant paraphernalia, glistening in their fine satins and silks, and coiffured to perfection.

The main supper room filled the enormous conservatory, and before the seat at the head of the table which had been set aside for the Prince Regent was a large, shell-shaped basin full of crystal-clear water which flowed into a simulated meandering stream along the table, flanked by banks of exotic flowers. Will-o-the-wisp gold and silver fish flashed mysteriously along the stream from behind small rocks and coloured stones.

Lucilla found it almost impossible to conceal her excitement behind the necessary unruffled facade of well-bred calmness. In her wildest dreams, she had never imagined such splendour. Even the servants in white powdered wigs and scarlet livery, their crested buttons gleaming like real silver, seemed like high-ranking officers.

Neither had she expected such a throng of people, and it occurred to her, as her uncle steered her expertly through their midst, that she would never find Geraldine in such a crowd; not even if she searched the entire evening.

Thankfully, the crowd seemed to thin out as they made their way through the vast reception hall, and once inside the ballroom, where two groups of musicians played alternately from a raised dais at each end, there was far more room. Everything was so luxurious and spacious.

Lucilla looked curiously around at the sea of unfamiliar faces. Apart from her uncle, she knew nobody. But, almost at once, she found herself the centre of attraction as her uncle introduced her to a whole host of friends, men and women of his own age with their sons and daughters.

"Meet Mr. Martin Reynolds," her uncle was saying, and a young man stepped forward from their midst, as handsome as anybody she had ever seen. "The son of one of my oldest friends," beamed her uncle. And Mr. Martin Reynolds smiled at her in such a way as to set her heart beating unexpectedly faster as he swept her on to the floor to dance.

His charm did not end with his smile, she soon discovered. He was amusing and witty, a delightful flatterer, in a most convincing manner, and a very attractive companion. He was obviously much taken with Miss Prior, and it was not long before she began to return his attention. By supper time, she could not keep her eyes from him, nor he from her.

"Lord — that's a lovely girl," declared the Prince Regent, sipping his iced champagne and languidly helping himself to a peach from the bowl before him which was piled high with exotic fruits. His roving eye had strayed to Lucilla on and off the entire evening.

The Duke of Sedgeley looked with interest in the direction of the Regent's gaze. "Hmm, you mean the golden-haired one, sitting next to Reynolds?" he said, searching his memory hard for her name, which he had quite forgotten. "She's the niece of Sir Ralph Stavely up from Surrey, I believe."

They lapsed into a momentary silence before going on to talk of other things as Martin Reynolds took Lucilla by the arm to join the other swirling couples in a waltz. But Lucilla, glancing up quickly, caught the look on the Regent's face, and had to turn her head away because she was so amused. She did not wish to be rude to the royal personage, and he might well have been offended had he seen her expression, for there was on his bloated face that fawn-like look which a pretty woman could usually be relied upon to inspire, making him look, thought Lucilla, like a besotted codfish.

Thus it was that Lord Childs, accompanying Geraldine back to the ballroom a little while later, entered the room just in time to see Lucilla being led on to the floor by a handsome young man whom he recognized at once as being Martin Reynolds, a person he did not like. Many eyes followed the couple admiringly, for they made a striking pair.

Lord Childs could not help being much taken by Lucilla's youthful beauty — for it was the first time he had seen her since leaving Langley House, and she had grown even more lovely since then — but his eyes narrowed disapprovingly at her partner, and his face darkened even more as he noticed the way in which Martin Reynolds gazed down at Lucilla.

"Drat the man," he murmured in a voice so low that nobody heard, only half realizing, himself, that he had spoken.

Later, when dancing with his cousin, Lord Childs made a

point of saying, "We must ask Miss Prior and Sir Ralph to join us for champagne, Geraldine. The evening is slipping by, and we have not so much as exchanged a word with them yet."

"Oh, yes, Rupert. Let us seek them out as soon as we have finished dancing, and introduce them to Sir David Clifton, for I should like Lucilla to meet him."

Lucilla was encircled by an admiring crowd who had been attracted by her beauty. Her large violet eyes sparkled with fun, and her face was alight with pleasure. She had not expected to enjoy the ball anywhere near as much as this. From time to time, her gaze wandered and caught the smile of Martin Reynolds, a knowing, intimate smile which thrilled her, and which she could not resist returning.

Then, through the crowd, appeared Geraldine, magnificent in her apricot silk and sophisticated coiffured hair. By her side came Lord Childs, and Lucilla was to remember the look in his eyes, as he gazed at her, for the rest of her life.

"You will take champagne with us, Miss Prior, I hope," he asked as he bowed formally, unable to take his eyes off her beautiful face, and extending a short acknowledging nod towards Martin Reynolds.

"And perhaps take a turn around the garden for a little conversation," said Geraldine, adding quickly, "Sir David Clifton is to join us."

Lucilla understood at once how eager her friend was to introduce them.

"I should be delighted," she said graciously, thoroughly enjoying a newly found air of sophistication which the evening had bestowed upon her, and then, more like the usual Lucilla, adding, "Let us go whenever you like, Geraldine — I long for some fresh air and a cool drink."

Since Lord Childs had not asked Martin Reynolds to join his party, that young man took his leave, bowing graciously to the ladies before doing so, and casting a quick, adoring look at Lucilla, to which she smiled prettily.

Lord Childs, noticing Reynolds' expression, glared at him as he departed, then, turning to Lucilla, declared, "Before we take our stroll, Miss Prior, will you not do me the honour of a dance?"

She looked at him in surprise but nodded agreement, and was about to say something when he stepped forward, and, taking her firmly by the arm, led her to the fringe of the dancers.

To her astonishment, he danced sublimely, far better than Martin Reynolds. She could scarcely remember when she had last enjoyed dancing so much. She hardly noticed the other couples as the two of them moved together in perfect harmony. It seemed that a magic ingredient had been added to the music. She glanced smilingly up at him, and saw again upon his face the look he had given her when they had first met. Was it her imagination, she wondered, or did he hold her just a little closer as they gazed into each other's eyes for a brief moment? Suddenly, he seemed to realize that he was staring at her. He glanced away, and began to engage her in light conversation.

She blushed a little, for she, too, realized that she had been looking at him in a way which might be considered unseemly. She wondered quickly why such a man as he had never married, and compared him in her mind with Martin Reynolds. Mr. Reynolds, she decided, was fun, while Lord Childs, although charming, was far too unbending.

To her surprise, she suddenly heard him say, "No doubt

everybody has told you how beautiful you are this evening, Miss Prior."

She looked up at him in amazement.

"Well . . ."

"Come now, Miss Prior, you are too modest. Admit it, for I think so, too."

"Ah! Now that you have said so, I begin to believe it then," she replied with a delicious twinkle in her eyes.

There was a spring in her step as Lucilla walked towards the carriage. She was on her way to see Geraldine, and, for once, was not accompanied by her aunt. That good lady had taken to her bed through sheer physical exhaustion, as she had declared, after so many outings and parties.

A week or so had passed since the night of the ball, during which time Lucilla had found herself bombarded by invitations from people of whom she had never even heard. Many of these Aunt Amelia would not let her accept, on the advice of Sir Ralph Stavely, who thought them inappropriate friends for Lucilla's tender years.

Today, she looked as pretty as a picture, bedecked in white muslin trimmed with crimson velvet points and a full, crimson skirt. On her head was a little dress bonnet of white crepe with a small circular opening on the crown, through which peeped a bunch of golden curls. Dangling from her slender arm, clad in elbow-length white kid gloves, was her new indispensable of crimson velvet, a present from her uncle, drawn together with a crimson ribbon and containing her handkerchief and purse.

A smile danced around her mouth as she sat in the carriage, for she was thinking as usual of Mr. Martin Reynolds. Already, she had seen him on several occasions, and he had paid court to her, in no uncertain terms, to such an extent that she could not wait to see him again. She was longing to confide in Geraldine as soon as she saw her.

Martin Reynolds was tall and of a slender build, with fair, wavy hair, and pale blue eyes which had a directness of gaze that sent a newly found thrill of excitement through Lucilla every time she encountered it. He was handsome, in an orthodox way, with good, even features and a slightly hooked nose. He laughed a great deal, although Lucilla did not always think what he said so very funny. However, she laughed with him because, somehow, he seemed to catch her up in his exuberance, and she also enjoyed the delicious feeling of sharing a joke that nobody else in the world knew about. What she liked most of all was the way in which he was so delightfully attentive, even over the smallest things, which made her feel so very special. When she looked into his eyes, she felt that she was the only woman in the world of any importance, and, certainly, Mr. Martin Reynolds lost no chance in telling her how singular she was as often as he could.

Lucilla had seen neither Lord Childs nor Geraldine since the night of the ball. She suspected that they had been even more caught up in the social whirl than herself, which was why she had not heard from her friend. When a messenger had appeared with an invitation from Geraldine to spend the day with her, therefore, she had accepted it with glee. Aunt Amelia had been grateful for a day in which to rest, and saw no harm in allowing her niece to go unaccompanied on such an innocent call.

Lucilla hummed a little to herself as the carriage progressed slowly through the congested streets around Covent Garden. She had not realized when she set out, for she was unfamiliar with such things, that it would be so crowded. Inadvertently, she had chosen the busiest time of the day. The main streets were crammed with cars of vegetables, fruit, and flowers, and trade was brisk.

She began to wish that she had not asked to be taken such a long way round, except that she had always wanted to see this area with its famous Drury Lane Theatre. Slowly, the horses moved forward a few steps at a time, and Lucilla peered from the window, watching the bustle and the brawls, the cheeky-faced street urchins, and the fashions of the fine ladies and occasional dandy.

Eventually, the carriage cleared the crowds, and set off at a constant trot for the palatial splendour of Lord Childs' house. Lucilla wondered whether Geraldine's romance with David Clifton had continued to flower as much as her own, and had returned to musing over Martin Reynolds again when the carriage drew to a halt outside Lord Childs' house.

She alighted quickly, and in so doing only just managed to avoid a large puddle, for it had been raining heavily during the night. In her haste to step past it, she did not look where she was going, and caught a swift blow on her arm as somebody, moving hurriedly from behind, bumped into her. She drew back in momentary pain, expecting an apology from the person, but none was forthcoming. Instead, a shabby-looking man made off at a run, spattering her with filthy water from the road.

Lucilla was so incensed that she felt like calling after him. She stood rubbing her bruised arm, glaring after the man who suddenly turned into the side entrance of the house which led to the mews at the rear. Without quite realizing what she was doing, Lucilla set nimbly off in pursuit. She knew that he would be cornered, once behind the house, and she intended to give him a piece of her mind.

Gathering up her long crimson skirt, she ran swiftly into the mews. He heard her footsteps as she turned the corner, for the enclosed area seemed to act as a sounding board. He glanced furtively behind, and she saw his face. It was only a brief glimpse, but enough to make her stop in her stride. The man was the gypsy from Dorking Fair.

Not knowing quite what to do, for she realized at once that he must have some clandestine appointment with Lord Childs, she stood hesitating for a moment. To follow the odious fellow would be silly, even dangerous, and she certainly did not wish for an encounter with Lord Childs. Quickly, she turned on her heel and began to walk hurriedly back to the front of the house.

She was just rounding the corner when a familiar figure strode towards her. She could not believe her ill-luck. A moment later and she would have missed the encounter. But, since there was nothing she could do about it, she braced herself, tried hard not to look uneasy, and prepared to face the questions.

"Great heavens!" exclaimed Lord Childs, amazed at finding her there.

Lucilla's chin went up bravely.

"What on earth are you doing here, Miss Prior?" he asked, bowing slightly.

"Oh, Lord Childs, I am so grateful to see you," she replied in a docile voice.

"Oh?"

"I was alighting from my carriage a few minutes ago and saw some rough fellow run into your mews — I am sure he might have been a thief. I followed him but did not catch him . . ."

"I see. And you would have taken it upon yourself to tackle the man once you had cornered him, I suppose," he said, in a sarcastic voice which implied how foolish he thought her.

"Oh, no, I would have called a stable lad or the groom, of course," she stuttered.

He watched her closely as she spoke.

"Take my advice, Miss Prior," he said sternly. "Do not rush headlong into trouble. Such men can be violent, as well you know, and, in any case, it might have been one of the stable men. Probably quite an innocent fellow, in any event."

She nodded meekly.

"I suppose it was rather silly of me," she said in a subdued voice, and made as if to pass him, but he took hold of her arm.

"Permit me to escort you safely to the house," he said, graciously but firmly.

"Thank you, Lord Childs," she replied, feeling that he suspected she had spotted the gypsy.

But his next words dispelled her suspicion, for he turned to her pleasantly and said, "Sir Ralph Stavely must be proud of you — you were a great success at the Duke of Sedgeley's ball."

"It is kind of you to say so, Lord Childs," answered Lucilla demurely.

"There is no need to ask if you enjoyed yourself," he continued. "Your face revealed only too clearly that you did — as indeed you should have, for it was a magnificent occasion, and the Prince Regent does not attend the first London ball of every young lady . . ."

"How gracious of the Prince," laughed Lucilla, "although

I doubt very much that he realized he was doing me such an honour.''

"Oh! Do not be too sure. He has a fine eye for a pretty face and scarcely misses anything exceptional . . . but, tell me, what did you think of the Prince?''

Lucilla hesitated. She did not wish to sound impertinent, but she could not resist from saying what was in her mind.

"Why, he has even more chins than Aunt Amelia!'' she declared. "La! You know full well, sir, that the Prince is old and fat," she continued bluntly. Her eyes were laughing as she looked up at him. "Surely he would be better matched to somebody of Aunt Amelia's years.''

"Hmph! So that is what you think, is it, Miss Prior?'' His eyes were twinkling and his lips twitched, then, all of a sudden, he was roaring with laughter.

Lucilla dimpled prettily.

"Yes, sir, that is precisely what I think," she said, with finality in her voice.

By now they had ascended the steps which led to the main double doors. Still laughing, he tugged at the bell, and the doors were flung open in seconds. He ushered her inside, then without saying more, he bowed and left her.

Geraldine had been waiting impatiently for Lucilla to arrive. Dressed in a tawny velvet gown, she had taken several agitated turns around the room, stopping from time to time at the window to see if there was any sign of Lucilla. At one time, she thought that she had heard a carriage drawing to a halt and had hurried to the window expecting to see Lucilla alighting from it, but, when she had got there, the carriage was already moving off and there was no sign of her friend.

She began to pace the room again, wishing that Lucilla would come. Her face was overcast and there was a worried look in her beautiful eyes. She sighed from time to time and dabbed her eyes ineffectually, for she had cried a little already, and felt that she might burst into tears at any moment.

Impatiently, she pulled the servants' bell which hung to the right of the vast fireplace.

"Has Lord Childs left the house?" she enquired anxiously when the footman appeared.

"Yes, Mistress, several minutes ago," the man replied. "He went to the stables to get his horse saddled for a ride in the park."

"Ah! Then he will not be here to take cordial with my guest and myself," said Geraldine. "Bring sufficient for just the two of us, with some of those little queen cakes and almond biscuits."

The footman hurried away, and Geraldine once again walked to the window. Then it was she heard Lucilla's light tread outside the door which had been left slightly ajar, and her friend suddenly appeared in the room.

Lucilla realized at once that Geraldine was upset about something.

"Why so sad?" she inquired. "I can see by your eyes that you have been weeping . . . whatever is it?"

"Oh, it's Rupert," cried Geraldine in despair, for once making no attempt to hide her true feelings. "He has been so horrid these last few days — quite impossible, in fact. His temper is appalling — I can't hardly get a civil word from him — and sometimes he will not speak at all. It is so unlike him," she added, the tears welling in her eyes, "that I fear he must be ill."

"But I have only just spoken to him," declared Lucilla in astonishment, "and he seemed in a perfectly good temper."

She quickly told Geraldine of her encounter with Lord Childs, taking good care not to mention that the man was the gypsy she had seen in Dorking.

"Well, you must have charmed him into a better humour, then," retorted Geraldine ruefully, "for he has said only a few words to me these last two days. It is as though he has some terrible preoccupation — always there to worry him."

And it is to do with that vile gypsy, thought Lucilla. For a brief moment, she considered telling Geraldine all about the gypsy, although her first instincts had been to remain quiet about it, but, remembering how Geraldine had reacted when she had mentioned the Dorking Fair episode, her courage failed her, and she decided to keep the matter to herself.

"Well, his humour seems much improved," she added lightly, in an effort to cheer up Geraldine.

"But what am I to do?" persisted her friend, "when it happens again."

"Nothing," Lucilla snapped, and then she said, more gently, "If he does have some sort of a problem, you will only add to it if you start fussing. Try to be a little more tolerant, Geraldine — don't just think of yourself." Lucilla did not really wish to be so blunt, but she saw no other way, for Geraldine was very self-centred on occasions.

"I suppose you are right," assented Geraldine, looking just a little annoyed at her friend's outspoken words. "But, all the same, I shall keep an eye on him, and call a physician if need be."

"Don't do that, for heaven's sake," exclaimed Lucilla. "You will infuriate Lord Childs by such an action. Just try and forget about it all, Geraldine. Let us make the most of this day together, for my aunt says that we must return to Surrey shortly," Lucilla added, in an effort to change the conversation. "She says that we must not abuse my uncle's hospitality by remaining in his London home when he returns to the country, and he is planning to do so shortly, for he adores his wife, who is bedridden. He will never leave her longer than he can possibly help. She is such a kind, dear person, Geraldine."

But Geraldine did not seem to be interested in Lucilla's aunt. "Oh, no!" she cried. "I couldn't bear you to leave London so soon," she declared with feeling. "I shall ask Rupert if you may come here and stay until the end of the month, at least."

Lucilla's face lit up at the thought. "That would be wonderful — I could see more of Mr. Martin Reynolds, perhaps."

". . . And I can give a dinner party and ask both Mr. Reynolds and Sir David Clifton," smiled Geraldine.

"Yes," breathed Lucilla, "we could see them both far more often in each other's company. Oh, Geraldine, I really do think that I am much taken with Mr. Reynolds . . ."

"And Sir David Clifton is always in my thoughts, too. Did you not consider him a fine man, Lucilla?"

Lucilla nodded vigorously.

"My uncle Ralph described him as a sterling man in every way," she said, to Geraldine's unconcealed delight.

"Well — I am sure the same can be said of Mr. Reynolds," declared Geraldine, beaming at her.

A most satisfied expression sealed the corners of Aunt Amelia's mouth as she folded the letter which she had just received from the Reverend George Prior. She had felt extremely torn when Lucilla had returned from Geraldine and told her that it was highly probable they would be asked to stay at Lord Childs' house.

On the one hand, she had wanted very much to remain in London for a while longer to give her niece the full benefit of the astonishing success she had made of her debut into society (for Aunt Amelia was growingly optimistic over brilliant marriage prospects for Lucilla these days), yet, on the other hand, she had also realized it was her duty to return to the rectory with Lucilla.

They had forsaken her brother for far too long already, she had thought, and it was selfish to continue indulging themselves in London. Her brother, she knew, missed his daughter greatly, and as for herself, well, she was virtually the mistress of the rectory with all its attendant responsibilities, and needed to be there soon to organize the social functions and niceties required of a local parson.

Thus, when she had received a formal invitation from Lord Childs requesting them to stay with Geraldine until the end of the month, she had written at once to her brother and pointed out that, despite the invitation, she would quite happily return to Surrey with Lucilla if he so required — at very little sacrifice to either of them. This was not quite true, for she really thought that Lucilla might be losing all sorts of exciting marriage prospects by quitting London before the end of the season. She had sighed as she finished the letter, and had hoped that her brother might be able to read between the lines.

To her delight, his reply came as an unexpected surprise. He had said that his old friend, the Reverend Alexander Ponsonby and his wife had written from York, where the Reverend Ponsonby held office, to say that they would be journeying to Winchester shortly, and would take delight in visiting their old friend for a while after they had finished their business there. Thus, Lucilla's father had written that he would be most happy for Aunt Amelia and Lucilla to remain in London.

Now of all the people in the world most disliked by Aunt Amelia, it was Clarinda Ponsonby, wife of the said Alexander. They had met several times before and detested each other. Aunt Amelia's normally mild disposition forsook her in the company of this prying busybody, and she quickly degenerated into quite a waspish shrew.

To discover that this loathsome creature was actually to stay at the rectory for even a day or two was sufficient to make Aunt Amelia invent jobs of importance at the other end of the village. Now to find that she was to be there while they were considering prolonging their stay in London, almost seemed as though fate was smilingly giving its approval.

"Is it not splendid, dear?" said Aunt Amelia, addressing Lucilla, who had been waiting anxiously to hear what her father had said. "Your dear Papa will not be alone after all if we accept Lord Childs' kind invitation. He is to have his old friend, the Reverend Alexander Ponsonby, to stay with him at that time — and Mrs. Ponsonby."

"Then you will accept?" cried Lucilla, clasping her hands with delight at the unexpected turn of events, for she had doubted that her aunt would do so until now.

"Of course, my dear . . . Why, your father will scarce have a moment to think of us. The house will seem quite full with Clarinda Ponsonby there!" Aunt Amelia permitted herself an expressive sniff at the thought.

Lucilla burst into a peal of laughter.

"Oh, Aunt. Thank goodness we shall escape that dreadful woman. She is too boring and prying for words. Why, I can remember a rhyme I wrote about her when I was quite small. It began: Nosey Parker Ponsonby looks like a crow — "

She was stopped in mid-sentence by her aunt, who held up her hand in horror to restrain Lucilla.

"That will do, niece. We should not mock another's shortcomings — however much they may infuriate us. But still," she added benignly, "I must admit that I am very happy not to be there while the lady is visiting."

"So you will write at once to Lord Childs," urged Lucilla, "for as soon as he has heard from you, we may go at any time — Geraldine said so."

"Yes, yes. Have no fear, I'll attend to the matter now, and you shall send the messenger with it immediately."

Without more ado, Aunt Amelia marched firmly into the small writing room and allowed Lucilla to place pen and paper before her before settling down to word the note.

Lucilla returned to the salon to read her own letter, which she had received from her father.

He wrote amusingly of all the village news, which Lucilla read with pleasure, chuckling at some of his descriptions. It was not until she had reached the final paragraph that the words brought the colour rushing to her face, for the Reverend Prior mentioned a band of gypsies who had been prowling around the neighbourhood, thieving anything of value upon which they could lay their hands. They had even, he declared heatedly, broken into one or two out-buildings of the rectory, and had taken all manner of garden implements, not to mention a pile of old clothes which Aunt Amelia had put aside for the deserving poor.

Lucilla read about the gypsies with growing unease. The news of them brought back, only too vividly, the memory of the afternoon she had so foolishly visited their camp. She sat biting her lower lip apprehensively, wishing that she had never gone to the wretched place, and still furious with herself for leaving the letter behind at the rectory.

She sat gazing into the fire, wondering whether she should tell Lord Childs about the letter. She did not much relish his fury when he discovered how she had come by it, yet discover her foolhardiness he must if he was to know of the strange document.

Perhaps it might be better to wait awhile, she at last decided, until she actually had the letter in her possession, for if the worst came to the worst, and she could not bring herself to face him, she could probably send it, then he would never know her reckless part in its recovery.

The idea did not please her, though. There seemed to be something cowardly and underhand about it. She frowned, poking a few dying embers, annoyed at her own indecision.

"You look worried," observed her aunt, reappearing at that moment. "Has dear father said something to upset you? — there was nothing of the kind in my letter."

Lucilla shook her head and tried to smile.

"Gracious me, certainly not, Aunt. His letter is a perfect catalogue of events, and most amusing. Here, read it yourself. You'll enjoy it." She picked it up and handed it to her aunt, who exchanged it only too readily for the sealed note containing her acceptance to Lord Childs. She sank contentedly down on to the large, comfortable sofa, reached for her spectacles, and began to read.

Lucilla summoned the footman immediately and bade him take Aunt Amelia's letter to Lord Childs. The man took it, a trifle wearily. He was quite worn out with all the extra work which the two ladies seemed to delight in finding for him, and secretly longed for their departure. Hardly a day seemed to pass that he was not sent somewhere or other, either with a message or to dress shops and haberdashers to collect numerous parcels. Sir Ralph Stavely, who lived quietly in London, was never so demanding.

"Aunt, I do not think we are popular with the servants in this house," observed Lucilla with a guilty laugh, when he had gone.

"Nonsense, dear, popularity does not come into it. Servants must do as they are instructed — I am sure Ralph pays highly enough for their services," declared Aunt Amelia autocratically.

"Why don't you go and start your packing?" she added quickly, for Lucilla was hovering around the room without any purpose. "And do it properly this time, Lucilla. I cannot keep repacking everything for you as though you were a child."

Her niece needed no second bidding. She went at once to her bedroom, summoned the maid to bring her valises, and immediately set about the loathsome task with her customary vigour.

"We are to have a supper party on Friday," declared Geraldine, as soon as Lucilla had arrived with Aunt Amelia, "and I have asked all sorts of people I know whom I am sure you will really like." She cast Lucilla a significant look as she spoke, and Lucilla realized at once that she had invited Mr. Martin Reynolds.

"How kind of you, dear," said Aunt Amelia, "but pray do not put yourself to any extra trouble on our behalf. We are indebted to you enough for asking us to stay."

"I should have had one in any case, I daresay," replied Geraldine nonchalantly, "and now that you are both here — so much the better."

"Have you invited Sir David Clifton?" Lucilla could not resist asking.

"Hush! Where are your manners, Lucilla?" exclaimed her aunt disapprovingly. "You do not quiz your hostess on her guest list."

"It is no matter, Miss Prior, I assure you," said Geraldine, amused at Aunt Amelia's sense of propriety, and exchanging at the same time a knowing look at Lucilla.

"Yes, Lucilla, his name has certainly been included — my cousin and I owe him hospitality, and he is so very popular as well."

"Ah! I shall look forward to meeting him again, then . . ." Lucilla's voice was polite to the extreme, for she did not want to give anything away in front of Aunt Amelia, yet her eyes twinkled.

Aunt Amelia looked at her sharply and guessed at once, however, that there was more to this supper than met the eye. Her instinct told her that the girls were planning something despite their innocent air, and she very much suspected that it had to do with the young man they had just mentioned. Aunt Amelia had seen how well her niece appeared to enjoy the company of Mr. Martin Reynolds at the various functions which they had attended, and, although he seemed a pleasant enough young man on the surface, she was not altogether sure that she trusted him. The thought, therefore, that this new gentleman, Sir David Clifton, might prove to be a possible beau for her niece pleased her enormously.

She had been mystified by the fact that Lucilla had apparently found nobody to her liking despite all the social gatherings to which she had been invited, and which had been positively bulging with what Aunt Amelia considered most eligible bachelors. It had been a source of disappointment to her and one reason why she was pleased to be able to stay on in London. Perhaps she had misjudged her niece after all, and there was somebody. She could not wait to make the acquaintance of Sir David Clifton if that were the case.

When Friday evening arrived, and Aunt Amelia observed Sir David across the long dining table, she was more than delighted with what she saw. As Aunt Amelia consumed successive helpings of boiled potatoes, first with the salmon, then with the turbot and smelts, then with several generous slices of saddle of mutton, and, finally, the dessert and fruit, her approval mounted at each mouthful, and she was in the finest of humours when she sailed into the grand saloon with the other ladies, leaving the gentlemen to their brandy and port.

Her approval did not extend to Mr. Martin Reynolds, who sat next to Sir David. Oh, dear no, for by now Aunt Amelia had decided that he was a young man who needed to be watched, if ever one did.

She turned to her niece as the ladies sat eating marzipan sweets, and said pointedly in a soft voice, "I can see why Sir David Clifton was asked to Geraldine's dinner party, my dear."

Lucilla turned to her with a merry smile.

"Oh, Aunt, I knew that you would understand — he really is so charming, is he not?"

"I am in full agreement over that," declared her aunt,

drawing her niece away from the other ladies so that they could talk more freely.

"But tell me, dear, how long has this friendship been so ripe?"

"Almost since the first meeting," replied Lucilla, "and it has — well, Aunt, really . . . er . . . thrived since the night of the Duke of Sedgeley's ball!" It did not occur to the young girl that her aunt imagined it was she — and not Geraldine — who harboured romantic notions of Sir David Clifton.

"I cannot understand why you did not talk to me about it, then," said Aunt Amelia warmly. She was about to say more, but the men were strolling into the room to rejoin the ladies, and there was no chance.

However, if Aunt Amelia chose to forget about Lucilla's friend, Lord Childs did not. Unlike Aunt Amelia, he had correctly assessed the position, and had seen at a glance that Geraldine and Sir David Clifton were enamoured with each other, while it was Mr. Martin Reynolds who was so much taken with Lucilla's charms.

This had irritated Lord Childs beyond reason. Martin Reynolds was a man he knew and did not trust. He was well known for his rakish life and countless affairs with the ladies, who seemed to find him irresistible. In fact, Lord Childs had only agreed to his name being included in the list of guests for the evening because Geraldine had requested it, and he had not wanted to disappoint her. Now he was annoyed with himself for permitting it.

Lord Childs was determined that Lucilla would not become involved with such a man. As soon as the last guest had departed, he decided to say something. Thus, when the footman had eventually shown the last person to the door, he turned to Aunt Amelia first and inquired if she had spent a pleasant evening, then, fixing Lucilla with a firm gaze, he added, "And you, Miss Prior, have you enjoyed the company here tonight?"

"Indeed, yes," replied Lucilla unsuspectingly. "It was quite the happiest evening I have spent for a long time. Geraldine chose such interesting and pleasant guests, that one would have needed to be in a very peculiar mood not to enjoy the conversation."

"Sir David Clifton was in good spirits, was he not?" asked Geraldine, looking a little flushed.

Aunt Amelia pricked up her ears and watched Lucilla.

"Sir David Clifton, Geraldine, can always be relied upon to be witty and entertaining at any supper party," replied Lord Childs calmly, taking a pinch of snuff.

"And Mr. Martin Reynolds, he, too, was in good humour, I thought," said Lucilla gaily.

At this, a glint of steel appeared in the eyes of Lord Childs.

"Hmph!" he ejaculated with a curl of his lower lip, and was about to say something when Geraldine, who had not seen the expression on his face, declared, "Mr. Reynolds seems much taken with Lucilla, Miss Prior. I should not wonder if he does not ask if he may call upon her."

Aunt Amelia looked utterly bewildered.

"Mr. Reynolds! But I thought it was Sir David Clifton," she declared.

"Indeed not, Miss Prior," said Geraldine, drawing herself up with dignity. "You are quite mistaken there. Sir David Clifton has already asked my cousin if he may call upon *me!*"

"But Lucilla . . ." Aunt Amelia turned to her niece accusingly. "I thought you said a little while ago that you thought Sir David very charming . . . and, well, you gave me to understand . . ." Her voice trailed off at the incredulous look on Lucilla's face.

"Why, Aunt, I gave you to understand no such thing," Lucilla declared indignantly. "I thought it was obvious to everybody how very much impressed he is with Geraldine — why, he cannot take his eyes off her." She gave an amused little chuckle. "You have the wrong man, Aunt, for it is Mr. Martin Reynolds that I like."

"Oh, no, Lucilla!" Her aunt said, thoroughly shocked. "He is not the sort of person of whom your dear father would approve for one moment, I do assure you."

"And rightly so, Miss Prior," said Lord Childs, joining in, having patiently awaited his cue. "However charming he may seem, Mr. Reynolds is not to be trusted. Your niece would do well to forget all about him."

"Why did you invite him here tonight, then?" demanded Lucilla rebelliously.

"The man is good enough for a supper party," replied Lord Childs with a shrug, "but he is not to be taken seriously."

"Oh! I will not listen to such talk," cried Lucilla angrily. "He has always appeared to me to be the most pleasing of gentlemen. Indeed, I should very much like to see more of him."

"Lucilla!" breathed Geraldine in a shocked voice, wishing with all her heart now that she had never asked him to supper. "Pray be warned by my cousin. He knows far more about these matters than you or I."

"Not necessarily!" declared her friend, with spirit. "As I am sure he will discover in the future!"

8

"Stuff and nonsense! Why, Geraldine, you sound like my Aunt Amelia — I am surprised at you." Lucilla turned to face her friend with a look of amazement on her beautiful face.

The two girls were visiting Geraldine's fashionable dress-maker for Geraldine to have the final fittings of the gowns which Lord Childs had insisted she buy. As soon as the carriage had clattered on its way through Grosvenor Square, Lucilla had proceeded to tell her friend of the wonderful afternoon she had recently spent in Vauxhall Gardens with Mr. Martin Reynolds.

Geraldine had looked at her askance.

"I am surprised that your aunt permitted you to go out at all with Mr. Reynolds — let alone by yourself. Did she not insist that you have a chaperone? The place is positively dissolute in some respects."

"Pray, do not alarm yourself, Geraldine," said Lucilla calmly. "Although my aunt was very much against the idea to begin with, she did eventually agree because we went in a party, at least ten of us, including Mr. Reynolds' sister, Clarissa. And, of course, Mr. Reynolds did take the trouble to come to the house and ask my aunt for her permission,'' she concluded with a trace of triumph, for she was determined to show that Martin Reynolds was not in the least the terrible creature which Lord Childs had painted him to be.

"Hmm — well, I suppose that it was all right. But I am glad that my cousin did not know of the outing all the same, for you know how he feels about the gentleman.''

"Oh, indeed. He has made his feelings crystal clear," said Lucilla with a shrug of her shoulders, "but I am not beholden in any way to Lord Childs, and I intend to continue my friendship with Mr. Reynolds. At least," she added with a laugh, "it cannot be said that he is a fortune hunter as well, for I am as poor as a church mouse.''

"There are more important things than fortunes," replied Geraldine waspishly.

Lucilla burst into a ripple of laughter.

"Come, Geraldine, do not be so prudish," she exclaimed in her forthright way. "No harm came to me, and I had a most exciting time — why, I actually saw a balloon take off successfully. Although I admit that the men in the basket beneath seemed to be having a little trouble getting it off the ground.''

"Oh," said Geraldine, a trifle enviously. "Now that is something I have always longed to see — but nobody would take me.''

"Why not come with us another time?" suggested Lucilla at once. "Perhaps Sir David Clifton will also join us. But apart from the ballooning gentlemen, it was *such* fun there, Geraldine, with a display of fireworks and wonderful music. Oh, I am positive you would have enjoyed it. Even the balloon was beautiful, all over coloured with mauve, pink, and palest green . . .''

"Did you, by any chance, see the blue man?" asked Geraldine curiously.

"Why, yes. He was there in the crowd watching the balloon rise, and it is quite true what they say about him. Every stitch of his clothing was in shades of blue. It is even rumoured," she added, with wide eyes, "that his rooms and all his furniture are in shades of blue also."

The blue man she referred to was one of London's leading and most eccentric dandies. He dressed extravagantly, entirely in various tones of blue, and was never seen in any other colours. He had become one of the sights of Vauxhall for whom everybody looked when they strolled there.

"They say," said Geraldine thoughtfully, "that the man is a little mad — did he look it?"

"Well . . . er . . . a little peculiar," assented Lucilla, and she gave her friend such a comical look that Geraldine could not resist smiling, and almost forgot the disapproval she felt for Lucilla's outing.

"And did Sir David Clifton call upon you yesterday?" inquired Lucilla decorously, making the most of Geraldine's good humour.

"Ah! He did," replied her friend with a happy sigh, "for he has been, as you know, in Hertfordshire for several days . . . I so missed him, Lucilla."

"I am sure he will ask for your hand in marriage any time now," declared Lucilla positively, "and then you will see him all the time. Think how wonderful that will be!"

"The thought is constantly with me," admitted her friend, "and I am so grateful that my cousin likes him — for think how dreadful it would be, Lucilla, if he did not."

Lucilla nodded. To herself she thought, thank heavens Lord Childs does not have to approve the man I wish to marry, or I should likely remain a spinster all my life.

When the carriage stopped outside Geraldine's dressmaker's shop, the two girls parted company for the time being. The shop was in a fashionable part of London, and there was little danger to which Lucilla could come wandering along the road, looking into the shops. She loathed tedious fittings for clothes, even though she loved the finished product, and was therefore very glad when Geraldine had suggested that she do some shopping on her own account instead of accompanying her.

Lucilla had hardly sauntered more than a few steps when she heard footsteps approaching briskly from behind. Something told her at once that the person was trying to catch her up, yet she could not imagine who it might be, and she did not wish to glance back, for not only would this be considered bad manners, but she would feel so silly if she was wrong. Very quickly, however, her curiosity was satisfied, for she heard a familiar voice bid her good morning.

"I did not think to see you abroad so early this morning, Miss Prior," declared Mr. Martin Reynolds as he removed his hat with a flourish. "Why, after yesterday's exertion at Vauxhall, most young ladies would have rested abed all morning."

"Not I, sir," said Lucilla with one of her dazzling smiles. "I do not fatigue easily, and, in any case, I had promised my friend to ride with her to the dressmaker."

"You are not by yourself?" he asked, looking disappointed.

"Indeed not, Mr. Reynolds. My aunt would hardly allow me to wander around London by myself. Why, you have no idea how hard I had to work to convince her that I would come to no harm during our innocent visit to Vauxhall Gardens."

"I see," he said with a short laugh. "But it is a pity all the same."

"A pity?"

"Yes — for I thought to ask if you would accompany me to the theatre one evening, Miss Prior. But I doubt now that your aunt would agree."

Disappointment rang clearly in his voice as he took her gently by the arm and guided her to a charming little lace shop on the corner of the road.

"It would be impossible, would it not?" he asked sadly as he looked down into her large eyes. "Your aunt would never allow such a thing . . . and something tells me also that she does not much care for our seeing each other, either."

"Oh, Mr. Reynolds," Lucilla whispered honestly, "I am afraid that you are perfectly right. But, as for myself, I should adore to come . . ."

"Then somehow we must seek to persuade your aunt," he urged. "Mention the subject tactfully to her, and if you think that she is likely to agree, send me a message at once that I may come and personally request her permission. What a delightful evening it could make —"

"I will try. Indeed I will."

He took her by the arm and turned her in the direction of the window of the lace shop.

"Look," he said, pointing at a set of delicate lace-edged handkerchiefs, the best to come out of Nottingham. "I noticed these as I passed by recently; they have the letter L embroidered in the corner. Please do me the honour of allowing me to present you with a dozen, Miss Prior."

"Oh, sir, I could not. It is not done," cried Lucilla despite herself, eyeing the handkerchiefs longingly.

"Let it be our little secret," he cajoled. "Nobody need know. They are so beautiful that they deserve a fittingly beautiful owner." He took her small gloved hand in his as he spoke, and gazed down at her.

Feeling as though she was walking on air, Lucilla permitted him to lead her into the tiny shop. He purchased the handkerchiefs, and presented them to her as soon as they were outside again.

"I shall think of you every time I carry one," she said softly.

"Ah! That is why I bought them, dear Miss Prior," he said, laughing softly. "To be constantly in your thoughts is all that I ask."

"I must go," said Lucilla, feeling that the eyes of passers-by were upon them. "Geraldine will be awaiting me soon."

Feeling rather flushed, she bid him good-bye and continued her window-shopping, although her meeting with Martin Reynolds had quite dispelled the placid enjoyment she had previously been reaping from the innocent exercise.

Geraldine glanced at Lucilla curiously when she met her at the dressmaker a little while later.

"You have a very high colour, Lucilla," she observed with surprise. "I think that you had better take a rest when we get home. You must have overtired yourself yesterday at Vauxhall Gardens. Either that, or you have a fever."

"Well, I do feel rather warm," agreed Lucilla, and was about to tell her of the unexpected encounter with Mr. Reynolds when Geraldine suddenly saw something in a shop window which caught her fancy, and she hurried inside for a closer inspection.

Neither was there much chance to tell her on the return journey in the carriage, for Geraldine was full of talk of the gowns which were nearly finished and looking superb. Twice, Lucilla tried to interrupt her with her own piece of news, all to no avail, and by the time they had arrived home it was too late for the time being, since Geraldine was accompanying her cousin to the house of a friend for luncheon, and had to go at once to her boudoir to attend to her toilette.

Lucilla was surprised that Geraldine had not asked her what her little parcel contained. Geraldine had glanced at it when they had met, and Lucilla had felt sure that she was going to ask her, but Geraldine's own acquisitions had seemed of paramount importance to her, so the matter was never raised. Lucilla gazed at the delicate little handkerchiefs admiringly as she placed them lovingly in her handkerchief sachet, the contents of which, until then, were of a more utilitarian nature, comprising plain cambric and cotton.

Meanwhile, Lucilla pondered over the best way to approach her aunt on the question of a trip to the theatre with Mr. Martin Reynolds. She felt sure that if her aunt could only get to know him more, her dislike for him would vanish. But that was a thing of the future, and Lucilla longed for the theatre now.

She wondered whether or not to broach the subject as she partook of a light luncheon with her aunt, but her instinct told her that this would not be a good idea. Aunt Amelia was not in the best of moods, for she had slept badly the previous night, and had one of her headaches, which always left her in a short temper.

"Why not rest in bed this afternoon with your curtains drawn together?" Lucilla suggested as she poured a small quantity of laudanum into a tiny glass and handed it to her. "Perhaps by teatime you will be recovered, and I will be able to order tea for you in your room."

Aunt Amelia placed a plump white hand on her aching brow.

"Yes, dear. I'll do as you suggest," she assented wearily, "although it is such a nagging pain I doubt it will be gone by teatime."

"Poor Aunt, then I shall not disturb you," said Lucilla gently.

Her aunt looked disappointed.

"Pray do, niece," she replied quickly. "There's no point in starving oneself for a mere headache — and make sure that they send up some seed cake from the kitchen, as well!"

Later that afternoon, when Lord Childs and Geraldine had returned from their luncheon, Lucilla was surprised to receive a terse summons from Lord Childs to attend him immediately. The footman who brought the message added a rider of his own when he saw the puzzled look on Lucilla's face.

"You'd best go at once, Mistress," he warned, "for His Lordship is in as black a mood as I've seen for a long time. Don't keep him waiting!"

Lucilla took his advice and sped to her room to tidy her hair and sprinkle her neck and palms with jasmine water. If there was to be a confrontation about something, she told herself spiritedly, she would go into the fray looking her best. She could not for the life of her think what could be so important as to necessitate the urgent command from Lord Childs, although she realized uneasily that it was something which must have rankled him deeply.

He was pacing the room impatiently when she arrived and turned abruptly in his stride to face her as she opened the door. His face was set and his eyes were cold.

She knew at once that she was in for some stern rebuke over something and prepared herself for the worst.

"I asked your aunt to attend on me also, Miss Prior," he began, motioning her to a seat, "but I understand that she is unwell, and, since this is a matter of some importance, I shall see you now and speak to her later."

Lucilla sank weakly back on to the settee, utterly mystified. She had not seen him look like this since their disagreement at Langley House.

"Your behaviour has been drawn to my notice, Miss Prior, and I am gravely disappointed in you," he began icily.

"My behaviour, sir?" exclaimed Lucilla, hardly able to believe her ears, since she could think of nothing that she had done to warrant the rebuke.

"Yes, Miss Prior, a disgrace to my cousin and to your good aunt, not to mention to myself."

"Sir?"

"You were seen in Vauxhall Gardens only yesterday in the company of Mr. Martin Reynolds — I have it on good authority, so don't bother to deny it."

Lucilla's fine eyebrows went up in defiance.

"Indeed, I shall do no such thing, Lord Childs. I admit I was there with the gentleman, and what is more, I greatly enjoyed myself. Where is the disgrace in that, pray?"

"You know full well that no reputable lady should be in such a place, with such a gentleman, unaccompanied by a chaperone," he retorted coldly.

"But, sir —"

"I am hurt and mortified, Miss Prior," he added, without

allowing her to continue. "You know full well how I feel about Mr. Reynolds, yet you go out of your way to ignore my feelings on the subject."

"If only you would let me say a word," declared Lucilla impatiently. "You have been incorrectly informed, Lord Childs, for I was not alone with Mr. Reynolds. There were at least ten of us — and his sister was acting as my chaperone. Also, and this may surprise you, sir, I had the permission of my aunt to be there."

Her words must have surprised him, yet his face did not soften. "And this morning?" he persisted, staring hard at her. "Did your aunt also give her permission for a shopping expedition with the man?"

"Oh, that!" Is it possible, Lucilla wondered to herself, to do *anything* in London without Lord Childs finding out? "You have only to ask your own cousin, sir, with whom I actually went shopping to see the folly there. While Geraldine visited her dressmaker for fittings, I indulged myself in a little window-shopping, and Mr. Reynolds happened to be there at the same time. He caught me up as I was walking by myself and we had a brief conversation."

"Huh! And Mr. Reynolds had not the slightest idea that you would be shopping by yourself this morning, I suppose," he said sarcastically.

"Oh, I suppose you think that I mentioned it to him before — that I made a clandestine arrangement," declared Lucilla, with an angry toss of her head, her temper flaring at his unreasonable attitude and his humiliating interrogation.

Not giving him time to reply, she added furiously, rising to her feet, "It is clear to me, sir, that you and I shall never agree. You seek the worst in me, and if it is not there, then you imagine it."

Her fiery retaliation staggered him.

For a brief moment, they stood gazing at each other. Lucilla's wide-eyed gaze was a combination of self-justification and youthful defiance, while that of Lord Childs was of a man who had somehow been caught in a snare of his own making.

"You could talk yourself out of almost anything, I should think, Miss Prior," he declared with a cynical laugh. "But, for all that, I am not sure that I am far from the truth. However," he added flatly, "if my words have upset you so much, then I apologise."

"What could you expect!" His unwilling apology had only fuelled her temper more. "How could you speak to me in this fashion as though I were some common slut?" Her eyes flashed as she declared, "Perhaps it will be best if I return home at once with my Aunt Amelia."

The passion behind her words had brought a charge of fire to her beauty which took his breath away. Lord Childs could only marvel at it as he replied, "There will be no need for that, Miss Prior. But if you love Geraldine as you say you do, would it not be a fair compromise to take your aunt with you in future when you are meeting Mr. Martin Reynolds? In this way nobody's reputation need suffer."

"Take my aunt with me — always?"

"Yes."

"Sir, my aunt is not young. She does not wish to see the places that I long to visit. Why, for a start, she would have loathed the crowds at Vauxhall Gardens . . ."

"On such an occasion, perhaps some other suitable arrangement could be made," he conceded. "Believe me, Miss Prior, I have only your welfare at heart."

"Oh, very well!" she said, a little ungraciously. "But I still wish to remind you that the two occasions of which you have just spoken did nothing to justify your accusations, Lord Childs."

Then it was that she saw a softened look come into his eyes which brought a slight flush to her cheeks. For the first time she had a twinge of conscience that, perhaps, after all, he was thinking of her.

"Perhaps it was unwise of me to converse with Mr. Reynolds so long in public when I was shopping," she admitted, "although I really could see no harm in it at the time."

He was about to reply when a servant knocked at the door and entered with a letter upon a dainty salver. The letter was for Lucilla, which she took under the suspicious gaze of Lord Childs.

"I will leave you, Miss Prior," said Lord Childs with the merest curl of disdain at the corner of his lips, for he seemed to have guessed already who had written the letter. "You will wish to pen a reply, no doubt."

Left to herself, Lucilla tore open the seal with such speed that she cut herself on the sharp edge of the paper, and a little cry escaped her as a dark trickle of blood oozed from the hairline incision. She thrust it against her cambric handkerchief as she hurriedly read and reread the letter, for Mr. Martin Reynolds had excelled himself in an art at which he was adept, and had written her the most perfect words of love.

She could not take her eyes from them, she was so entranced. Then she suddenly realized that the messenger was waiting for a reply, and, pulling herself together, sat down to answer the paragraph in which Martin Reynolds had asked her to accompany him to Drury Lane Theatre the following evening. He also asked when it would be appropriate to call upon her aunt to seek that lady's permission.

Before her confrontation with Lord Childs, Lucilla would have unhesitatingly suggested that the following morning would be a most suitable time for Martin Reynolds to visit Aunt Amelia. But now she sat, biting the tip of her quill, uncertain what to do. If she were to act as Lord Childs had requested, it would mean taking her aunt with her to the theatre, which was utterly ludicrous, since obviously, no harm could come to her in such a crowded place. And also, Aunt Amelia disliked the theatre, so there was little likelihood that she would agree. And yet refuse Martin Reynolds' invitation, Lucilla could not.

Again she read the words of love which had flowed from his pen with such apparent depth of feeling. She was convinced that no man could write in such a way unless he was truly sincere. Without turning the matter over more in her mind, she put pen to paper and accepted his invitation. To take Aunt Amelia, she decided, would only be utter nonsense, since no young lady would surely be in need of a chaperone at the theatre, and certainly Lord Childs could not have meant her to comply with his request on such an occasion. In any case, Lucilla had no intention of searching him out, after their recent argument, to discuss such an inflammable subject. She was still piqued that he should take it upon himself to advise her on the choice of a beau, in any case, and was more determined than ever to prove that he was wrong about Martin Reynolds.

Aunt Amelia remained in bed the following day because of a slight chill which had developed after the headache, so that Lucilla saw her only for a brief moment in the morning. For the rest of the time, Lucilla was entirely alone, since Lord Childs had taken Geraldine off for the day to see an elderly relative who had certain business commitments which affected those of her late father.

The evening could not come fast enough for Lucilla, and she roamed the massive house impatiently, longing for the day to go. She began her toilette far earlier than she would normally have done, after trying on two or three gowns before making a final choice. Having never been to the theatre before, she was not quite sure how to dress, which added to her indecision, although she full realized that she must look her best, since Drury Lane Theatre was the haunt of the fashionable.

She emerged from the house at precisely the time that Mr. Reynolds' carriage drew up outside the front door, for she had been watching for it from the window. She wore a pale blue satin dress with a flow of small bows down the centre of the corsage, graduated in size to larger ones upon the skirt. A simple string of pearls adorned her slender white throat, and around her shoulders she had flung a deep blue velvet cloak, edged with white fur.

Martin Reynolds' eyes kindled when he saw her. Lucilla was one of the most beautiful girls he had ever set out to seduce, and a prize well worth all the extra effort he was having to take.

"I should not really be here," said Lucilla with a guilty little laugh as she sat by his side in the carriage.

He turned to her, looking puzzled.

"No — you see, my aunt was too unwell for me to trouble her today, or for you to come and see her, and Lord Childs has more or less forbidden me to meet you unless accompanied by a chaperone. Still, I am sure that a visit alone with you to a crowded theatre would be permitted."

"Lord Childs takes some of his old-fashioned, quaint notions a step too far," assented Martin Reynolds with an amused tone in his voice.

"But he is only trying to protect me," declared Lucilla hurriedly, for in her heart of hearts she knew this to be true. "It is just that he takes too much upon himself — after all, he is not a relative of mine, and, until a few months ago, I had not even made his acquaintance."

She did not see the look of impatience pass over Mr. Reynolds' face in the gloom of the carriage.

"Let us forget about Lord Childs," he said tersely. " 'Tis as good as having him here with us if we continue to talk about him . . ."

He had drawn closer and his lips brushed against her cheek as he spoke.

"Let us make the most of our precious time together — Aunt Amelia might be with us another time," he added.

She drew slightly back from him — a quick, shy movement.

"I am very fond of my aunt," she declared, defensively.

"A charming lady, I agree," he drawled, releasing her a little, for he had slipped his arm around her, "but surely you are happy that she is not with us at this moment?"

"Perhaps," she admitted coyly.

"If your feelings are the same as mine, you will have longed for this moment all day."

"Oh . . ." whispered Lucilla, delighted and thrilled at his boldness.

She did not have time to say more, for he pulled her gently to him and said in a low, soft voice, "You are the most beautiful girl I have ever seen, Lucilla, and I have loved you from the moment I set eyes upon you."

Then he kissed her, long and lingeringly, and Lucilla responding, tried hard not to let the image of Lord Childs come between them.

Throughout the play, Lucilla's thoughts dwelt on that kiss, and she could hardly keep her mind on what the actors said. She told herself she was blissfully happy, yet, lurking at the back of her mind was just the slightest disappointment that Martin Reynolds' kiss had not meant more to her. She wondered what it would be like to be kissed by a man like Lord Childs, and felt her cheeks burning at the very thought.

From time to time during the play, Mr. Reynolds reached out and took her hand. Lucilla permitted him to do so with a half smile playing around her pretty mouth. Lord Childs, she knew, would heartily disapprove of such flirting and the thought filled her with a rebellious, mischievous delight.

Even in the foyer afterwards, which thronged with people from the fashionable set, she did not object when Martin Reynolds stole a quick kiss. She also made herself determined to like the friends to whom he introduced her, peacocking dandies for the most part, whom she would normally have rejected with disdain.

Later that night, as Lucilla brushed her hair before going to bed, she fell to wondering whether to tell her aunt of the latest developments with Martin Reynolds. Her first instinct was to go straight to her and confide in her. But something deep inside Lucilla prevented her from saying that she was actually in love with Martin Reynolds, for, although he fascinated her and she found him fun to be with, she was not really sure if her feelings, even though she sometimes thought them to be so, could truly be described as being in love.

When she arrived home, she had seen nobody, for Geraldine and Lord Childs had both departed to their beds upon their return to the house, expecting Lucilla to have been asleep hours ago, and so, as yet, she had spoken to nobody about her evening at the theatre.

It seemed that hardly had she dropped off to sleep than somebody was gently shaking her by the shoulder. In a half doze she opened her eyes and looked into Geraldine's face. Her friend was peering anxiously down at her.

"Wake up, Lucilla. Oh, do wake up."

"What is it? Is something wrong?" Lucilla sat up with a start, rubbing her eyes. "It is still the middle of the night, surely."

"No, indeed it is not. It is past eight in the morning, and, although it is so early, I *had* to come and see you. There is something I have been longing to tell you all night!"

"Mmm — must be very important, then," mumbled Lucilla, drowsily reaching for her bed wrap and shivering slightly.

"Only in the most wonderful way!"

"Oh?"

"*He* is going to ask my cousin for my hand in marriage!" declared Geraldine, her face aglow. "You see, after we had finished our business matters with my great uncle yesterday, we went to Lady Hartingdon's for dinner. Sir David Clifton was there . . . it was so wonderful . . . we strolled in Lady Hartingdon's garden afterwards, and, well, he proposed to me . . ."

"Oh, Geraldine, how marvellous!"

"I'm so happy, Lucilla. But David thinks that it would be

only right and proper to ask my cousin's consent, even though I am of age. I should not wish to hurt Rupert in any way. What do you think?"

"Of course you must — and he will be only too pleased to give it. Oh, Geraldine, I am so happy for you," declared Lucilla, kissing her friend as she spoke. "Sir David will make you a perfect husband, and I know that you will be very happy with him. When will you arrange the marriage?"

"As soon as possible," exclaimed Geraldine unhesitatingly. "For there is no point at all in waiting. Oh, Lucilla, it is sheer agony being apart from him for a single second. I just live for the times that we are together."

"Believe me, I understand only too well," replied Lucilla warmly, and then she added shyly, "I really think that I know with all my heart how you are feeling . . . I should feel the same if I were in your happy position, dearest Geraldine."

Geraldine, despite her elation, caught the wistful note in Lucilla's voice, and, interrupting her, declared affectionately, "Ah, Lucilla, the right man will come along for you — you will soon discover a suitable beau. Why, you always have an admiring crowd of young gentlemen around you when we go out to supper or to a soiree."

"But they are just . . . well . . . somebody to talk to in a pleasant fashion. It is so difficult to find somebody who pleases one on all points, and even more so to know if one is really in love," retorted Lucilla seriously, for she was thinking of Martin Reynolds, and had been ever since Geraldine told her the wonderful news. Not for anything in the world would she have mentioned his name now, however, lest Geraldine think that she was seriously inclined towards him, and of that she still was not sure.

"Hmm," exclaimed Geraldine, giving her a curious glance, for she was surprised to see her friend in such an unusual mood. "You'll know perfectly well and very quickly when the right gentleman appeals to you, Lucilla. Of that I can assure you."

"And did you know quickly with Sir David Clifton?" quizzed Lucilla pertinently.

Geraldine coloured up a little. "I always found him most mannerly and attentive," she said cautiously.

"Is *that* all!"

"No — of course not."

"Well, then?"

"Oh, really, Lucilla! How you do probe!"

"Only because I am so keen to know," persisted Lucilla appealingly.

"Well, then," conceded Geraldine in final exasperation, "to be perfectly honest, I knew almost at once but did not want to admit it to you lest you thought it sounded too flippant — for I do not really believe in love at first sight, although, in my case, it was very nearly that. It was a sort of mutual understanding. An instant delight in each other's company . . ."

"And you really *knew* with all your heart so soon that he was the person with whom you would most like to spend the rest of your life?"

"Yes! Oh, yes!"

"Even so," declared Lucilla with an old-fashioned look upon her young face, "I daresay it does not take everybody in the same way. Others may need longer to make up their minds." She was thinking again of herself as she spoke, although Geraldine failed to catch the tone in her voice which implied this. "And perhaps, too," she added, "not all gentlemen would declare themselves so quickly."

9

Lucilla stood staring forlornly at the tables arranged with exquisite tea and dinner services. She had accompanied her aunt to the fashionable Wedgwood showrooms because Aunt Amelia, who had long been awaiting this opportunity, wished to replenish parts of a broken tea service used at the rectory.

Normally, Lucilla would have enjoyed a visit to such a splendid place, for there was much of beauty to see, but today there was something on her mind, and she took small pleasure in either the wares or observing the distinguished ladies of taste who came there.

Lucilla had left behind a tearful Geraldine, whose elation of the previous day had turned overnight into bitter resentment. Lucilla could still hear her friend's choked words in her mind as she stood there. She had never seen Geraldine so beside herself.

"My cousin has refused to give his consent to our marriage," Geraldine had sobbed, "and he will give no really good reason. It is absurd! I think he must dislike David as much as he does Martin Reynolds . . ."

Geraldine's statement had stunned Lucilla. She could see

no sense in Lord Childs' refusal. She had led Geraldine gently to the sofa near the fire and bade her lie down and try to calm herself. She had then rang for some cordial and patted her friend's tear-stained face dry with one of her own plain handkerchiefs.

"Try not to sob," urged Lucilla kindly. "You will only make yourself ill. Tell me exactly what happened."

"There is little to tell," her friend had whispered as her fingers writhed together. "David asked Rupert for my hand in marriage, and, instead of Rupert giving his consent as we both thought he would do automatically, he said that the idea was out of the question . . . that we had not known each other long enough, and" — her voice had begun to falter again — "we should not be behaving like excited children over such a serious step. We must wait longer so as to be completely sure."

"So he has not positively refused?"

"No — but you have not heard the worst," Geraldine had retorted. "When David asked him what he considered would be a sensible time, he said . . ." Geraldine had begun to cry again at the mere thought.

"Well?"

"He said — perhaps a year! Depending on how things materialized."

"Whatever did he mean?" scoffed Lucilla. "Depending on how things materialize? Why, they cannot materialize any better than they are at the present, for you love each other."

"I know," Geraldine had wailed. "My cousin must be mad! I never thought that I should say such a thing about him, but I am sure he is absolutely *mad!*"

"He is being ridiculously unreasonable," Lucilla had

agreed, more mystified than outraged. "I cannot understand what he has against an early marriage. Why, Sir David
is a gentleman of whom any person would be really proud.
He has every quality which Lord Childs admires, and he is
certainly not after your fortune, Geraldine, for I gather he
has more than enough of his own."

"The match is perfect. Perfect in every way," Geraldine
had sobbed. "But it is still not perfect enough for my cousin,
it seems. And if we are to marry with his consent, we must
wait. Oh, Lucilla, what shall I do?"

"Why — marry without his consent, of course," Lucilla
had declared with spirit.

"I know," Geraldine had murmured wretchedly. "It is
what David says — and yet I loathe the idea. I do not wish to
cross my cousin. He is not a man who easily forgives and
forgets, and I should hate to lose his friendship, Lucilla."

"Come — I doubt that anything so extreme as that would
happen."

"You did not see his face," Geraldine had said disconsolately. "He looked so hard and unyielding — I have never
seen him like that before."

Lucilla had not replied. She was thinking that, although
Geraldine may not have seen that granite expression on the
face of Lord Childs, she was well acquainted with it herself.
It had also crossed her mind, although she would never have
said so to Geraldine, that perhaps there were other reasons
why Lord Childs did not want the marriage to take place so
soon.

"Perhaps he will relent if you give him a little time,"
Lucilla had at last said, not very convincingly.

"No — he seems determined to wreck my happiness."

"Let me go to him."

"It will do no good."

"You cannot tell. He may be regretting his hasty words already. Come, let me try. I can do no harm, at least."

Geraldine had at last agreed, adding warningly, "Be careful, though, for he is in a monstrously bad temper."

"Ho! I do not care. I have seen him in a bad temper before," Lucilla had exclaimed stoutly, "and his black moods don't frighten me. I shall go and see him this very moment!"

She had left her friend immediately, before Geraldine could change her mind, and had gone in search of Lord Childs. But he was nowhere to be found, and she had reluctantly had to forego, for the time being, the doubtful pleasure of yet another confrontation with her friend's cousin.

"He will be back later this afternoon, Miss," Lord Childs' manservant had informed her when Lucilla had eventually tracked him down.

"Then kindly inform your master that I wish to speak to him, and would be grateful if he could wait upon me at five of the hour in the library," Lucilla had declared crisply. "And tell him that it is a matter of the utmost importance." She had left the man staring after her with raised eyebrows, for it was almost unheard of for a person to leave a directive like this for his revered master. But Lucilla had ignored the questioning look on his face, and had left the room, head high, an expression in her eyes which had silenced the man.

Now, as she wandered around the fine Wedgwood show-room with her aunt, she suddenly realized what she had done. She had actually been audacious enough to summon Lord Childs upon a matter which was not really her concern at all.

"Lucilla — you are not paying attention," declared Aunt

Amelia testily. "You did not hear a word I said — come, admit it."

"I'm sorry, Aunt," replied Lucilla, trying to gather her thoughts together. "You asked my opinion — which pattern I liked — the one on this table or the one in that showcase . . ."

"Yes, indeed. I asked you twice. Now will you give me an answer?" Without waiting for a reply, she made off to another table where she had just spotted something else which she liked.

Lucilla followed her unhurriedly, still thinking of her forthcoming meeting with Lord Childs. Her courage was very near to ebbing as she thought of exchanging angry words yet again with this unpredictable, moody man. And yet, he was not always so difficult, she told herself, remembering brief moments of his gentleness.

"Lucilla!"

"Oh, Aunt. I am coming," Lucilla called impatiently, feeling that all eyes were upon her, for she knew of old how Aunt Amelia's voice carried.

"I might not have brought you with me for all the help you've been," grumbled her aunt.

"Well you see, Aunt dear, I have quite made up my mind already which pattern I like the best," declared Lucilla coolly (as indeed she had, for she had seen the very pattern in the home of a friend many months before and admired it).

"Hmph! You surprise me," exclaimed her aunt, unconvinced, "or I would have said that your mind was anywhere but in this showroom, young lady."

"Yet, *I* have managed to make up *my* mind, Aunt, and you have not," replied Lucilla teasingly.

"Indeed? Well, be so good as to tell me which it is, then."

"Why, this, of course," said Lucilla, pointing to a delicate, floral pattern in soft shades. "Without doubt, it would look really well in our small drawing room at home."

"How very remarkable," declared her aunt with delight, " 'tis the very one I had in mind. I shall go and place an order for it now."

She promptly left her niece and made her way to one of the assistants whom she proceeded to engage in conversation for several minutes about the quality of the ware and the number of pieces she needed.

Lucilla sauntered around the tables with her mind still only half on what she saw. She was working out the best way in which to later broach the subject of Geraldine's marriage. She was impatient to be getting home, for it was already well into the afternoon, and she had no desire to be late for her meeting with Lord Childs. She was much relieved, therefore, when her aunt eventually appeared at her side.

"That is finished, niece," she declared with triumph, puffed out with success that the order had at last been placed.

"And now for home," said Lucilla delightedly.

"Oh, no. We aren't finished yet, my dear. There is still another call to be made," replied her aunt briskly as she ushered Lucilla through the door.

"But, Aunt —"

"It will not take long."

"Must we do whatever it is today?" pleaded Lucilla, "Cannot it possibly wait for another day?"

"Don't be impatient, dear," scolded Aunt Amelia. "It is just a quick visit to that lovely wallpaper shop we passed on our way here. I have it in mind to write and ask your dear father if he will consider some of that flocked paper for the walls of the dining room."

"But it is so expensive, Aunt. You know he will never agree."

"Ah! Not necessarily, for this is being offered at a special price. I caught a glimpse of the notice saying so as we passed by, so I really think it would be worth while our paying a short visit."

"Very well, then," assented Lucilla lamely, "but nowhere else, I implore you, Aunt."

It had taken all Lucilla's powers of persuasion to get her Aunt Amelia out of the wallpaper shop within the hour. There was so much to see that her aunt had stood in the middle of the shop, her homely countenance shining with pure delight at the sight which met her eyes. Not only was there every conceivable kind and quality of wallpaper (including the most exotic to come from France), but there were, as well, charming plaster cornices and friezes, and all manner of other ideas to add a touch of elegance to the more modest home.

"Just think of it, Lucilla. We could completely transform the plain interior of the rectory with just a few of these ideas," Aunt Amelia had said, gazing with admiration at everything.

"Ask to see the flocked paper," Lucilla had urged. "Look, there is a salesman free now — over there." She had taken hold of her aunt's arm and marched her firmly in the man's direction before Miss Prior could waste any more time.

Finally, Lucilla had managed to get her out of the shop by promising to return with her immediately after they heard from her father giving his approval to Aunt Amelia's suggestions.

As soon as they arrived home, Lucilla had consumed her tea hastily, which had not been difficult since Geraldine had taken to her bed for the day, and her aunt had been anxious to go to her room and remove her tight shoes. She had hurried to the library just as the clock was striking five of the hour.

Luckily, Lord Childs was late. She stood alone in the vast, book-lined room wondering uneasily whether he would actually come. There was no guarantee that he would be back in time, and even if he were, he might not deign to appear.

She stood for a fraction of a moment with a slight frown on her brow, wondering how long she should wait for him. Then she noticed that somebody had already been there before her, for there was a cup and saucer upon one of the side tables and a plate with crumbs upon it. Obviously, Lord Childs had taken tea in the library, so he was at home.

It was while she was glancing at the empty cup and saucer, not yet cleared away by a servant, that her gaze began to wander along the immaculate, book-lined shelves. There was not a book out of place, each standing at precisely the same distance from the edge of the shelf like soldiers on guard, never expecting to be read, but prepared, just in case. Shelf upon shelf was the same.

She walked over to those near the chair where Lord Childs had been sitting to take his tea, and, as she did so, she stumbled upon the protruding leg of a chair. She half fell, but managed to stop herself by grasping wildly at the library steps, upon the top of which were balanced a few books. As she jolted the steps, one or two fell with a loud report to the polished floor, and she bent hurriedly to retrieve them.

Then it was that she noticed an untidy pile of documents thrust to the side of the books on the bottom shelf, and her gaze wandered over the topmost piece of paper. It did not at first look like anything important. Just a rough sheet with a few scribbled words upon it. But then Lucilla noticed, to her surprise, that Geraldine's name appeared on the first line, and, moreover, it was spelled with a J instead of a G.

Amused, and thinking it to be some sort of a joke, she could not resist reading on, gradually realizing that the scribbled note had more serious implications than she could possibly have suspected. Brief and illiterate — for it had scarcely a single word spelled correctly or a single sentence properly constructed — it had obviously been penned on behalf of a person who could not even do so well as the ignorant writer, since he had signed the note with a cross and a crudely formed B.

But it was the contents which filled Lucilla with horror. Difficult to read though it was, Lucilla soon deciphered the scribble. The writer claimed that Geraldine's mother had not died at childbirth at all, but had run away shortly afterwards with a former gypsy lover to join the band of whom he was leader. Lucilla was just about to read more when she heard a sound behind her, and realized that Lord Childs had entered the room.

For a moment, she stood transfixed to the spot. To be found by Lord Childs reading such a note was just about the worst thing that could have happened to her, come as she was to plead Geraldine's cause at a time when she had prayed he would be in a good temper. At that moment, she suddenly saw in a flash a possible reason for Lord Childs' strange attitude to Geraldine's marriage. Perhaps what the note said was true? But whatever the reason, she needed to act quickly and calmly now.

Mustering up all her bravado, Lucilla turned to Lord Childs with one of her most beguiling smiles, and walked graciously across the library to meet him. She made no attempt to conceal the scrap of paper as she thanked him for having the courtesy to attend on her.

"It was an unusual request, Miss Prior," he said coldly, "but since it appeared so urgent and I returned home earlier than I anticipated, I am happy to be here with you."

He glanced down at her hand as he spoke, and for the first time noticed the piece of paper which she was still clutching. At first, he did not appear to recognize it. Then, suddenly, a wave of fury swept over his features and he seized the paper from her.

"What are you doing with this?" he half shouted.

"I found it on a pile of documents over there," replied Lucilla with a nonchalant little wave in the direction of the papers. "It was the only small scrap I could see. I was just about to write a note to you, for I did not think you were coming. Why? Is it of importance? Is something written on the other side?"

He cleared his throat uncertainly.

"Of course there is, or I should hardly have been so annoyed," he replied brusquely.

"I am sorry."

"It is of no matter," he said guardedly, "merely an impertinent note from some fellow who seeks to make trouble."

"Ah! Well, no doubt you will be able to deal more than adequately with that, Lord Childs," said Lucilla sweetly.

He hardly seemed to hear her, but continued to gaze

abstractedly at the note, a pucker on his brow, raking his hand through his dark hair.

"Would that I could," he mumbled, almost to himself.

She cleared her throat.

"I wish to apologise in advance, Lord Childs," she began diffidently.

He looked up, startled, as though her words had brought him back to reality.

"What was that?"

"I said," began Lucilla again, "that I wished to apologise in advance for what I am about to mention."

He smiled wryly.

"Proceed, Miss Prior. I am all ears."

"Sir, I love Geraldine dearly, as you are aware, and it grieves me beyond measure to see her so bitterly unhappy because you will not give your consent to her marriage with Sir David Clifton. I have come to plead with you to change your mind and to reconsider . . ."

To her astonishment, he was not angry. Instead, he paced the room for a few moments as if deliberating over his reply.

"Believe me, Miss Prior, I do not take exception to your request," he declared eventually, "and, knowing your love for my cousin, I quite understand the extreme of the feelings which compelled you to leave such a . . . directive with my servant." He paused, and Lucilla breathed a sigh of relief to see the merest twinkle in his eyes, although it was gone the next moment as he continued sternly, "But I cannot change my mind about Geraldine at this moment."

"Oh, Lord Childs!" The disappointment was strong in her voice.

It seemed to soften him, for the next moment he added, "You must not breathe a word of this to another living soul, but certain matters have arisen which must be completely cleared up before Geraldine can marry anybody."

"Sir — I do not understand."

"No, and neither can I tell you more at this moment. I ask only that you will trust me, Miss Prior, and help me if you will by comforting Geraldine as best you can. Believe me, I am as upset as you are at this wretched state of affairs. I could not have wished for a better man than Sir David Clifton to ask for my cousin's hand in marriage. God willing, he may still have it, yet."

"Are you sure there is nothing I can do to help?" she asked gently.

"I do assure you, Miss Prior," he replied, looking touched by her offer, "that there is nothing you can do. Nothing at all, except to console my cousin. The problem is such that I alone can unravel it."

"Not before too long, I hope," said Lucilla. "I fear that Geraldine will not wait too many months."

"She will have to wait," he interrupted. "There is no other way."

"Then why not explain to her about these . . . er . . . problems?"

"I cannot." The finality in his voice amazed her. Geraldine must never know any of this — not so long as I can help it, that is."

"Well," said Lucilla weakly, "at least I shall be able to put her mind at ease as regards one point, for she thought you had something against Sir David."

"Oh, no. I have already said how I feel about him."

"Ah, yes. You have said to me. But *she* does not know it. Geraldine thinks that perhaps you dislike him in the same way as you do Mr. Martin Reynolds!"

"Huh! What an absurd notion! Why, there is no comparison. Mr. Reynolds is a philanderer, Miss Prior. Forgive me, but I must tell the truth, even at the risk of upsetting you. The two men are leagues apart in every possible way."

Lucilla's colour had mounted violently at his hard words. Her eyes began to glitter, and she held her head at that angle which meant trouble.

"Pray remember, sir," she said defiantly, "that you cannot influence me against Mr. Reynolds. Moreover, I shall continue to feel the way I do about him until positive proof of the things you say come to light. I shall never listen to mere words against him — when he is so kind and charming in reality."

Lord Childs listened to her coolly, and then shrugged and walked away.

"It is up to you, Miss Prior," he replied with his old aloofness. "I am not your guardian, so it is not my duty to approve or disapprove your choice. I can only advise you as a friend, thank God!"

"Well, sir," said Lucilla bristling, "you have certainly done that often enough, and I am still not completely sure of your true motives."

"Motives? I have no motives, you foolish girl," he exploded.

"Your vehemence towards Mr. Reynolds leads me to think otherwise," she replied tactfully.

"Indeed!"

"I think that you two have crossed each other's paths in the past, and that there is some old animosity between you," she threw at him, "for you could not dislike him so outrageously unless there were."

A cynical laugh escaped him.

"There is no *single* incident, I do assure you, Miss Prior," he exclaimed with a granite expression upon his face, "for several spring instantly to mind when Mr. Reynolds has behaved in a far from commendable way."

"Sir!"

"In any case, I will discuss this matter no more," he declared, glaring at her. "I would not have said this much if you had not provoked me!"

"I would not stay to hear more," she retorted at once. "I will withdraw immediately to console your poor cousin if you will kindly allow me to pass."

He stood coldly aside without glancing at her, and she swept from the room in silence, her face flushed and a rebellious glint in her beautiful eyes.

She went straight to her aunt's room, for Aunt Amelia had decided on a short nap after her arduous shopping. However, before she had loosened her stays and slipped off her tight shoes, she had sat down at the small writing table, and written in glowing terms to the Reverend George Prior of all they had seen at the wallpaper shop. After this, she had climbed thankfully into the high four-poster, and dropped off to sleep in no time with a tranquil smile upon her round face, dreaming of decking out the modest rectory like a veritable palace.

Lucilla found her sitting up and much refreshed, tying the strings of her cap and humming to herself. She did not appear to notice Lucilla's flushed cheeks or the old look of defiance smouldering in her niece's large eyes.

"Aunt, you must come with me to Geraldine's boudoir," declared Lucilla testily. "If she is as upset as she was this morning, I shall need your support."

"Perhaps Lord Childs is right, dear," said her aunt sagely,

"Marry in haste, repent at leisure, my dear. It's an old saying, but it has a lot of truth in it, nonetheless."

"Nonsense, Aunt," exclaimed Lucilla tersely. "You know as well as I do that in this case the match is a perfect one."

"Well, if that is so, Lord Childs will give his consent soon enough, I daresay."

"Hah! That remains to be seen."

Aunt Amelia gave her a puzzled look. She said nothing, for she could see that Lucilla was in the kind of mood which only grew worse if she tried to reason with her. But of one thing she was sure, that it was not only Geraldine's problem which had upset her niece that afternoon.

"Pass me my shoes, dear," she said resignedly, "the old ones that don't rub against my bunion — then I'll come with you."

She carefully eased her feet into the well-worn shoes with many ooh's and ah's, while Lucilla stood glowering at her, still thinking of Lord Childs and how much she detested the man. His remark concerning Martin Reynolds had so incensed her that she had quite forgotten the strange note which she had found scribbled on the rough piece of paper.

It was not until her aunt had finally completed her short toilette and was heard to say, "He may have his reasons — Lord Childs I mean, dear, for not giving his immediate consent," that Lucilla suddenly remembered it.

"Reasons, Aunt? What on earth do you mean?"

"I feel that something is in the wind," said her aunt uncannily, screwing up her face in pain as she moved gingerly from her seat at the dressing table, for her bunion ached horribly.

"Fiddlesticks!" declared Lucilla, slightly amazed that her

aunt should be so shrewd. She picked up one of her aunt's silver-backed brushes, and gave her gleaming hair one or two impatient swishes with it. "Be very careful what you say to Geraldine, Aunt. For heaven's sake don't hint at anything like that . . . you'll upset her no end if you do. She weeps at the least provocation."

"I think," said her aunt tartly, "that I can be relied upon to handle Geraldine properly. Look to yourself, Miss, and make sure that *you* don't provoke her."

"Oh, there is no danger of that," said Lucilla confidently, as they left the room together. "I would rather die than see her upset any more — I cannot tell you how sorry I am for her."

They found Geraldine pale and wan lying on top of the richly embroidered counterpane of her bed. She barely glanced up as Nurse Hargreaves ushered them into the room. She had not bothered to dress, and still wore her silk negligee trimmed with fine lace and caught up under the bosom with a wide ribbon bow.

"Geraldine — I have seen Lord Childs," burst out Lucilla, "but he will not change his mind, I'm afraid. Still, he says that he greatly respects Sir David — in every way."

"I told you not to waste your time," she muttered crossly.

"Come — things are not so gloomy as all that," declared Lucilla, in an effort to cheer her up. "Since Lord Childs thinks so highly of Sir David, I am sure that he will come round soon."

"But *when?*" demanded Geraldine, raising herself on her elbow and beckoning her old nurse to arrange her down-filled pillows so that she could sit up properly.

"As soon as he is sure . . ." said Lucilla, her voice tapering off, rather.

"Lucilla is right," joined in Aunt Amelia.

"I have told her so all the morning," mumbled Nurse Hargreaves, "but she won't listen. I've never known her take anything so badly."

"Why not get dressed, Geraldine, and join us in the drawing room?" urged Lucilla. "Lord Childs would think so much better of you for showing a little spirit. We can tell you all about our shopping expedition to the Wedgewood shop — and the wallpaper man — I'm sure you'll be interested. I would be, anyhow, if I were soon to be a bride," she ended firmly.

A low sigh escaped Geraldine. She did not seem to be tempted by Lucilla's suggestion.

"You cannot stay a bed all day and every day sulking like that, Miss," grumbled her old nurse.

"Sulking? I am not sulking," declared Geraldine grandly, giving the old woman a withering glance.

"Of course you are," said her nurse, ignoring it, "just like a child, instead of a young lady thinking of marriage."

Geraldine coloured up with annoyance.

"La, Nurse, how you do go on," she said, affecting a bored sigh. "I shall dress for dinner presently, meanwhile I think I should like some tea sent up — nothing to eat though," she added hastily, lest her nurse should think that she had scored some success in rousing her. "It is just that I feel so thirsty and fatigued."

"Fatigued, indeed!" retorted Nurse Hargreaves, clucking her tongue with disapproval as she hobbled to the door to carry out her young mistress's orders. "Fatigued — with not so much as six steps taken across the room the entire day!"

"Would you like us to leave you, dear?" inquired Aunt

Amelia, anxiously wondering if perhaps Geraldine might really be unwell.

"No," replied Geraldine hesitating. "But perhaps, if you could spare Lucilla for a while," she added tactfully.

"Of course, dear," said Aunt Amelia, rising at once to take her leave. "Lucilla will be only too happy to stay with you, will you not, niece?"

She shot Lucilla a quick look as if to say, do what you can to make her see sense, and departed immediately, leaving in her wake a perfumed trail of bergamot and lavender.

"Oh! Thank goodness they have both gone," exclaimed Geraldine. "Now tell me, word for word, what my cousin said."

Lucilla assembled her thoughts, and gave Geraldine as near as possible a verbatim report of her short conversation with Lord Childs, taking good care to omit the strange problem which he had mentioned. She also wisely made no mention of the illiterate note she had found in the library.

"I shall tell David when I next see him," said Geraldine, "that at least my cousin has nothing against him . . . I suppose that is something."

Lucilla was looking at her friend strangely. She had hardly heard what Geraldine had said, for she had been thinking of the note she had read so hastily in the library before Lord Childs had apppeared. It now occurred to her that it must be connected with the gypsy who haunted Lord Childs, and, moreover, with the letter she had found in his caravan. She determined to get hold of the letter without more ado, and give it to its rightful owner.

10

Lucilla was in fine fettle. She had written the note and dispatched it, and felt as though a great burden had been lifted from her shoulders.

All through the night, she had pondered on the best way to get hold of the letter addressed to Lord Childs, tossing and turning until dawn. It was not possible to ask her father to send it, for lengthy explanations would be needed. Neither would it be sensible to take a stagecoach herself, although for a few moments she had recklessly toyed with the idea. Eventually, she had decided to write to cook, whom she knew could read and write in an elementary fashion.

Cook had worked at the rectory for the past ten years, and adored her young mistress. Lucilla felt sure that she could be trusted to keep a secret, and had written to her asking her to slip into the bedroom and retrieve the letter from the chest of drawers. Then she was to send it to Lucilla without delay so that it could be given to Lord Childs.

Lucilla had decided to brave Lord Childs yet again, and to tell him the whole story when she handed him the letter. She prayed with all her heart that he would try to understand the spirit of adventure which had taken her into the gypsy's caravan, and that somehow it would help him with the strange problem which involved Geraldine.

The note having been dispatched, she turned her attention to her next problem, which concerned her own life, and that of Mr. Martin Reynolds, for she was worried that Lord Childs might well write to her father and warn him that she was seeing more of this man than was in her best interests. She intended to sort out her feelings towards Martin as soon as possible, before Lord Childs had time to intrude in any way. She longed to see Martin, and daily waited impatiently either to hear from him or meet him unexpectedly out in society.

An unexpected stroke of luck brought her just such an opportunity far sooner than she had expected. Geraldine sought her out the following day, wearing a slightly conspiratorial expression.

"Would you not care for some fresh air, Lucilla?" she asked sweetly. "It is a most beautiful day, and the first really fine one we have had the entire week. A walk would do us both good."

Lucilla looked at her in surprise. Geraldine was not one for too much fresh air, and she did not much care for walking, either.

"Where had you in mind?" inquired Lucilla cannily.

"Ah, well . . ." Geraldine seated herself elegantly opposite her friend and offered Lucilla a sugared almond, which Lucilla loved. "I had in mind to visit St. James's Park with Sir David Clifton, but since we are not betrothed, my cousin prefers me to take a chaperone . . . and I wondered —"

"— if I would be the chaperone," finished Lucilla for her. "Bosh! As if *you* needed a chaperone. Why, Lord Childs has chaperones on the brain. What harm can possibly come to you with a gentleman like Sir David, I should like to know, in a crowded place like St. James's Park?"

"It is for the sake of propriety, Lucilla," declared Geraldine disapprovingly, "and if you will not come, I shall have to ask somebody else — Miss Prior, perhaps. That would not be nearly so pleasant as having you."

"What is wrong with my aunt, pray?" demanded Lucilla, raising her pretty eyebrows and looking shocked, even though there was a mischievous twinkle in her eyes.

"Nothing! Nothing at all," said Geraldine hurriedly. "Miss Prior is the kindest of souls, and I am most fond of her. But quite apart from anything else, she does not walk far, and I should dearly love to stay with David for an hour or so, and perhaps even take tea with him."

"Oh, very well," laughed Lucilla, "I will come — and delighted to do so, as well you know!"

Quite apart from the fact that she was helping out her friend, Lucilla liked the idea of a walk in St. James's Park herself, for there was much to see in the park at the moment. To celebrate peace — for Napoleon's empire was now in ruins — the Prince Regent had proclaimed that great celebrations should be held in all the London parks. Fun, on a grand scale, was in the air, and Lucilla longed to be part of it.

Oriental temples, towers, pagodas, and bridges were in the course of being built, and Lucilla wanted to see them for herself. She had overheard two ladies talking to each other in a shop about them, and her imagination had been fired immediately.

"It will be wonderful," she declared with glee, "to catch a glimpse of the Chinese bridge. I wonder how far they have got with it. I hear that the whole thing will be illuminated on the night of the celebration — do you think that Lord Childs will take us, Geraldine?"

"He does not really care for the rabble!" declared Geraldine snootily, "but, perhaps if we caught him in a good mood, he might be persuaded."

"Oh, do ask, Geraldine! If anybody can persuade him, you can."

"I'll see," replied Geraldine guardedly. "But, for the moment, if we are to go for our walk after luncheon, I must send a message right away to Sir David."

She went at once, to write the note, leaving Lucilla alone to brood yet again over Mr. Martin Reynolds. Now that she had agreed to go for a walk with Geraldine, it meant that yet another day would pass before she saw him. Sighing to herself, Lucilla searched out her aunt to tell her of the arrangement she had just made with Geraldine.

As she sauntered through the vast house, she wondered whether she dare write a short note to Martin Reynolds. She told herself that if she were careful, she could word it in such a way as not to appear too eager for his company, but just pleasantly so. Lucilla's pride would not allow her to appear too enamoured with him before he had made more positive declaration of his feelings.

She walked slowly towards the library, intending to pen a subtle letter, but once there, somehow could not bring herself to do so, and had already turned away to retrace her footsteps in the direction of her aunt's room, when Lord Childs appeared with a guest. He nodded towards her in a brusque fashion but did not stop, and there was something in his manner which told her that it would be a long time before he forgave her for their recent conflict.

She heard the library door shut behind them, and sighed

with relief at the narrow escape she had had, for it would have been painfully embarrassing to be caught penning an illicit note to Martin. Even though Lord Childs would not have known to whom she would have been writing, he was so shrewd, and she would never have been able to conceal her feeling of guilt, that he would probably have guessed at once. She consoled herself by hoping that Martin would write to her, never suspecting what was in store that afternoon.

Geraldine did not appear again until it was time for Sir David Clifton to call upon them with his carriage. Then she sailed forward into the wide, marbled reception hall looking so exquisite that Lucilla gasped in admiration.

"Well — I wondered where you had disappeared to hours ago," she said with a smile. "Now I see — you have spent all this time preening yourself for Sir David. And a very good job you have made of it, too."

"La!" replied her friend languidly, "how you exaggerate, Lucilla. I merely washed my hair and got Nurse to arrange it to the best effect beneath my bonnet. One's toilette always takes time — if it is done with care," she added significantly, since Lucilla was usually inclined to rush hers.

"Wearing a beautiful gown like that helps, of course," declared Lucilla unabashed, studying the finer detail of her friend's expensive dress. It had been delivered fresh from the dressmaker only that week and was utter perfection in every way.

Made of the finest silk in a delicate shade of pink, it was caught demurely up under the bust, as was the fashion, with a rufflike collar of a deeper tone which matched the frilled cuffs of the long sleeves. The bonnet, with its tall crown, was ruched in the same shade of silk and tied beneath the chin with a wide pink ribbon. Over Geraldine's arm hung a dainty indispensable, and she carried a frothy parasol in the other hand.

"Perhaps — but you also look very pretty this afternoon," remarked Geraldine kindly, rather pleased that her dress had made such an impression. "You always look very well in that shade of lilac. Why, I do not see how it could be much bettered."

And, in a way, Geraldine was right. For what Lucilla's gown lacked in style — the dress had only been made by the local seamstress at home — it made up for in the flattering colour and its simplicity.

Lucilla had exquisite taste with colours, and seldom made a mistake when selecting stuffs for new dresses, unlike Geraldine, who seemed to have no instinct in such matters. Lucilla had learned early the hard way, for money was short, and she had to wear her dresses whether she liked them or not once she had received them from the seamstress. Therefore, she chose simple styles and had developed her natural ability with colours.

Today, her lilac-coloured gown complemented to perfection her delicate rose-coloured complexion and blonde hair. And, although she was not so immaculately turned out as Geraldine, her simple dress and fetching bonnet set off her beauty so well, that many a head turned as she sauntered through St. James's Park. The sparkle in her deep-violet eyes and general air of fun and vivacity were so infectious that she soon had Sir David laughing heartily as the carriage conveyed them swiftly in the direction of the park.

"Lucilla wished to see the Chinese bridge they are building, David," explained Geraldine. "She takes a positively childish delight in such things. For myself, I am not the slightest bit interested, for the crowds spoil it all for me."

Sir David cast his beloved an adoring look.

"I quite understand, dearest," he said gently, "but if you could bring yourself to tolerate the masses for a while, I truly think you would find it worth the effort. It will be a sight never likely to be seen again in London's parks, I do assure you. . . . There is also to be a mock naval battle on the Serpentine . . . and fireworks, such as one can hardly imagine, in Green Park."

"Oh, go on! Do tell us more," urged Lucilla with shining eyes.

"You like fireworks, Miss Prior?"

"I adore them, sir," Lucilla replied with a gay ripple of laughter.

"Aha — well, it is said that in Green Park alone there is to be a grand transformation scene, some hundreds of feet high, called the Castle of Discord, which will portray the horror of war and all its ensuing destruction — ending in a final curtain of smoke."

"Oh, how awful," exclaimed Lucilla.

"Not so," laughed Sir David, "for out of the shroud of smoke will waft another revelation — a beautiful Temple of Concord!"

"Oh! I simply *must* go and see it."

"How do you know all this, David?" quizzed Geraldine, amazed that he should be so well informed of something she considered to be trivial.

"Ah — I was with the Prince just after he had finished discussing the ideas for these incredible celebrations," admitted Sir David, "and he could not stop talking about them, he was so delighted."

'Well, perhaps if society is to take them so seriously, we

should participate, Lucilla," said Geraldine thoughtfully, turning to her friend. "I shall certainly speak to my cousin about the matter."

"Oh, there will be all sorts of events to which you will both be invited, I am sure," declared Sir David. "Everybody seems to be planning some sort of a party, and I gather that one can scarcely get hold of any musicians, for they have all been booked well in advance."

"How marvellous," exclaimed Lucilla in rapture at the idea, "to waltz away the evening in such splendour. I cannot imagine a better way to celebrate victory."

"We should practise the waltz more assiduously," said Geraldine seriously, remembering that they had both had little experience of the dance, and were comparatively clumsy compared with the way some ladies glided around so effortlessly.

"You will not be alone in your pursuit of perfection," remarked Sir David. "Many of the fairer sex practise the entire morning as often as they can, they are so determined to look well on the ballroom floor."

"There, Lucilla!" Geraldine spoke in her elder-sister tone. "What did I say?" She turned to Sir David, "I am so glad that you told us, for now I see that we simply must devote more time to our dancing if we are to master the waltz completely."

"It cannot be too difficult," retorted Lucilla quickly, for she had no intention of spending hours and hours with a tedious dancing master. "Why, it is simply a question of moving gracefully in time with the music."

"And that is not as easy as it sounds," said Geraldine firmly. "We do not wish to appear like clodhoppers from the country — we have seen enough of them in our time in Surrey."

Lucilla said nothing, but she smiled to herself at Geraldine's grand manner, for, until very recently, those same unassuming people had been Geraldine's main source of friends, and had seemed to please her well enough then.

"It looks as though we are not the only ones curious to see how the work is progressing," said Sir David, changing the subject, for he had been looking out of the window intermittently, and was surprised to see so many people.

The carriage had already stopped, and the door was being opened for them to alight.

"Oh, dear! I had no idea it would be so busy," said Geraldine, looking disappointed, for this was not her idea of a place for a romantic stroll.

"I think it will improve once we are inside the park," said Sir David a little anxiously. "There are always those who wait to meet their friends about here."

Geraldine looked a little pacified, and drifted into the park at a serene pace on the arm of Sir David. Lucilla hung back uncertainly. At that point, there was not room to walk three abreast, and, anyway, she thought it would be pleasant to let the two lovers stroll alone together for a while. She decided to follow a little way behind, near enough not to be thought by passers-by to be on her own, yet far enough away as to give them both the feeling that they had a little privacy.

Hardly had she gone a few steps than she beheld striding towards her, dressed splendidly in russet-coloured frock coat, dazzling white cravat, and pale cream breeches, none other than Mr. Martin Reynolds. She could not believe her good fortune.

"Good afternoon to you, Miss Prior," he said, removing his hat with his customary flourish, and smiling at her with that charm which suggested that he had seen nothing that day until he had set eyes upon her beauty. "Out walking alone in St. James's Park — 'tis not what I would have expected of you! What would your aunt say if she knew?"

"You have it wrong, sir," replied Lucilla with an amused smile, "for I am not alone. See" — and she waved her parasol gaily in the direction of Geraldine and Sir David — "I am with my friends . . . and . . . believe it or not, it is I who am the chaperone today!"

"Tut tut!" he exclaimed with a droll expression on his handsome face. "I should not have thought that either of those friends would need any such thing."

"For propriety's sake, Mr. Reynolds," she said prudently, copying Geraldine's expression. "You know how Lord Childs is a stickler for such matters."

"Oh, indeed, Miss Prior," he replied with a short, sarcastic laugh. "Lord Childs is as good as a mother and father and a whole family of elder sisters to you both!"

She could not resist a quick smile, but turned her head away so that he could not see his remark had amused her. In a strange way, she felt loyal to Geraldine's moody, punctilious cousin, although she could not for the life of her understand why.

Geraldine and Sir David had slowed to await Lucilla, and now saw with astonishment with whom she was walking.

"Mr. Reynolds and I have just met," explained Lucilla as they exchanged greetings with him. "I was just about to call you," she added, "before Mr. Reynolds went on his way."

"But I am in no great hurry, Miss Prior," Martin Reynolds said pleasantly, "and if you would permit it, I should consider it a great pleasure to walk with you for a while."

Geraldine glanced uneasily at Sir David as if seeking his approval without actually asking.

Like Lord Childs, Sir David distrusted Martin Reynolds, yet, as no harm could possibly come to Lucilla while they all remained together, he could see no reason why he should not stay for a while.

"Would you like that, Miss Prior?" he asked kindly.

"Well, it would be pleasant to talk to Mr. Reynolds for a few minutes." Lucilla confesssd tactfully, and Sir David saw at once that it was rather lonely for her without a companion of her own.

"Then do join us, Reynolds," he said briskly. "Take a turn with Miss Prior if you wish, by all means, but stay close by, for we shall be returning to my house to take tea in a while."

Lucilla noticed that Sir David did not invite Mr. Reynolds, but she did not care. She was only too happy to be in his company during the walk.

"What a beautiful afternoon this is turning out to be," said Lucilla happily.

"Quite by chance, too," added Mr. Reynolds, "for I am really on my way to Richmond, and only dropped by to see these splendid decorations planned by our Regent."

"Richmond! Oh, then I must not delay you," exclaimed Lucilla.

"There is no hurry. A few minutes will make little difference," he replied easily. "I am only going to my house there, and will probably stay but a few hours to attend my business before returning to London."

"It's a long way to go for just a few hours — what energy you have!"

" 'Tis nothing, my dear Miss Prior, when one's time is one's own, and one is a lonely bachelor."

Lucilla was about to reply, but instead let out a short cry

of pain, for she had not been looking where she was walking and had turned her ankle on a small step.

"Oh, how silly of me," she cried, biting her lower lip as she tried to walk on the foot. "I should have seen it; everybody else did."

Martin Reynolds took her by the arm and helped her along a few paces, but she soon stopped, for she had wrenched the ankle quite badly.

"I think, if you don't mind, Mr. Reynolds, I should like to sit down for a while," she said. "Just a small rest may help."

Luckily, they were passing a seat which had at that moment been vacated by three ladies, and Martin Reynolds guided her towards it.

"I'm sure it will recover quickly now that I am sitting," she smiled, "but would you be so kind as to run and catch up Sir David and Geraldine, tell them I will rejoin them as soon as possible, if they would care to take a turn around the park and come back for me."

Almost before he had returned, Lucilla noticed that the ankle was swelling, for she had taken several furtive peeps. She sat gazing ruefully at the passing crowds, annoyed with herself for not seeing the step. It was the same ankle that she hurt at Langley House, which, no doubt, meant there was some weakness there.

"How is it?" asked Mr. Reynolds as he rejoined her.

"Looking rather swollen, I am afraid," replied Lucilla in a crestfallen voice. "I have just taken a peep."

"Does it pain you much?" he asked anxiously.

"No, not a great deal as I sit here, but later, when I walk, it may."

"It might be better than you think," he declared optimistically. "Sometimes a rest can work wonders — unless you prefer to return home."

"Oh, dear, no. I was so enjoying myself."

"I could take you if you wished. My carriage is waiting for me in any case, so there would be no delay . . ." He left his sentence unfinished as Sir David and Geraldine were seen hurrying towards them.

"I am so sorry to upset your walk in this silly way," called Lucilla as they drew near.

"My dear Miss Prior, think nothing of it, as if you could help such a thing," said Sir David sympathetically.

"Poor Lucilla, does it hurt much when you walk on it?" asked Geraldine.

"I have not tried yet. Let me see." Lucilla rose unsteadily to her feet. "Ooh . . . it is a little better, I think. Perhaps if I were to walk very slowly . . ."

"Nonsense, Miss Prior," declared Sir David firmly, "you will only do more harm than good. I think you had better return home at once."

"Oh, no! I could not stand the thought of spoiling your afternoon," cried Lucilla, looking mortified.

"If it would help, Sir David, I could take Miss Prior for you. My carriage is already waiting to collect me — she would be home in no time."

Geraldine glanced uneasily at Sir David. She did not like the thought and neither did he, and yet, since Sir David had instructed his own carriage to return much later, it seemed a sensible thing to do.

"Oh, I think it would be an excellent idea if I were to accompany Mr. Reynolds," said Lucilla. "In that way you can continue your stroll, and your afternoon will not be completely wrecked."

Sir David looked uncertain. He thought for a while, then noticing how pale Lucilla looked, he at last agreed.

"Very well, Mr. Reynolds. Perhaps it may be the best thing to do. It is most kind of you. But make sure," he added, turning to Lucilla, "that you call a physician as soon as you return home, Miss Prior."

The two couples bade each other farewell, and Lucilla walked very slowly back with Martin Reynolds to his carriage. She trod gingerly at first, and then gradually her pace quickened until, by the time they came in sight of the carriage, she was almost sure that the foot was well on the way to a full recovery.

In the carriage she lifted her skirt surreptitiously when Mr. Reynolds was looking out of the window and took a quick peek, and, even though the ankle did not hurt anywhere near so much, she was annoyed to see that it was still quite swollen.

"How are you feeling?" asked Martin Reynolds, turning his attention to her.

"Much recovered, thank you," replied Lucilla with one of her beautiful smiles, "but the ankle is still swollen, I fear."

"Mm . . . if you feel better," he said thoughtfully. "What a pity to return straight home on such a fine afternoon."

"Mr. Reynolds — what can you be suggesting?" she asked in momentary surprise. Then a mischievous little chuckle escaped her as she inquired, "Had you something else in mind?"

He drew closer and took her hand.

"Nothing that will pain your ankle, I assure you, dearest Lucilla," he whispered, brushing her cheeks lightly with his lips.

"Then, what, pray, Martin?"

"The view is superb from the top of Richmond Hill," he whispered, "with the river winding its way far below, and the meadows and trees so green."

"Richmond!" exclaimed Lucilla in horror. "They would miss me at home and be frantic with worry — the idea is impossible."

"No, I do not think so," he replied calmly, "for they know that you are safe with me — why, Sir David Clifton himself permitted you to ride with me. And just think what a wonderful drive it would make. We could go close by the river, it is so beautiful this time of the year . . . while Richmond Hill is like the top of a little world of its own . . ."

"Mmm . . . it does sound lovely."

"Well, then, we shall do it," he cried, and tapped smartly on the side of the carriage to give fresh instructions before she could say more.

"I think my ankle has completely recovered," she laughed excitedly as the carriage turned round and moved swiftly in the opposite direction. For once, she had quite forgotten Lord Childs, she was so carried away by Martin's enthusiasm.

"You shall have plenty of time to rest it on the journey to Richmond," he replied, slipping his arm around her. "Meanwhile, let us enjoy each other's company."

As Martin Reynolds had said, the view from Richmond Hill was more than delightful. To Lucilla's romantic eyes it was utterly beautiful, and she stood gazing at it from the window of Martin's house, quite entranced. Already he had ordered from the housekeeper a small tray of simple refreshments, which she now brought and placed before them. Of other servants Lucilla had seen none, for only a very few were kept to maintain the house, since Martin scarcely used it.

They sat munching the cold chicken legs and thick, crusty bread as Martin poured more wine.

"You like it here?" he asked thoughtfully, as they later stood by the window, watching the river snake by below.

"It is wonderful . . . so beautiful," replied Lucilla with an ecstatic sigh, as she sipped the wine.

"Would you like to live here?" he said quietly.

She turned to him in surprise. She could not understand the expression on his face. It was strange, and she had never seen it before.

He took her glass from her to replenish it.

"I think I have drunk enough of your excellent wine," laughed Lucilla nervously. "I seldom take this much." She covered her glass with her hand to restrain him, for already she felt flushed and strange.

"Just a little more," he persuaded, as he bent and kissed the top of her head. "Let us celebrate the fact that we are alone together at last."

She conceded with a tender smile and withdrew her hand. They said little as they sipped their wine in the stillness of the room, gazing from the window.

"Would you like to see the rest of the house?" Martin asked.

"Have we time? I thought you had some business here?"

"I had, but the gentleman I was expecting is no longer able to keep the appointment — my housekeeper told me when we arrived. Did you not hear?"

She shook her head, for, although she remembered that there had been a conversation between the elderly house-keeper and Martin, she had wandered away to the window and paid little attention to it. Because of this, she had not observed Martin's relief at the news. She was not to know that the man had been coming to collect gambling debts long accrued, and that Martin was temporarily low on funds.

"Well, then, I should love to see the house," she replied happily, "especially if all the rooms are as charming as this."

He took her gently by the hand and led her from the drawing room. Everything she saw delighted her, for the furnishings and decoration had been carefully chosen by Martin's mother, a lady of great taste, although, sadly, nothing had been done to them since her death years before, and everything looked rather shabby now. Martin had little real interest in the house.

The bedrooms were in a similar condition, all except the last to which he eventually led her. This was the one which Martin occupied, although Lucilla was surprised to see that it did not look at all like a gentleman's apartment. The taste was more in line with something which a married couple would choose, including the two dressing rooms, one on either side, and a small boudoir through which one first entered.

"Ah! This is very pretty," declared Lucilla, eying the white and pink counterpane and the delightfully flounced tester.

"I thought you would like it," he laughed, as he slipped his arm around her waist and drew her to him. Before she quite realized what was happening, she found herself enveloped in a passionate embrace. Its suddenness caught her off her guard, and she responded only halfheartedly. This seemed to annoy Martin Reynolds and he held her tighter, covering her face, neck, and bosom with passionate kisses. She tried to draw away but he would not let her go.

"Don't play the coy young miss with me, Lucilla," he mumbled roughly, his ardour increasing. "I know you cannot wait to lie with me!"

Then, suddenly, with a quick, deft movement he flung her onto the bed, pinning her down with his arms.

Terrified, Lucilla struggled to free herself, and began hammering him hard with her fists. But he merely laughed, and ignored the feeble pounding. Before she realized quite what he was doing he had torn at her bodice and ripped part of it away from her bosom.

Biting back a sob of half fury and half fear, she suddenly saw how stupid she had been in not heeding the well-meant advice of Lord Childs. The thought of Lord Childs seemed to bring her courage, and, summoning all the strength in her body, she thrust her fist into Martin Reynolds' face, tore at his hair with all her might, and scratched his cheek viciously.

A cry of anguish escaped him as he drew back with his hands on the smarting scratches which were already trickling with blood. Lucilla did not wait for more. In a flash, she was off the bed, out of the room, and running as fast her legs would carry her through the house and down the stairs, hardly looking where she was going, her heart thumping against her ribs and her cheeks flaming.

In moments, she was out through the front door and running down Richmond Hill at a pace she had not known since a child. She was hardly aware of the amazed expressions on the faces of passers-by as she ran on blindly.

Eventually, as she neared the foot of the hill, a pain which she had ignored in her panic, and which had been shooting from her ankle to her foot, seemed suddenly to envelop the whole of her leg, forcing her to bite her lip in agony and to lean against a wall for support. She had entirely forgotten her wrenched ankle in her terror. At the same time, her full predicament dawned on her, for, although she was safe from Martin Reynolds, Richmond was a strange town to her. She knew nobody there, or where to go for help.

Desperately she looked around. Strolling along on the opposite side of the road was a soberly dressed couple who were looking at her curiously. Taking her courage in both hands, she hobbled to them.

"Pray, excuse me," she began politely, "for intruding upon you in this way, but I am a stranger to Richmond town and need help . . . Is there a stagecoach to London or anything that will convey me there . . ."

They both gazed at her in utter amazement, especially the man, whose eyes went at once to Lucilla's torn dress.

"You must help me," Lucilla burst out tearfully. "I know nobody in Richmond and I have just escaped from the most horrible . . ." Her voice began to break, and the tears streamed down her face. "I must get back to London tonight," she sobbed.

The woman stepped forward and took hold of Lucilla's hand.

"Calm yourself, young lady," she said gently. "People are looking at us. We have not said that we will not help — have we, Charles?" she said, addressing the man.

He shook his head, for he was heartily embarrassed and was sure that Lucilla was a harlot, but his young wife was of a kindlier disposition.

"Here, take my shawl," she said, " 'tis only a cheap one, but it will cover that torn dress. You can't travel in a stage like that. Now wipe your face with this handkerchief and stop trembling so. You are safe now, and in luck, too, for the last stagecoach stops for passengers only a few minutes' walk away."

"Thank heavens!" murmured Lucilla as she tried to carry out the woman's instructions, although her hand quivered so that she could hardly control her movements as she dabbed with the handkerchief.

"Have you money?" demanded the woman, for she had noticed that Lucilla did not have a reitcule.

Lucilla glanced down, and saw with horror that she had left her indispensable behind. She shook her head wretchedly.

"Charles, give her the fare," commanded the woman.

He did so, but with ill grace.

"I will return it, I promise," said Lucilla, realizing that the man could probably not afford to part with the money. "Please tell me where you live — I will see that it is sent."

"You shall do no such thing," said the woman gently. "If we cannot afford to help a person in distress, we are indeed poor, and I hope that we never reach that sad state!"

So saying, she took Lucilla firmly by the arm, and set off smartly in the direction of the main hostelry, where a jostling crowd already awaited the arrival of the stagecoach for London.

11

The house was in a turmoil. As Lucilla slipped into the hall, she could hear from the small adjoining saloon Aunt Amelia's hysterical sobs in rising crescendo; Geraldine's voice, low and breaking, endeavouring to comfort her; and Nurse Hargreaves clucking over them both.

It had been a nightmare of a journey from Richmond with the other passengers either snoring or drunk. A bleary-eyed lecher who was sitting near Lucilla had actually leaned across to her, put his hand on her knee, and suggested that he take her home for the night. Lucilla had glared at him, ignoring the affront, at once petrified and furious. Luckily the man had dropped off to sleep shortly afterwards and did not awake for the rest of the journey.

When she had eventually alighted from the stage at Piccadilly, she had half run, half limped all the way home, quite sure that she would be robbed or murdered on the way. But, mercifully, she had reached the house in safety, her hair matted and tangled, for it was a ferociously windy night, and her tear-stained face was smudged and grimy.

The servants who let her in stood gaping at her, aghast.

"Miss Lucilla — whatever has happened?" the girl

declared involuntarily, and then, casting a hurried glance in the direction of the saloon to make sure that nobody had heard Lucilla enter, whispered, "Go upstairs, Mistress, as fast as you can. I'll give you time to wash your face and tidy your hair — and to change that dress — before I tell them you're back safely."

Lucilla shot her a thankful look and ran across the hall to the staircase, but she was not quick enough. She had just put her foot on the first stair when the library door was thrown open and Lord Childs stood there, a look of incredulous disbelief on his face as he took in her bedraggled appearance.

She saw the expression and felt so humiliated that, for once, she could think of nothing to say. She lowered her eyes, unable to face him. Staring miserably at the floor, she vaguely wondered why she could not remain still, since both she and it seemed to be swaying from side to side like a boat at sea.

Lucilla glanced up at Lord Childs and tried to say something. She moved her mouth but no words would come. A slight gasp escaped her before she began to fall, caught in the nick of time by Lord Childs. She was aware of his arms around her, but knew no more until she opened her eyes a few minutes later and found herself lying on the sofa by the fire in the library.

As soon as he had observed the ashen colour of her face and the glazed expression in her eyes, Lord Childs realized that she was near to exhaustion. He stepped forward to support her and caught her just as she swooned. He gathered her up like a child, and carried her into the library, kicking the door closed behind him, for he had no intention of allowing the hysterical women to see Lucilla in her present condition.

He slipped off his coat and covered her gently, then he took hold of her frozen hands and warmed them in his own and waited patiently for her to recover, as he knew she shortly would in the warmth of the room. When her eyes fluttered and she regained consciousness, he tilted her head and poured a little brandy into her mouth. Slowly, she came fully to, her head in the crook of his arm as he knelt on the floor by the side of the sofa.

"Don't talk, Lucilla," he whispered, and, although she was only half conscious, she dimly realized that it was the first time he had ever called her by her Christian name.

"Keep still," he urged, "you are safe now. Try to rest for a while."

She did as she was bid, still in a state of shock, her spirit so diminished that all she wanted to do was to close her eyes and forget the horrible ordeal through which she had just passed.

Eventually, she opened her eyes and gazed around the familiar room. It was then that she saw Lord Childs was still supporting her head. He had not stirred from her side. She tried to raise herself, and he gently eased her on to the down-filled cushions of the sofa. She sank wearily back with a little sigh.

"I don't know where to begin — how to tell you . . ." she whispered, looking up at him as he poured them both more brandy. He handed Lucilla her glass, and took a quick swig of his own. "There's no hurry. As soon as you feel better you shall go straight to bed. Explanations can wait until the morning."

She shook her head.

"No. I shall tell you now. It is the least I can do . . . but my aunt . . . I cannot face her!"

"There is no need," he replied. "Miss Prior has been informed of your safety and has been requested to retire for the night. Although," he added with his old twinkle, "I had a little trouble in keeping her out of this room."

"Thank heavens! I could not bear anybody to see me like this," Lucilla whispered in consternation. "It would be too degrading for words." She looked down at her torn dress as she spoke.

"There is no fear of that, for I have sent everybody to their beds," he said firmly. "The ladies have been upset quite enough for one day."

"All because of my stupidity."

'No — because of your inexperience," he said unexpectedly.

"I had no idea that Martin Reynolds would be so utterly evil," she burst out. "Before, he was always so kind and gentle, but I see now that you were right, and he is nothing but a . . . womanizer."

He listened with a face set like granite as her story unfolded.

"I'll find him if it's the last thing I do," he muttered, almost to himself, "and then justice will be done — by my own hand, it will!"

"He must have thought me so very stupid," said Lucilla, sitting up and sipping her brandy with a little of her usual spirit. "I thought, well, that he was growing fond of me." She dared not add that she had been sure he was falling in love with her, or that she had almost imagined herself to be in the same state of mind.

"Hah!" His fury prevented him from speaking for the moment.

"I did not realize," she added, her voice breaking, "that he was merely playing with me as though I were a simple child."

"Don't talk any more now," Lord Childs said, biting back the abuse on his lips, and seeing how deeply disturbed she was. "Go to bed, and you will feel better in the morning after a good night's rest."

"I am so ashamed of myself," she murmured, "and yet it did not seem so terribly wrong at the time. My ankle did feel much better . . . Martin Reynolds made it all seem so plausible."

Lord Childs took a step forward, for he thought she was about to faint again. Lucilla had turned pale and her voice trembled.

" . . . instead, oh — how could he!" she said, turning to Lord Childs imploringly.

"Try to put it all out of your mind," he urged. "For at least you managed to get away, and thanks to those kindly people, you secured a seat on the stage."

"Yes, I am lucky."

"And when you alighted at Piccadilly," he said, flinging a log on the dying embers, "you, no doubt ran all the way back."

She nodded.

"Well, you have paid dearly for your lack of judgement," he continued, brushing his hands clean, "and now, my dear, you really must go to your bed. Do not mention any of this matter to your aunt or to Geraldine. I will deal with them myself in the morning. We shall not talk of it again."

Without saying more, he offered her his arm and escorted her slowly to her room. She accompanied him in silence, for by now she was utterly drained of energy, although so relieved at the way in which Lord Childs had reacted that she felt strangely becalmed.

As he opened her bedroom door and she bade him good night she caught sight of an unfamiliar figure preparing her bed.

"What are you doing here?" demanded Lucilla as soon as he had bid her good night and returned to the library, for she was surprised to see that it was the young serving wench who had let her in when she had returned.

"Don't be angry, Mistress. I know I had no right to come, for I am not a chambermaid, but, well, you looked all in when I opened the door just now, so I waited my chance and slipped up here to warm your bed and help you undress. All the chambermaids have been abed this past hour or more . . ."

"I'm hardly likely to be angry at such a kind thought," declared Lucilla, flinging herself on the bed and kicking off her shoes. "Did I see you warming the bed?"

"Aye, Mistress, right properly. I've been at it this past fifteen minutes, so you'll be as warm as toast tonight. But hurry and undress, Mistress, or it will be getting cold again."

The girl was already unfolding Lucilla's nightdress as she spoke. Lucilla had started to unbutton her dress, but the girl hurried to assist her, dealing with the tiny buttons as fast as her clumsy fingers would allow. Lucilla let her complete the task even though she could have done it far quicker herself, for the wench was so anxious to help.

"There's warm water in the basin, too," added the girl proudly. "I brought it up in a kettle from the kitchen myself — said the master had ordered it."

"Tut! You should not have told an untruth for me,"

scolded Lucilla, half asleep as she splashed her face with the deliciously warm water, a rare treat even in Lord Childs' sumptuous home.

"Well, it was only a little lie," pleaded the wench, "and downstairs they were all going on so — what with the sobbing and the vapours, nobody thought much about helping you. Not a single one of 'em gave any orders to even warm your bed — so I saw to it myself."

"My poor aunt," Lucilla murmured. "She must have been beside herself with worry."

"Aye — that she was. And when she did discover you were safe home, well, it was as much as the master could do to stop her from rushing into the library at once. But he can be very stern, can the master, and I don't think she dared cross him."

"Thank goodness!" said Lucilla, as she held her arms above her head for the girl to slip her nightdress over her shoulders.

"You'd best let me try and get some of those tangles out very quickly," the girl said, looking at Lucilla's matted hair. "It will be a real crow's nest in the morning if I don't. And something else for the ladies to gossip about!"

Despite her overwhelming fatigue, Lucilla was quick to see her point.

"Very well," she assented. "I am so tired that I am past caring anyhow. But for heaven's sake hurry, and pass my bed shawl to put around my shoulders, for I'm turning to ice."

The girl nodded, tucked the shawl around Lucilla, and began with deft movements to brush the matted hair. She hardly hurt at all, her touch was so instinctive and sure.

"What is your name?" Lucilla asked.

"Mandy is what I'm called by, Mistress. But my real name is Liza. When my mother died, we all went to live with my aunt, but she had a Liza of her own, so she called me Mandy. I was lucky to get this job in Lord Childs' fine house," she added proudly, "and there's talk of promotion already, for I'm to be made a proper parlour maid soon."

"What on earth were you doing opening the door to me?" demanded Lucilla, slipping in between the soft, warm sheets. "Where was the butler?"

"I don't know — I was passing the door at the time, so I opened it. Silly not to."

"The butler would be furious if he knew," said Lucilla, amused at the girl, "but I am glad it was you, all the same, for that crusty old man would not have made anywhere near such a splendid lady's maid!"

There was a little flushed spot of temper on Aunt Amelia's plump cheeks as she moved in a rustle of taffeta along the corridor towards the library. Her placid nature had been aroused, and she had determined to have words with Lord Childs, for he had sent a message to her early that morning positively forbidding her to question her niece on the previous day's happenings.

Lucilla was to be left entirely alone as long as she wished, he had instructed, and on no account were either his cousin or Miss Prior to visit her to discuss what had occurred. Any explanations would come from him, he had added adamantly.

"Hmph! We shall see about that, indeed!" she had declared indignantly as she read the note, and had swept out of the room immediately to see him.

Aunt Amelia was annoyed to discover that Geraldine was

with Lord Childs, who rose in his usual mannerly way as she bustled into the room.

But for once she was not charmed by his graciousness.

"Lord Childs," she exclaimed, sitting poker stiff on the edge of the chair to which he had motioned her, "I find your attitude intolerable. I have every right to visit my niece when I please, and for you to tell me not to talk to her about yesterday is ridiculous. Why should you try to keep secrets from me, pray? I *must* know what occurred, and I have every intention of finding out. It was outrageous enough of you to forbid me from seeing her last night, but now, this . . . well, I cannot accept it."

Having delivered her tirade, she sat back and glared at him.

"Pray calm yourself, Miss Prior," replied Lord Childs soothingly, taking a thoughtful whiff of snuff as he spoke. "Nobody has forbidden you to see your niece. You may go to her as soon as she awakes, if she so desires. And as for my keeping what occurred a secret, I have no intention of doing any such thing. I merely ask of you to show a little charity, and not to question her on such a painful experience."

Aunt Amelia did not reply. She was a little taken aback by his placating words. But she continued to glower at him, nonetheless.

"The fact of the matter is," he went on, "that I have the unpleasant duty of telling you that your niece was abducted by that villain — Martin Reynolds. He took her to Richmond to seduce her, Miss Prior, but, happily for all of us, your niece managed to escape."

At these words, Aunt Amelia gasped and clasped her hands together much like a small child at prayers. Geraldine had turned a putty colour, and clutched the arms of her chair in horror.

"All is well," he continued quickly before either of them fainted, "for, luckily, apart from the shock of it all, your niece seemed little the worse for her ordeal, despite her tousled appearance when she entered the house — which was another reason why I wanted neither of you to see her."

He paused and cleared his throat, giving them time to recover.

"Now, perhaps, you will both understand why I do not want such an excruciatingly painful experience discussed with her. And as for Martin Reynolds," he concluded darkly, "you may safely leave that vile scoundrel to me. This time he has gone too far! I do not think that he will dare raise his head in society for many a year by the time I have finished with him."

A blush of mortification had spread over Aunt Amelia's face.

"Lord Childs, how will you ever forgive me? I should have realized that you had good reason for your requests, however unreasonable they seemed to me. Oh, dear, my poor Lucilla! What a horrifying thing to happen to such a sweet, innocent child! Whatever shall I tell her dear father?"

"Nothing!" snapped Lord Childs. "There is no need to mention the matter to anybody, since it is over and done with — to dwell on it will only exaggerate its importance."

"My cousin is right, Miss Prior," said Geraldine in a small voice, speaking at last. "The only way to help Lucilla will be to ignore this unmentionable incident. As for myself," she concluded righteously, "I shall do exactly as he says and shall forget the matter completely, even when dear Lucilla feels well enough to talk."

Lord Childs cast her a gratified look, while Aunt Amelia dabbed ineffectually at her nose with her cambric handkerchief as if grappling with her own thoughts on the subject. Presently, she seemed to have settled things in her mind, however, for she turned to Lord Childs and declared, "You are quite right, sir, and I shall comply with your requests. What a mercy it was that you were here when this dreadful business occurred. Without you, I cannot imagine how I should have coped. As it is, you have come to my niece's rescue in such a way as to render her eternally grateful to you — and I pray with all my heart that she fully appreciated what you have done."

"Come now, Miss Prior, please do not exaggerate my part in the affair," replied Lord Childs with a dismissive gesture, sounding a trifle embarrassed.

"Perhaps," he added as an afterthought, "you would set yourselves the task of prescribing something to gladden young Miss Prior's heart. See to it that a maidservant is sent out for her favourite flowers — something like that. Meanwhile, I shall track down Martin Reynolds and deal with him in my own way."

In fact he had already sent the groom, a burly fellow, and two muscular stable lads off to Richmond to lie in wait for Reynolds and to bring him back, but he had little hope that they would meet with success, since he was convinced that the wretch would have gone into hiding. He was right. Martin Reynolds was no fool, and had quickly realized that in Lucilla's case he had overstepped the mark. He suspected, and rightly, that Lord Childs would not rest until justice had been done.

Reynolds had therefore lost no time in leaving Richmond, and, once at his London residence, he had stopped only long enough to collect all the money he could lay his hands on, and to throw a few clothes into a valise. Then he had made off posthaste to the coast. Here he had taken a boat for France, and journeyed on to Italy. He travelled in that country extensively before being forced into marriage with Sophia da Vicca (her elder brothers having discovered their love affair), who subsequently made his life a perfect misery by her constant nagging and bad temper.

It was not until well into the morning that Lucilla eventually opened her eyes and remembered the terror of the previous day. For some time she lay quite motionless, staring straight in front at the wall, churning the events over in her mind. It was only when she recalled the gentleness of Lord Childs that her taut expression softened, and she felt a soft glow of warmth spread through her body. His kindness had been so unexpected that it still staggered her.

As she lay quite still in bed, concerned with her own thoughts, the door silently opened, and Mandy crept into the room. She bore a tall vase of flowers which she placed on the chest of drawers, then stood back to admire them with her hands clasped behind her back. Suddenly she turned round and saw Lucilla watching her.

"Lord, Mistress, I did not know that you were awake," she declared, going pink. "These are the blooms which I fetched myself from the shop on the corner — Miss Prior and the young mistress bade me get them. But I believe," she added, casting Lucilla a sly look, "that the master suggested it."

Lucilla raised herself on her elbow and looked at them.

"They're lovely, really beautiful, but how is it that you are here waiting on me again?"

The girl chuckled.

"A bit of luck, Mistress," she confided with glee. "My aunt works at the flower shop, and when I heard that the footman was being sent, I asked if I could go instead. When they heard why, they soon agreed — they knew I'd get the best flowers."

Lucilla smiled at Mandy's puckish delight.

"Shall I say that you need some hot chocolate and toast?" the girl inquired, edging from the room, having propped up Lucilla with a bank of pillows.

"I'm not hungry, but some coffee would be nice," Lucilla said, adding, "I don't suppose you know what is going on in the house — if everything is quiet, and the ladies calmed down after yesterday?"

Mandy shook her head.

"Sorry, Mistress. I only came with the flowers as a special privilege because I got so many good blooms from my aunt. I'm not really supposed to stay with you for a single moment. Still" — and a mischievous look appeared in her grey eyes — "I could do a bit of scouting for you, if you wished. Daresay nobody would notice me."

"Well, perhaps very quickly, then, on your way to the kitchen to tell them about the coffee. But mind, don't do anything stupid. I should hate to think that I was the cause of your losing your job."

Mandy was gone in a flash, returning after about twenty minutes, flushed with her reconnoitering.

"The coffee is on its way, Mistress, and you could hear a pin fall in the house. Everything is that quiet."

"Have you seen the other ladies? And is Lord Childs at home this morning?"

"Heavens, yes! The master has been with the ladies in the

library, giving them a talking to — or so it seemed," she added hastily, colouring up, for she had not been able to resist putting her ear to the keyhole.

"I see," said Lucilla, her lips twitching at the girl's guilty expression, but, before she could say anything else, there was a brisk knock at the door, and a chambermaid appeared bearing the coffee on a silver tray, and propped up next to it a note addressed to Lucilla in Lord Childs' handwriting.

The chambermaid glared at Mandy, and was about to reprimand her for being upstairs with the young mistress when Lucilla came to her rescue.

"The girl brought me something at my instruction," she said, "but she may return to the servants' quarters now."

The chambermaid looked appeased, and poured Lucilla's coffee.

As soon as she was alone, Lucilla reached for the letter and broke the seal. A look of relief spread over her face as she read the short but thoughtful message, stating that, as soon as she felt fit enough — and to make sure that she really did feel fully recovered — he would be grateful if she would wait upon him in the library.

"Ah! He is still in an understanding mood," she whispered to herself, for she had doubted that his kindness of the previous night would continue. It seemed too good to be true.

Lucilla sipped her coffee thoughtfully, glancing at the elaborate French clock on the chest of drawers. It said eleven of the hour. Without more ado, she rang for the chambermaid and requested pen and paper, wrote two polite lines thanking Lord Childs for his concern, and then added that she would be delighted to join him at midday. She had every intention of speaking to him before seeing her aunt or

Geraldine, for she wanted to know precisely what he had told them.

Lucilla finished her coffee and sprang out of bed. She peered apprehensively at herself in the mirror, and was pleased to see that, despite her ordeal of the previous day, she looked little the worse for it, the night's sleep having completely restored the colour to her cheeks. Only the torn dress, thrown across a chair by Mandy, who was not trained in tidiness for my lady's chamber, remained to remind her of the hateful episode. She looked at it with repulsion and rang for the maid, instructing the girl to dispose of the garment. Then she splashed her face with water, brushed her long, golden hair, and reached for her favourite dress, a simple gown of hyacinth blue which her father always admired.

Praying that she would not meet either her aunt or Geraldine in the corridor, she made her way swiftly to the library, and arrived just as the clock in the alcove next to the door was striking twelve of the hour.

Lord Childs was standing lost in thought by the window with his back to the door. She coughed discreetly to attract his attention, for he did not hear her slip quietly into the room. He spun round to face her, and noted at once by her appearance that she had completely recovered.

"Good morning, Lord Childs," Lucilla spoke quietly, for she was a little unsure of his attitude, despite his kindly note.

"Miss Prior — good morning to you," he said with a broad, uncomplicated smile. "I trust that you are none the worse for your unfortunate adventure."

"None the worse, at all, thank you, Lord Childs — although very much wiser," she replied with a contrite expression. Then she added anxiously, "I have not seen my aunt or Geraldine yet."

"Oh, you need have no fear," he said with a wave of his hand, as though they were both of no importance whatsoever. "I have dealt with *them*. I told them briefly what had happened to you and asked them not to mention the subject again. I do not think you will be troubled by Miss Prior at all! And as for my cousin, she is too fond of you to want to raise the matter, realizing how painful it would be to you."

"Thank heavens!" exclaimed Lucilla, turning to face him with gratitude in her voice. "I have much to thank you for, Lord Childs — and I am truly sorry that I have been stupid over so many things in the past. I see now that you are usually right, and . . . well . . . you probably have your usual sound reasons even for delaying Geraldine's betrothal to Sir David."

She stole a quick look at him as she spoke to see how he had taken her remark. She had vowed to herself that she would raise the vexed matter of Geraldine's marriage if she found him in an approachable frame of mind. To her delight, the remark did not appear to ruffle him.

He crossed the room and sat beside her on the sofa.

"I have indeed very sound reasons, Miss Prior," he said in a low voice.

On the spur of the moment, she took her courage in both hands and said daringly, "Will you not confide in me, Lord Childs, and permit me to share this worry with you?" Her enormous violet eyes were fixed on him appealingly. He found it difficult to resist her.

"Ha! Worry is too mild a word," he ejaculated bitterly, "for there seems no way out of this . . . this . . . threat that has dogged me ever since I stepped inside Langley House."

"The gypsy — it has something to do with that odious vagabond, has it not?"

He nodded, and lapsed into silence. Suddenly he seemed to make up his mind to confide in her, and began to speak in a bitter, dry voice.

"The day after I arrived at Langley House, that vagabond sent me an impertinent note asking to meet me at the Fair. I would not have gone but for one thing. He enclosed a miniature of Geraldine's mother with the note. I could take no chances if Geraldine was threatened in any way, so I went. Forgive me, Miss Prior, for denying your story," he added. "I was horrified when I discovered that you had seen me, but I could not admit to it for Geraldine's sake. Anyway . . . from that day to this, my peace of mind has been at the mercy of that wretch with whom you saw me. My dear cousin's happiness and her entire future are in jeopardy. You see, Miss Prior, Geraldine's mother did not die at childbirth as she believes — I know this because her father told me — Geraldine's mother ran away from home only a few weeks after Geraldine was born . . ."

He paused uneasily, groping for words.

"She was a wayward girl, and had encouraged the advances of some rogue of a gypsy — heaven knows how they ever met, but he seemed to have some hold over her, for she was obsessed with him. She left Geraldine's father for this man — joined his tribe and was never seen by her family again."

Lucilla was silent. Utterly lost for words.

"The man with whom you saw me knows this sad story, and is demanding money to keep quiet. Even worse. He claims that Geraldine is really the gypsy's daughter, and threatens to tell her so unless I keep him quiet with gold.

Oh, do not think that I mind parting with the money," he added, despair heavy in his voice. "I do not. But there can be no future in such blackmail. Geraldine will never be safe until I have somehow managed to prove that she is the legitimate daughter of her legal father — something practically impossible to verify since both parents are dead."

"Oh! It is all horrible," exclaimed Lucilla in dismay, recalling with unease Geraldine's dark good looks. "That odious man — how I hate him."

All the time, she had been thinking of the letter for which she had sent, wondering whether she should mention it now to Lord Childs. Yet, to raise his hopes would be cruel, and, after all, she did not know what the contents might be. She glanced at him shrewdly, and decided that it was not the time to tell him, he was far too distraught. Better by far, she decided, to wait until she had the letter in her possession.

"If all else fails, I shall have to tell Geraldine of the man's evil theories," he said, rising to his feet wearily. "She will be shattered, but at least it will free her from blackmail. But I pray to God it does not come to that."

"She must never know," cried Lucilla passionately, realizing how such a hateful revelation would affect a proud person like Geraldine. "She must never be told — it would shatter her!"

Lucilla's voice had become quite shrill, and she clutched her hands together so hard that the knuckles bit into her flesh.

Lord Childs saw how pale she had become, and said, tenderly, "I should not have burdened you in this way, Miss Prior. You have been through enough already. Pray, try to dismiss it from your thoughts, for there is nothing you can do. At least you understand now why Geraldine cannot at the moment become betrothed."

"I do — only too well," she replied unsteadily. "But I implore you not to lose heart — something good will come out of this evil, I am sure."

Her words, sincere though they were, seemed of little comfort to him.

"You had best go now and see your aunt," he said flatly. "That good lady will be quite beside herself with worry if you do not show yourself to her soon."

She nodded, and although she felt quite at a loss to know how to console him, she searched her mind fervently for some small way in which she could be of help to Lord Childs. Inside her was a growing desire to prove herself worthy to him after her shameful behaviour. Suddenly, it seemed more important to Lucilla than anything else in the world that he should think well of her. She took her leave of him praying with all her heart that Cook would not delay too long in sending the letter.

12

When old Madge Potter, the rector's cook, had received Lucilla's strange note, she had sat down by the kitchen range for a full half-hour, puffing out her ruddy cheeks with concentration as she painstakingly spelled out each word to herself and pondered over the strange request. Read she could, but only with great effort, and since she got precious little practice at the art, it seemed to get more difficult each time.

Squinting a little, and turning the letter towards the light, she had made out the name of her young mistress at once, for, since she rarely received a letter, she could not wait to see who had written to her.

Lucilla's name brought a bewildered look into her mild grey eyes, for, although she was fond of her young mistress, Madge realized at once that something was afoot, otherwise why should Miss Prior write to her? A thing she never did.

Having read the note at last, she sat rocking herself gently in the same old pine rocking chair where she had once dangled Lucilla on her knee, cogitating over the peculiar request which her young mistress had made.

She could not fathom the reason why Lucilla should ask

her to find the letter which was addressed to Lord Childs. Why had she not written to her father? Slowly, the old cook had worked out that Lucilla wished to keep the matter a secret from the rector. She had sat, shaking her head from side to side, a worried frown upon her wholesome face, for she adored her master, and hated the thought of doing anything which might in any way be disloyal.

Still, there was such a strong note of desperation in the letter that even Madge's unsubtle mind could not fail to feel it, and, since Lucilla had an open nature and would never dream of doing anything underhanded to upset her father, Madge at last reconciled her conscience, and decided to help her young mistress.

It had not been easy. Madge, being the cook, was seldom seen in the main part of the rectory. She had no reason to go there, since she presided over her own domain, the kitchen, and had no need to be anywhere else, unless, of course, Miss Prior sent for her. However, since Miss Prior was away with her niece, even this possibility was eliminated.

As she had rolled the pastry for the big game pie, so beloved by the rector and his guests, and kneaded the bread with her large, deft hands, Madge had slowly decided upon a scheme. The village painters were working in the rectory at that time, come to give the rambling old house a lick of paint where it was most needed. The rector was careful with his money, and hated spending it on such things, but he was under pressure from his sister who had even written from London about, of all things, expensive flocked wallpaper. To please her, therefore, he had directed the painters to work in both his sister's room and that of his daughter.

Happily, when the painters were in the house they were

usually instructed to use up any leftover paint on the servants' quarters. This time, Madge thought to herself, she would ask the rector if the servants' staircase could be freshened up a little. The paintwork was all chipped and scratched, and had not seen a paint brush in all the time she had worked at the rectory. If the rector agreed, then all the servants — including herself — would need to use the main stairs for a day or two and it would thus be quite a simple thing for her to slip into Miss Lucilla's room.

As soon as she had put the bread to rise by the fire, she had wiped her floury hands clean on the coarse, cotton cloth hanging by the flour bin especially for the purpose, and had set off in search of the rector. He was in the middle of preparing a sermon, but nonetheless patiently stopped to hear her request. To her delight, he had agreed at once, and Madge had returned to the kitchen with a quiet glow of satisfaction, treating herself to a quick nip of elderflower wine before making a sustaining bread-and-butter pudding for herself and the two housemaids.

She had only to wait until the end of the week before the painters would be free to start on the narrow staircase which wound its way up from the rear entrance close by the kitchen to the small rooms in the attic set aside for the servants.

As soon as they had moved in with their ladders, she had lost no time in making her way to Miss Lucilla's room to look for the letter. However, on entering, she had discovered to her consternation that the bow-fronted chest of drawers, which usually stood in the far corner of the room, was no longer there.

"Lor! What'll I do now?" she had declared out loud. Obviously some of the furniture had been moved to other rooms (of which there were eleven) to facilitate the painters. The chest might be in any one of them.

She had made her way heavily back to the kitchen where she had brewed up a pot of tea as she slowly decided on her next move. There was nothing for it but to search every chest of drawers (since they were all practically identical) in every spare room.

So, as time had permitted, Madge had creaked daily from room to room, making sure never to be away from the kitchen for too long lest she aroused suspicion, emptying out the contents of the drawers, and searching painstakingly for the letter as described by Miss Lucilla.

Finally, on the third day, just as the painters had been completing their task, she had tracked down the right chest of drawers in a room which had been locked, and to which she had only recently located the key.

"Thank the Lord!" she had uttered, with a deep sigh of relief. A little groan had escaped her as she had knelt on creaking knees to open the drawers. Since these drawers were interchangeable, and had been taken out during the moving of the chest, she was obliged to search them all.

On the final drawer, Madge was near to exasperation, for, if the letter did not reveal itself here, she would not know where to look. But there was nothing. She had gazed at the scattered contents in disbelief, and then a thought had occurred to her, and she had started to remove the green lining paper. Her tenacity had been rewarded, for there lay the letter in the very spot where Lucilla had hastily thrust it so many weeks ago. Lucilla had quite forgotten that she had tucked it beneath the paper when she had written so hurriedly to old Madge.

Getting slowly to her feet with a grimace of pain as her stiff old joints righted themselves, Madge had placed the letter carefully in the capacious pocket of her apron and hobbled back to the safety of her kitchen.

That night, when she was alone, she had sat down at the well-scrubbed kitchen table with quill and paper, treated herself to the luxury of burning two tallow candles, for her eyes were failing these days, and written with great deliberation and immense care: "Dear Mistres, I have the leter of Lord Childs and send it to you at wuns. I coold not find it at ferst. Pleas forgiv dilay." After signing her name slowly and fastidiously, for Madge was extremely proud of the fact that she could write her name so well, she sat back and thought for a bit before adding the rider: "Nobodi doth no."

From the packet of cheap envelopes which she had purchased at market many years previously, she selected one big enough and strong enough to seal the package containing the letter addressed to Lord Childs and her own short note, addressed it with infinite care, and hid it in a drawer until morning, when she intended to give it to the boy to attend to with particular speed.

Lucilla was beside herself with anxiety. Days and days had passed, and she still had not heard from old Madge. She began to wonder whether the old cook might be ill, or even worse, perhaps dead. She could not see, unless some such reason existed, why Madge had not written.

Once again the reckless idea occurred to her of going herself to the rectory. A plan was already forming in her mind, and she had practically decided upon putting it into action when, late one morning as she sat in her room moodily brushing her hair, there was a tap at the door, and a chambermaid stood before her with a clumsily sealed package upon a silver salver.

Lucilla's heart gave a jump. She saw at once by the ill-formed characters of the writing that it could be from none other than Cook, and that quite obviously it contained the all-important letter. Her hand trembled slightly as she unfolded Cook's short note and read the contents, smiling to herself with relief on old Madge's ability to keep a confidence, and, thankfully, she had come well up to expectations.

Now that Lucilla came to examine the letter addressed to Lord Childs more carefully, this being the first time she had ever held it for any length of time, she was puzzled at the appearance of the document. Not only did it look dirty, which was to be expected since it had come from the gypsy's filthy caravan, but it gave the impression of being quite old, the colour of the paper having grown yellow, and the ink faded to a dull brown. She could not understand it. Still, since she now had it safely in her possession, she dismissed the worry as being trivial, and decided to lose no more time in handing it over to its rightful owner.

She went in search of Lord Childs at once, the letter safely concealed in a velvet reticule she used for lengths of silk for embroidery. She dangled the reticule casually on her arm, and sailed out of the room with a disarmingly innocent air, looking for all the world as though she was on her way to sew a neat seam in the saloon.

Lord Childs was not in the library, neither was he to be found in the writing room, the drawing room, or the painted room. His elusiveness annoyed Lucilla, and, without wasting any more time on the fruitless search, she made her way impatiently to Geraldine's room, for Geraldine usually knew what her cousin's arrangements were for the day.

Tapping lightly on the door, she hardly waited for an answer before peeping quickly inside, since the girls only gave a perfunctory tap on the door when they visited each other. She was just about to speak when the empty scene before her curbed the words. She could see through the open, gilt-decorated doors of the boudoir into Geraldine's sumptuous bedroom, and there was no sign of her friend. Indeed, the bedroom was immaculate, and looked as though it had not been disturbed since the servants had made the bed, and tidied and dusted.

Lucilla stood in the middle of the vast room casting an impatient glance around for any clue that might reveal Geraldine's whereabouts. But there was nothing. Not an item of clothing had been left out by the servants, which was a pity, for it might have given some indication of where Geraldine intended to go that morning.

There was nothing for it but to go in search of Nurse Hargreaves, for she would certainly know of Geraldine's whereabouts. The old nurse slept in a room on the same floor as Geraldine, not in the servants' quarters, owing to her more superior position and length of service. Lucilla sped along the passage, and thumped loudly on the door of her room. When the old woman did not answer, Lucilla's suspicions that Geraldine had gone shopping accompanied by her nurse were confirmed.

Crossly, she returned to her bedroom, placed the reticule under lock and key in her travelling chest, and wandered downstairs to the main drawing room. She had her hand on the handle of the door when a loud commotion coming from the direction of the hall stopped her from turning it.

To her horror, she discerned Nurse Hargreaves' voice crying out shrilly in a hysterical voice for Lord Childs.

Lucilla gathered up her skirts, and ran swiftly to the hall. The old woman was in tears, wringing her hands with despair, sobbing and babbling incomprehensibly.

"Calm yourself, Nurse," said Lucilla gently, placing her arm around the old woman's frail shoulders which were shaking with convulsive sobs. "Tell me quietly what the matter is — I cannot understand a word you are saying."

"Oh, Miss Lucilla, she's been kidnapped!" shrieked the old nurse, omitting to say who. "She's gone — dragged away by two murderers — I'll never see her again!"

Alarmed beyond words, Lucilla helped her into a chair.

"Tell me slowly . . . how did it happen where and when?" she demanded.

"In a narrow street off Piccadilly," whispered Nurse Hargreaves, the tears streaking down her parchment-lined face. "We had gone there to look in the window of Giles the silversmith — Miss Geraldine had it in mind to order something for her cousin's birthday. Well, we had hardly got there when there was a rattle of a decrepit carriage behind us, and two rough villains leaped out, seized my young lady, and thrust her inside . . . that was the last I saw of her." The old nurse's sobs grew out of control at this point.

" 'tis grave, Mistress," said the butler in a low voice to Lucilla.

She gave him a scornful look for his unnecessary remark, and promptly turned to address the crowd of servants who had somehow gathered around them.

"Does anybody know the whereabouts of Lord Childs at this moment?" she demanded.

Some shook their heads. Others mumbled frightened

thoughts. Lucilla looked at them in despair. "Surely some-body knows! Go and fetch his valet," she instructed the nearest footman.

Suddenly a small voice spoke up from the back of the crowd.

"I can tell, Mistress!"

"Come forward at once, Mandy," ordered Lucilla, for she had recognized the young girl's voice immediately, "and speak up quickly."

"Begging your pardon, Mistress," she said, bobbing a quick curtsy and colouring up rather at the curious stares of the other servants, "I would have spoken sooner — but I did not want to do so out of turn." She cast a worried look at some of the older servants, for she knew how hostile they could be. "His Lordship is gone to the shoemaker in Cran-bourne Alley, and he has taken his valet with him."

"Did he say when he would be back, girl?" demanded Lucilla.

"Nay, Mistress. I know no more," replied Mandy un-easily, fearing that she had drawn too much attention to herself already, and worried that her habit of eavesdrop-ping, which accounted for this information, might be detected.

Lucilla guessing this, could see that nothing further would be got from Mandy, and dismissed her. At the same time, she turned to the other servants and said, "Go about your duties now — I am sure we shall soon have Miss Geraldine back with us."

Then she instructed that a messenger should be sent at once to the shoemaker to impart the news to Lord Childs, and that another should escort Nurse Hargreaves to her room.

"As for you," she said, addressing the butler. "You are to tell Lord Childs this terrible thing as soon as you open the door to him, just in case the messenger misses him. Do not waste a second if I am not here myself at that moment."

"Yes, Mistress," he replied with his customary stiff bow, "I will acquaint His Lordship with everything immediately."

"— and," continued Lucilla, "send word to the head groom to prepare fresh horses and another carriage, and to have it awaiting His Lordship's pleasure at the front of the house — for he may need to use it at once upon his return."

Having given her instructions, and racking her brain to make sure that she had not overlooked anything, Lucilla returned at last to the small drawing room which the ladies sometimes used when they were by themselves, and helped herself to a much-needed cup of hot chocolate.

She stood nervously sipping the steaming beverage by the window watching anxiously for the return of Lord Childs. She could not face telling her aunt the dreadful news until she had restored her own equilibrium.

She had just consumed the last of her second cup, when the rattle of a carriage brought her hurrying to the window again. To her astonishment, Lord Childs swung out of it almost immediately. She could scarcely believe her eyes, for the messenger could not possibly have got to the shoemaker so swiftly. Then she realized that Lord Childs had returned without encountering him, and that he was still in ignorance of Geraldine's abduction.

Lord Childs had already disappeared from view and entered the house. Even now, if her instructions were being followed, the butler would be telling him. Lucilla put down her cup with a hasty rattle, and ran from the room, through the maze of corridors and adjoining rooms to the main hall. It did not take her more than a minute or so to get there, yet, when she arrived, she was astounded to discover that Lord Childs had already departed again.

She called to the butler who had his back to her and was withdrawing in the direction of the servants' quarters.

"Lord Childs — where is he?" she cried.

He turned round in surprise at the tone of her voice.

"Gone, Mistress. He went at once when I told him about Miss Geraldine."

"But where?" demanded Lucilla. "Where did he go? How did he know where they've taken her?"

The butler gazed at her stonily.

"I did not inquire," he replied baldly. "I had hardly finished when His Lordship turned on his heel and went."

" . . . and he gave no clue?"

"No Mistress . . . except . . . "

"Well?"

"Just as I was closing the door, I did hear him instruct them to go with all speed to a tavern in the city . . . "

"Which tavern? Did you hear the name?"

"It sounded like the Old Rising Sun, Mistress."

"Which carriage did he take?"

"The one in which he returned."

"Ah! I thought so, for they would not have had time to harness the horses for the carriage I ordered," exclaimed Lucilla in triumph, "and with any luck they will be bringing it from the mews soon. Send a girl for my pelisse," she ordered, "I'm going after Lord Childs."

His mouth opened and shut again as though he was going to say something but thought better of it, on seeing the expression in Lucilla's eyes and the firm set of her mouth. In seconds, a servant was sent scurrying to Lucilla's room, leaving Lucilla to pace the hall floor impatiently as she peered from the windows to see if the carriage was yet brought round to the front of the house. As it happened, both the carriage and the servant with her pelisse arrived at the same time, and Lucilla was out of the house in a flash, still struggling into the simple garment as she ran.

Lucilla's luck was in, for there was little traffic to detain them along the Strand, and the carriage, with its fresh, fast horses, moved at a cracking pace towards its seedy destination. Lucilla sat biting her lips with agitation, trying to work out Lord Childs' mysterious reaction to Geraldine's surprising abduction. It was quite obvious to her that the gypsy was at the bottom of the affair, and that possibly Lord Childs knew the tavern, to which they both now raced, to be a favoured haunt of the gypsy and his accomplice.

The door of the Old Rising Sun was surrounded by a motley group of the most wretched vagabonds Lucilla had ever seen. They lounged sullenly against the walls, staring with hostile curiosity at the carriage as it ground to a halt. She drew a deep breath, stepped nimbly down from the carriage, and, head held high, passed through their midst.

The tavern was dim inside with small, dusty windows, and no candles. The place stank of ale and beer, long spilled on the floor and rough trestles, and never mopped up, just left to seep into the wood. When her eyes had grown accustomed to the gloom, she saw to her relief that not all the inmates appeared quite so sinister as those lounging outside. These seemed for the most part to be ordinary tradesmen and working men. And then her heart gave a jump. Standing in a corner, with his back to her, head and shoulders above the rest, was Lord Childs. With him, as she had half expected, was the vile gypsy.

Now that she had found Lord Childs, she was suddenly nonplussed as to what to do next. She had gone after him on the spur of the moment without really knowing why — except that in some strange way, she had thought that she could help in Geraldine's recovery. But she did not have time to ponder. To her dismay, Lord Childs suddenly seized the gypsy by the throat and hurled him to the floor. Next moment, he was on his knees shaking the man with such fearful vehemence that Lucilla was sure he meant to kill him.

She ran towards them in terror. Everything seemed to be happening so quickly.

"I'll kill you — and happily swing for it," breathed Lord Childs, furiously, his powerful frame towering over the cringing gypsy. "Speak now if you want to live!"

A small circle of men had begun to gather around them, but not one of them intruded. They could see that the fine gentleman had things well under control, and since it was not their fight, the gypsy could fend for himself. They watched from idle curiosity with blank faces.

"Are you going to speak?" demanded Lord Childs between gritted teeth, "or will you die for your deed?"

Lucilla could see that the gypsy would not be able to speak even if he wished, since Lord Childs held him so tightly around the throat.

The gypsy shot a sly glance around the bystanders to see if anybody might come to his rescue, or if his accomplice had arrived back, but, as he saw no sign of either, he gave Lord Childs a brief, malicious look, and began to splutter out some incoherent words.

"He wants to say something — lessen your grip on him,"

urged Lucilla, who had crept up beside them.

Lord Childs did not even look up, his rage was so overwhelming. However, despite his amazement at Lucilla's appearance, he seemed to understand the sense of what she said, and released the gypsy sufficiently for him to be able to utter a faltering sentence or two.

"The girl's here," the man ejaculated. "In the back, yonder!" He jerked his head in the direction of the rear of the building. "She's safe — unharmed — nothing touched. Not a hair on her head. I only wanted to show you that I meant business if you didn't pay up!"

Lord Childs did not wait for more. He let the man go with such a violent push that the fellow cracked his head against the floorboards with a sound like a pistol report.

Lord Childs was through the back door in a couple of strides with Lucilla running after him. She dare not speak; he seemed like another creature in his rage, hardly aware of her existence. At the rear of the shabby tavern were piles of rotting barrels and filthy rubbish. A rat or two scuttled off at the sudden intrusion. To one side was a small stable with a mean outbuilding attached to it. Lord Childs threw himself at the door of the outbuilding with all his strength, but it did not stir. Seizing a plank of wood, he began ramming it.

Lucilla watched his fruitless effort in silence. Then she had an idea. She caught Lord Childs by the arm and pleaded with him to stop. She calmly walked to the door, lifted the wooden latch, and opened it. Lord Childs watched her in amazement, for the door had not been locked from the start, which was not so surprising, since the prisoner could never have escaped. She lay prostrate like a corpse in the corner on some straw, bound and gagged, with only the terrified expression in her large brown eyes to reveal that she was alive.

Lucilla was across the floor in a moment to comfort her friend, wrestling with the knot of the gag as nimbly as she could, her fingers all thumbs in her agitation. As she worked at it, Lord Childs was cutting Geraldine loose from the ropes which bound her, rubbing the life back into her numb limbs.

"You're safe — your cousin has dealt with that vile gypsy who kidnapped you," whispered Lucilla tenderly as she unravelled the final knot of the gag. "There's nothing to fear now — you will soon be home."

It was only then that Lord Childs turned to Lucilla as if seeing her for the first time.

"How on earth . . ." he began.

"Did I know that you were at the tavern," she said quietly, as he gathered Geraldine up in his arms and carried her back to his carriage.

"The butler overheard your destination — I followed you," she explained coolly.

"You could have come to grief yourself," he replied in a low voice, "they would have stopped at nothing . . ."

"I cannot understand why they should choose to kidnap me at all," Geraldine whispered, still dazed, as Lucilla sat with her arm around her friend in Lord Childs' carriage. "Do you think they mistook me for somebody else?"

"Don't talk," commanded her cousin.

"Lord Childs is right," urged Lucilla. "Sit quietly. We can discuss this horrible matter when you are fully recovered. Their motives are not important, anyhow," she added, "so long as you are safe again."

"I was terrified," whispered Geraldine with a shudder. "It all happened so quickly — I thought they were going to murder me."

"Hush! Think no more about it. Put it out of your mind."

"What happened to those odious men? Did they get away?" pursued Geraldine.

"They will not trouble you again, have no fear," Lord Childs replied in a hard voice as he stared stormily from the window.

"May I speak to you, Lord Childs?" asked Lucilla meekly, "when we are safely home and have put Geraldine to bed," she added quickly, for she had no desire to raise the matter of the letter with him in front of her friend.

"As you wish, Miss Prior," he answered absently. "Come and see me as soon as you have escorted my cousin to her room, by all means."

The rest of the journey was made in silence. Lucilla was occupied with thoughts on the best way to tell him how the letter came into her possession. Geraldine lay back against the cushioned interior of the carriage with her eyes closed fast, while Lord Childs sat with his face like a mask of clay, his eyes unforgiving, and his mouth in a tight, grim line.

It did not take long to hand Geraldine into the safe care of Nurse Hargreaves once they were home. The old woman was so staggered and relieved to see her charge alive and little the worse for her adventure, that she shooed Lucilla away immediately, intent upon having her precious young mistress entirely to herself. She was already undressing her like a child, and had set the chambermaid to work with the warming pan on Geraldine's bed.

Lucilla slipped thankfully from the room, and went at once for the reticule which contained the letter. Lord Childs was partaking of a meal of cold meats when she joined him, and she saw that a spare plate had been set aside for her. She did not feel at all like eating, but thought it might look churlish not to accept his invitation to take a small, late luncheon with him. She therefore helped herself to some cold beef and ham, and sat down opposite him.

He poured her a glass of burgundy, replenished his own glass, and said slowly, "I did not think the wretch would go so far as this — even though he threatened it. I've refused to give him any more money, you see, so I must take the blame for my cousin's hellish experience. Thank God, we found her safely!"

He looked so tired and worried that Lucilla's heart went out to him. He gazed wearily at the food before him, pushing his plate away and leaving it uneaten. He was grown so thin of late that Lucilla wondered how nobody but herself had appeared to notice it.

"But what will happen if he tells Geraldine?" she asked hesitantly.

"It will not matter," he replied firmly, "for I shall tell her first. My mind is made up. I will not suffer this dastardly blackmailing one moment longer."

Lucilla cleared her throat a trifle nervously.

"Lord Childs — I have a letter in my possession which is addressed to you, and I wish to give it to you now."

He looked at her questioningly, but before he could speak, Lucilla hurried on. "I came by it in a strange way — you see, I found it in the gypsy's caravan before I came to London."

"What! How on earth came you to be in such a place?"

"Oh! I was there of my own free will, have no fear," she reassured him. Then, facing him squarely, she proceeded to tell him precisely what had happened.

He listened with a frown, but she did not give him the opportunity to say how foolish she had been, as she was sure he would, for she was already producing the document from her reticule and was handing it to him. Her head was bent, and she did not see the softened look which had come into his eyes at her quick, nervous speech.

He took it from her with no more than a nod, yet a tenderness had already crept over his face. Before he broke the seal, he spent time studying the writing. At last he looked up and said, "Lucilla — whatever this may contain, I thank you from the bottom of my heart for trying to help. It was a silly, reckless thing to go inside the caravan, of course, but I have long since decided that nothing will cure the daring side of your nature — and, as for writing to your cook to avail yourself of her assistance . . . well, thank goodness your judgement was sound, and you knew who you could trust."

A flush had spread over Lucilla's face. For the second time in his life, he had used her Christian name, and, moreover, the look in his eyes spoke more than any words. She had only seen it once before, when he had asked her to dance at the ball. She lowered long lashes as she replied, "Pray open the letter, sir, I cannot bear the suspense any longer."

There followed what seemed to Lucilla to be an intolerably lengthy silence. Lord Childs seemed to be reading the contents exceptionally slowly as she sat on the edge of her chair fighting hard the desire to run across and read the letter over his shoulder. Finally, he got up and walked thoughtfully to the window, examining the signature with care in the light. At last he seemed satisfied, and turned to face her.

"This letter was not intended for me," he said slowly.

"But — it bears your name. I do not understand . . . unless," and as she spoke, it flashed upon her what a fool she had been; for of course, by the very appearance of the document, she should have guessed that it had not been recently written.

"Some other Lord Childs . . ." she exclaimed. "It is old — intended for somebody now dead."

He nodded.

"I knew as much before I opened it," he replied, "and deliberated as to whether I should read the contents of a letter not intended for me. But, bearing in mind where you had found it — and the situation we find ourselves in, I decided I would read it."

"And . . . what does it say?"

He walked back from the window and sat down opposite her again.

"It solves our problem," he said quietly, "thanks to your dreadfully curious nature, my dear, for the letter was written by Geraldine's mother upon her deathbed only a few years ago — a broken woman. The poor wretch did not reap much happiness from her wayward romance, I'm afraid. She says so in no uncertain terms, but the main reason for the letter is to ask forgiveness for her selfish act in leaving her infant daughter in so cruel a way . . ." He paused before continuing. "And yet, she cannot have been all bad, for she seems to have realized the dangerous situation in which Geraldine might one day find herself if rumours were spread about her true father. In this document, she gives her word that the gypsy was never her lover until she eloped with him — she swears upon the Bible that Geraldine was the offspring of her legal marriage."

"Oh! I cannot believe my ears," cried Lucilla. "But how sad that the letter was never sent to its rightful owner."

"Even more remarkable — if fate had not led you to the

gypsy encampment at that moment, this document would have ended its days as ashes, and the truth concealed forever."

"Shall you tell Geraldine, since the letter is from her mother after all?"

"*Never!* She shall not know of the poor woman's tragic story — it would be like betraying her to tell Geraldine, and her daughter would only be made unhappy by the knowledge. All the same," he added cautiously, "I shall keep this document safely under lock and key — just in case it should be needed in the future."

"And now, of course, there is no reason why Geraldine should not be betrothed as soon as she wishes," declared Lucilla with a delighted smile lighting up her lovely face.

"No reason at all, Lucilla," he replied, relaxing into a grin. "I shall tell her at once that I give the marriage my blessing."

Preparations for Geraldine's marriage to Sir David Clifton had begun almost immediately, and the day had already been arranged. There never was such a bustle of activity, as Geraldine, Lucilla, and Aunt Amelia sent tradesmen and craftsmen of all types about their jobs in a flurry of excitement to meet the exacting demands for such a fine social occasion.

Lucilla was so happy for Geraldine's sake that she had scant time to think of her own unfortunate experience with Martin Reynolds, of whom no sign had since been seen in London. As soon as the couple were married, Lucilla and her aunt were to return at once to the rectory, a thought which did not please either of them, since Aunt Amelia had hoped that Lucilla would find herself a husband while in London, and Lucilla dreaded the thought of the dullness of the country life.

Lucilla saw Lord Childs often. He had completely softened towards her, yet there was with him always a slight restraint, which meant that she was always on her guard with him, and careful what she said, and meant that she would never have admitted, not even to herself, the fact that she was very quickly falling deeply in love with him.

In any case, she was sensible enough to put such romantic notions right out of her mind, for when he did marry, she realized he would choose somebody who had far more to offer than herself. So, while enjoying his company on the occasions which were becoming increasingly more numerous — for he always made a point of joining the ladies after dinner these days — she took good care never to allow her true feelings to show through.

Thus things were continuing in this state, when, owing to a lapse of memory on Geraldine's part, Lucilla's entire life was suddenly altered.

Geraldine sent Lucilla hurrying back one day to the vast salon where the grand wedding supper was to be held, and where they had just been deciding with the housekeeper how to seat all the guests already invited by Lord Childs. Geraldine had accidentally left behind a swatch of Nottingham lace, from which she had been selecting the covering for the tables.

Lucilla entered the room quickly, not expecting to find anybody there, since it had been empty when they left. But, to her surprise, Lord Childs was standing in the middle of the huge room gazing intently up at the lavish paintings of classical scenes on the ceiling.

"Oh, Lucilla," he called the moment he saw her, for these

days he had taken to always calling her by her Christian name. "What do you think of the ceiling? I am trying to make up my mind whether it could do with a little regilding around the edges before my cousin's marriage."

To Lucilla's eyes, there looked nothing wrong with it, but she knew what a perfectionist Lord Childs was, so she stopped a while and peered up hard at the exquisite colours of the paintings framed by the gilded friezes and cornices.

"Well?" he asked expectantly.

"In truth, Lord Childs, I can see nothing out of order," she confessed with a ripple of laughter. "I can see no blemishes, no smuts of dirt or any of the like — it all looks perfect".

"Hmph! Well, if you are really sure, perhaps I shall leave it then," he replied, still a little uncertain.

She turned to smile up at him as she added, "The room is beautiful and will look even more so when the tables are laid ready for the guests with this fine Nottingham lace which Geraldine has chosen." She held up the lace which she had retrieved from a nearby table to show him, and he nodded in casual masculine approval, his mind still on the ceiling and architraves. She turned and began to walk towards the door.

"Don't go," he called after her.

She looked round in surprise, for a different tone had crept into his voice; an urgent, compelling tone.

"There is something else . . . he added, a serious expression on his face.

She walked back to him expectantly.

"Lucilla . . ."

"Yes, Lord Childs?" There was a questioning look in her large, violet eyes.

"Lucilla — do you think — that is, I want to ask you

something, and it is difficult." He seemed to be groping for words.

She took an instinctive step towards him and her closeness seemed to dry up his words altogether. For a brief time he looked helplessly down into her beautiful face, then, before she realized what was happening, he reached out and took her hands in his. The look in his eyes held her in a timeless moment before he swept her into his arms, and enveloped her in a long, passionate kiss which seemed to breathe a new life into Lucilla, as his warmth and passion tingled through her veins and united them.

"Oh, how I love you," he at last breathed.

"Why did you never say?" she whispered, so happy that she could scarcely believe what was happening.

"I dared not even consider that you might feel the same," he said. "The thought that you might reject me tortured me so that I delayed this moment — had I but realized . . ."

"I, reject you?" she interrupted, sounding incredulous, "but I love you, dearest, dearest Rupert." She buried her head in his shoulder so that he would not see the tears that were gathering in her eyes. The suddenness of it all had quite overcome her.

But she did not deceive him. He began to cover her closed eyes with soft kisses, murmuring bemusedly as he did so, "Come now, I will not have any tears spoil my proposal of marriage. Will you become my wife, darling Lucilla? Say yes, I beseech you."

"Yes, oh, yes, Rupert," she whispered with one of her beautiful smiles, the tears having mysteriously disappeared.

'Well, then,' he declared with a long sigh of relief, "let us go together at once and tell your aunt and then Geraldine — before you have time to change your mind!"

"And Papa — when shall we see him?" she asked anxiously.

"Today, of course, my darling. We shall have the carriage brought round immediately after luncheon, so that I may seek your father's permission just as quickly as the horses can convey us there."

And so it was that further arrangements had to be speedily put into action for the day of Geraldine's marriage, since now a double wedding was planned, when the Reverend George Prior would lead his only daughter to the altar to marry the nephew of his late and dearest friend.

"Do you remember the gypsy, Lucilla?" asked Geraldine as the two brides were completing their toilette on the day of their marriage.

Lucilla stopped in the middle of what she was doing, aghast at the thought. Mandy, who had become her personal maid, was just handing her mistress her silver-fringed wedding slippers.

"Gypsy!" exclaimed Lucilla in horror. "How can you possibly mention that vile man now, Geraldine? This is a happy day."

"No — I am not talking about that wretch who abducted me," said Geraldine, turning and smiling at her, "I mean the old fortuneteller." She cast Lucilla a sly look from her deep brown eyes. "I hope you will remind my cousin how avidly he disbelieved her prediction — later in the day when you have become his wife!"